Whiter Than Snow

A Novel By

Miranda Shisler

ISBN 978-0-9965619-3-8

Cover art copyright © 2016 Kathleen Kirtland Photography
kathleenkirtlandphotography.wordpress.com

Published in the United States of America by Miranda Shisler
mirandashisler.blogspot.com

For Tanya, who loves those enslaved. May they be set free, and may we not rest until it is accomplished.

And when he came to himself... he arose, and came to his father. But when he was yet a great way off, his father saw him, and had compassion, and ran, and fell on his neck, and kissed him.

And the son said unto him, Father, I have sinned against heaven, and in thy sight, and am no more worthy to be called thy son. But the father said to his servants, Bring forth the best robe, and put it on him; and put a ring on his hand, and shoes on his feet: And bring hither the fatted calf, and kill it; and let us eat, and be merry:

For this my son was dead, and is alive again; he was lost, and is found.

Luke 15

Little Sicily, Ohio

1905

Prologue

They lied to me.

Kathleen's throat constricted as she held the flimsy, yellowed letter with trembling fingers. "My whole family lied to me."

Her entire nineteen years had been spent believing her family loved her enough to tell her the truth. She could see now she had been wrong to trust them so implicitly.

She sat back against the wall of the attic alcove, her eyes blurry with unshed tears. How long had the old trunk, filled with her baby things, been up there, hidden under the stairs? She'd never noticed it before. The letter had been in an addressed envelope, on top of the pile of blankets and clothes.

She stared at the words on the page, written in the small, hurried script of Uncle William.

"Kathleen?" She heard her mama's voice on the stairs. "Are you up here?"

Kathleen tried to swallow, but a lump sat in her throat. "In here." Her voice was strained.

Mama peeked around the corner and found her sitting under the alcove next to the open trunk. "I'm sorry we quarreled, Kathleen."

Kathleen didn't answer. She watched Mama's face turn pale when she saw what Kathleen was holding.

"You knew this was in here, didn't you, Mama?"

Mama didn't answer. She came to Kathleen and took the weathered letter from her hand. "I'd forgotten."

"What does it mean?" Kathleen asked the question, hoping with all her being that her mother might give a different answer than the one she expected to hear.

Her mama read the words silently. Kathleen could imagine them on the page. They would be forever burned into her memory.

Amy,

We have arrived in Portland and are spending time with Amelia's father and sister. Her mother's funeral is Sunday. Amelia is doing as well as can be expected.

I'm writing to you because we had a long talk last night, and I believe we have made a decision concerning Kathleen. I realize you have been waiting for my decision and she is six, so it is time to make up my mind.

I've decided to leave my daughter in your home. I think Clara would approve. You and Connor can continue to let Kathleen think of you as her parents, and I will be her uncle. I think this will be best for everyone concerned. Amelia understands my reasoning, just as we have already discussed with you.

We'll be staying through the month. Amelia is afraid, with Harvey being so young, that he will not tolerate another long train ride so soon.

Thank you, Amy. We'll see you when we return.

William

"Why didn't you tell me the truth?" Kathleen managed around the lump that had formed in her throat.

Mama folded the letter and pressed her fingers along the crease, as if doing so might erase the words inside. "It is a complicated explanation, Kathleen. And one only your uncle can really answer."

"Who is Clara?"

Amy pressed her lips together. "She was your mother. Clara McCloud. She was a saloon girl your uncle fell for."

"Everything makes sense now," Kathleen said dully.

"What makes sense?" Mama leaned against the doorjamb and gave a small sigh. Kathleen didn't blame her. It had been a hard week. Kathleen's older sister, Jennifer, all-around model daughter and upstanding citizen, had become engaged. As usual, Kathleen had felt the need to compete for her parents' attention, jealous of her sister. She desperately wanted her Mama and Papa to be as proud of her as they were of their oldest daughter who organized the local chapter of the Anti-Saloon League, taught Sunday school and helped the schoolteacher with lessons. Jennifer was beautiful, polite, friendly and kind. Kathleen never seemed to fit in anywhere, no matter how hard she tried.

"Why I never felt like I belonged in this family. Why everything seems to work out right for Jennifer and nothing comes easily for me. This wasn't my true home."

"How could you say that?"

Tears shone in her Mama's eyes, causing Kathleen to feel guilty. But she wouldn't back down. "You always take Jennifer's side. You compare me to her. I don't want to march for temperance or get married. I just want to ride my horse and tend the garden. Why isn't that enough? Why couldn't you have just loved me without expecting so much out of me?"

Her mother stood straight, confusion in her wounded expression. "Kathleen, we have ever *only* loved you that way. So has your uncle."

Anger bubbled to the surface, and Kathleen felt an overflow of heat. She stood, her fists clenched at her sides and her face hot. "*Father*, not uncle! I hate you all for lying to me!"

Kathleen went straight to her room she shared with Jennifer and packed her belongings.

Her mother followed. "Kathleen, don't go. We can work this out. We'll talk with William – just don't do anything rash."

Kathleen scoffed. "Isn't that what I always do, Mama? I might as well be true to my character. Don't worry; I won't be a burden to you all anymore. I'm leaving for good."

Her mama begged her to stay. She said Kathleen would break all of their hearts if she went. But Kathleen could not escape the ugly truth, and they were a constant reminder of it. She didn't belong. She had never belonged.

She wasn't worth telling the truth.

One

Dempsey, Ohio
September, 1905

Kathleen had grown accustomed to the screaming. She was surprised it jarred her awake after weeks of living in the saloon. She sat up, prickles rushing over her skin as she heard frantic voices and saw shadows moving past her door. Moments later, she heard the sharp tapping of Rita Dolsen's boot heels on the floor outside her room.

Kathleen pulled on a thin robe and went to her door. She cautiously pushed it open.

"The little wretch!" Rita spat as she looked into the room everyone gathered around. "Did she have any idea how much this would cost me?"

Kathleen felt a lump in her throat. The room was Lucy's.

Lucy was young. She'd been fourteen when she'd knocked on the back door of Rita's saloon, asking for scraps. It had been winter and she'd been starving. Rita, who never missed an opportunity to make money, saw the girl's potential for beauty and offered her a contract to work for at the saloon. Lucy had agreed. Maybe she didn't think she had another option.

Kathleen didn't think Lucy had any idea what kind of place she'd consented to work. For the weeks Kathleen had known her, the girl was nothing but miserable.

Kathleen dreaded peering around that corner and seeing the reason for everyone's gawking. But she needed to know. She leaned around the other girls and gasped in horror.

Red. It was all she saw. Blood, dried and dark, smeared across the floorboards. Soaked into the white silk fabric of the nightgown, staining it forever crimson. The same stain Kathleen felt on her soul, spreading and darkening all the goodness she had once assumed was there.

Lucy's angelic face was frozen in pained contortion. Her glossy black hair spread out on the floor around her. Her almond-shaped eyes stared, unseeing, at the ceiling, as if she petitioned God for something better than she was handed here.

Kathleen saw the razor lying on the floor next to Lucy. She swallowed back a sob as she realized what the girl had done to escape the life she couldn't bear. She felt a stab of guilt, for she had noticed scars on Lucy's wrists. How many times had the girl attempted to take her life before she succeeded?

"Clean up this mess." Rita gestured impatiently. "And if any one of you ever tries something so stupid, make sure it works, or I will make you regret it."

"If you live in a saloon, you'll have to act like a saloon girl sooner or later."

Rita's words bit like a bad taste on Kathleen's tongue. She couldn't get rid of the taste, just like she couldn't get the stain off her soul. And though it had been a week since Lucy had killed herself, Kathleen still saw the image of her lying in the pool of blood every time she closed her eyes. Was it a peek into her own future? Was there no other escape?

She finished the Friday night dancing act and scurried off the stage of the Iron Horse Saloon and Theater in Dempsey, Ohio. The other girls giggled and pulled their skirts up to their knees as the men cheered, raising their glasses in appreciation. The atmosphere in the smoky building was raucous and completely foreign to anything Kathleen had known in the life before she came here.

Her idyllic childhood in Little Sicily seemed like a dream now. A dream that was fading away with the harsh reality of her present existence.

Kathleen had hoped she might become accustomed to the dancing and suggestive routines she and the other girls were forced to perform. But as time went on, she became more unsettled. She could not help imagining the shock Mama, Jennifer or Aunt Amelia would feel if they saw her now.

They would be devastated.

She returned to center stage for the final act, the only part of her nights she never minded. As the piano played the opening chords of the song, she closed her eyes and pretended she stood on a stage in a respectable music hall.

She's only a bird in a gilded cage,
A beautiful sight to see,
You may think she's happy and free from care,
She's not, though she seems to be.

The words always comforted her. She may have no choice in anything else, but at least she could make her declaration in song, night after night. It was her only solace.

She saw melancholy glints in the eyes of several of the other girls. Kathleen knew some of them had been sold to Rita when they were only children. Some of them, like Lucy, had come through the doors because they were hungry and homeless. Others needed work, and Rita was the only one who would hire them.

Yet Kathleen had willingly walked through the doors at Rita's request. Why? Partly because she had been deceived. But she couldn't deny she'd also done it to spite her family.

They had lied to her. Every day she had been alive for nineteen years, the people she loved had forced her to live a lie.

"There's my little bird."

Kathleen felt panic at the sound of Bill Logan's voice. The man sat on a barstool as he did every night, leering at her as he chewed the end of his cigar. His unsettling beady eyes followed her wherever she went as his fingers raked through his greased hair.

"I have drinks to serve," Kathleen said, trying to sound cheerful. She gulped back her apprehension as Ames, the barkeeper, eyed her with warning. All the girls knew he was in charge when Rita was in her lounge. Kathleen wouldn't get away with refusing Logan again.

When Kathleen left Little Sicily, she went first to the saloon where her mother, Clara, had worked in Indianapolis. Kathleen hoped to know more about the mother she had not known existed. When she was offered a job at her mother's saloon, Rita had stepped in and told Kathleen she owned a concert hall in Ohio. She had gushed when Kathleen sang for her, and made the job offer seem like the best decision Kathleen could ever hope to make for herself. Rita had promised Kathleen would never have to do anything that made her uncomfortable.

She only came to know the true Rita after she had signed the contract. She had been a tool Rita needed to further her own agenda. The first time Kathleen flatly refused to serve the men their drinks, Rita had given her a warning. The next time, Kathleen had endured a beating from Ames, and the naïve girl she had been before died in those horrifying moments. Back at her home, she had been cherished. Here, she quickly understood she was nothing more than a slave.

As Logan leered at her, Kathleen knew he was well aware of that fact.

Two

Joshua's cow would be spitting mad.

He'd been sitting at the desk in his office at the jail for nearly two hours. The good reverend, the mayor and he had listened to Mrs. Elizabeth Cooke run her mouth for most of that time. Enough was enough. They weren't getting anywhere, and Joshua had things to do.

"Mrs. Cooke, I don't think you understand that we *agree* the saloon should be closed. You're preaching to the choir."

"Then why does it remain open, spilling its filthy influence into our town night after night?" Mrs. Cooke's voice was so high-pitched and whiny he wondered if the human ear was meant to take the abuse. He tried to imagine being married to someone like her and subsequently felt a little sorry for Mr. Cooke.

She wasn't finished. "The Anti-Saloon League's campaign before the last election caused the vote to go in favor of shutting down the saloon on Sundays, but the doors are still open on the Lord's Day. Men are still drinking and gambling away their hard-earned money and partaking of evils better left unsaid."

Joshua waited for one of the other men to answer. The room was silent. He sighed. "It's just the sheriff and me here in Dempsey. Who exactly did you expect would stay outside the saloon all day Sunday and make sure it stayed closed? The folks that want to see the place

9

closed are in church."

"Isn't it your duty, Deputy Whitley?" Her voice was breathless with her barely concealed emotion.

He swallowed back his frustration. "I help out the sheriff, Mrs. Cooke. But I have a farm. I have a grumpy old cow that's waiting on her milking as we speak. I've already neglected the planting and hay harvest. I can hear Grandpa grumbling from his grave. I don't have time to babysit the saloon."

"That is why we are forced to take matters into our own hands," Mrs. Cooke replied in a desperate tone. She crossed her arms with a loud sniff. "We care enough to see the law upheld, even if our officials do not."

Joshua stood and went to the hat stand to grab his Stetson. "I understand wanting to solve the problem. I do. But you go about something in the wrong way, you just cause more problems than you solve."

He headed for the door and opened it, ushering them all out. "I'm not a man to go back on my word. Violence and destruction of property will be dealt with. I know you think you're morally superior to Rita Dolsen, but you're not above the law."

Mrs. Cooke followed him out, her mouth still a thin line of disapproval. "Deputy, inaction is the same as agreement. I suggest you consider what you can do to see that saloon close its doors for good."

Joshua softened when he saw the tear in the corner of her eye. It was no secret her husband and son were both regulars at the saloon. "Mrs. Cooke, I know better than you realize what those places do to people and their families. I *will* see this through. You can help me most by praying."

She gave him a last glance before she walked away. He didn't feel like he'd gotten through to her. Violence in Dempsey was about to escalate, and it would only make his mission to get that saloon closed more difficult.

❈

Logan hooked his boot heel on the chrome rail that served as a footrest on the bar. He stared at Kathleen. She could tell he was angry at being refused again, but she could also see he liked the challenge.

"I can go ask Rita what she thinks." He grabbed her arm and pulled her closer. Her stomach turned with fear as she smelled his sour breath near her face. He scoffed. "A woman like you, thinking you're too good for me? You've got one use."

She wrenched her arm away from him and reached for a tray of drinks. "Now, now, I have work to do. Why don't you go on upstairs and find yourself some company?"

He stood up, forcing her back against the bar so hard her breath caught in her throat. She glanced at Ames, but he made himself busy wiping out a glass.

"Just wait, little girl," he said next to her ear. "You're going to regret telling me no."

He slammed his drink on the counter so that the contents sloshed over the side and landed on her dress. Then he turned and went to the stairs, but it wasn't five minutes before he returned and went into Rita's rooms. Not long after that, he left the saloon, smiling at her with a sick triumph in his expression.

Kathleen tried to hide in the crowd and keep busy, but as she expected, Rita soon beckoned to her from the door of her office.

She had no choice but to obey. Her feet felt heavy on the rough wooden floorboards as she weaved through the press of bodies and passed by Rita into the room.

Rita closed the door and turned, her delicate, gloved hands on sculpted hips.

"You can't refuse that man any longer." The older woman's dark eyes flashed with irritation.

Rita exemplified elegance in a silk dress with black lace edgings. Though she had to be nearing sixty, she was still beautiful in an exotic, mystifying way. Her office boasted rich tapestries, a thick rug and a mahogany desk. Gifts Kathleen assumed Rita had been given by adoring customers lined her desk. Everything in the room spoke to Rita's ability to exercise control over others.

Kathleen didn't answer. She crossed her arms over her chest and looked out the window, seeing her reflection in the dark pane. The sight disgusted her. The image in the window couldn't be Kathleen Able of Little Sicily, Ohio. She saw a "prairie dove," dressed suggestively in a costume designed to draw attention to her body. She was a "lady of the night." Both polite ways to refer to women whose profession was sin.

She looked down in shame and fought back the sting of tears unshed for too long. "I think he means to hurt me."

Rita scoffed. "This isn't a business rich in likable fellows." She took a step closer and Kathleen heard the tap of her black boots as she stepped off the Persian rug. "No one cares how you feel about your situation. No one in here and no one outside this building, or you wouldn't have come through the door in the first place. The only reason I have been patient is because you look and sound like Clara McCloud when you sing. There are a hundred other saloons between here and Indianapolis that would love to boast about having her daughter on their stage. She was legendary. But don't think I'm going to keep clothing and feeding you if you refuse to play your part."

Apparently not interested in Kathleen's response, Rita waved her away. Kathleen hesitated only a moment before she returned to the noisy room of gambling and carousing. The stage had been possessed by young men dancing with saloon girls. Feathers and boas shook in the air as the raucous laughter warred with tinny music from the player piano.

"There you are."

Her throat went tight at the sound of Logan's voice. He grabbed the flesh of her arm, his nails biting as he jerked her back against his body.

She fought the hold he had on her and cried for help, but the sound was drowned out by the noise around them. He wound his arms around her waist and picked her up, heaving her toward the door.

Nobody spared her a glance.

He dropped her when she got too heavy, dragging her along the boards of the front porch and down the stairs by her hair. She fell on her hands and knees when he threw her into the alley next to the saloon. He closed the gate as she tried to push herself up off the ground and failed.

"Rita doesn't think you're too good for this." Logan roughly pulled her up and pushed her back against the brick wall, and forced his mouth against hers. She tried to scream as his hands slid down her body. Desperate for air, she brought her heel down on his foot and tried to push him away. His laugh was harsh. He hit her in the face. She fought to remain conscious, for she knew if she fainted she would most likely never wake up again.

"I'll make you sorry you ever dared to tell me no."

He reached for the knife on his belt. She cried out again and tried to escape as he held both her wrists in his free hand.

"Please, don't," she whimpered. He raked a boot under her feet so that she fell, hitting her head on a crate. He dropped to his knees and aimed the knife at her face. She desperately tried to wriggle away and felt sharp pain down her leg as the knife made contact.

"Don't worry. I'm not going to kill you yet. But by the time it happens, you'll want to die."

"No," she cried.

"Hey!"

At the sound of another man's voice, Logan jumped off her and dropped the knife. Kathleen didn't wait to see the face of her rescuer. She held her bleeding leg and ran for the back door of the saloon that led through the kitchen and up the small service stairs to her room. She crumbled into a heap on the other side of her door and cried.

Three

Joshua saw the glint of the knife as Logan threw it behind him into the woodpile. He saw a trail of blood as well, and knew the escaping saloon girl had been injured.

"What are you up to, Logan? Did you hurt her?" Joshua put his hand on his holster in warning.

Logan shrugged and flashed an amiable smile. "Aw, Deputy, you know I'm about as angelic as they come. I wouldn't hurt a flea."

"I know you all too well." Joshua went to the woodpile and fished out the knife, keeping an eye on Logan.

"This yours?"

Logan shrugged. "Never seen it before in my life. I just came out here to have a smoke in peace."

Joshua prayed for patience, lest he shoot the man on the spot. "I can lock you up, and we'll discuss it in the morning with a judge if you'd rather."

Logan laughed. "You think a judge will care what happens to one of her kind?"

Joshua knew the vile man had a point. Even a shifty, no-good character such as Logan would win against a saloon girl.

"If I see you hanging around here again, you'll be in my jail cell, no matter what any judge says or doesn't say. I won't have you disturbing the peace or harming folks."

Logan tipped his hat to Joshua before he disappeared into the night. Joshua saw the hard glint in the man's eyes. He'd recognized it well enough in his years as deputy. He had no doubt the man would kill to get what he wanted.

Joshua walked around to the front of the saloon. The sight of the place was like the stench of a dead animal. Disgusting. He hated it. He hated everything the saloon stood for, and all the trouble it caused his town. He was dead-set against it because of all the families that had suffered. Including his.

Pain swelled up within his chest as he pushed back the memories that tried to take hold in his mind. He pasted a passive expression of authority on his face before he pushed open the swinging doors.

Joshua sauntered to the counter, knowing all eyes viewed his journey. He put his hands on the bar and eyed the barkeeper.

"What are you drinking, Deputy Whitley?" Ames wiped out a glass and set it in front of Joshua.

"Heard there was trouble tonight. Someone got hurt."

Ames shrugged, the long sides of his moustache twitching. "I haven't heard anything of the sort."

Joshua heard the dishonesty. He twisted his mouth and refused to look away from the man's challenging stare. "I'm sure Rita won't mind if I have a look around. Just in case."

Ames raised an eyebrow. "You don't have a reason to be in here if you aren't drinking or partaking of our services."

Joshua could argue or call the man's bluff. He stared past the bar to the line of bottles along the ornate mirror behind the counter. "I sure could go for a sarsaparilla."

Everyone in the vicinity laughed. Ames shook his head and made a show of trying to locate such a beverage. "Sheriff's boy here wants himself a sarsaparilla. Anyone else man enough to join him?"

Joshua took the glass after Ames filled it, raised it to the mockers, and downed it with one breath, giving an exaggerated sigh of appreciation. He set the glass down hard on the counter and bowed to the scattered applause.

"Where's Rita Dolsen?"

Ames nodded toward Rita's rooms. Joshua flipped a coin on the counter and tipped his hat. He made his way through the crowded room. A young woman approached him and smiled suggestively at him, grabbing his arm and walking with him. He quickly looked away to avoid the eyeful her dress offered.

"Now, Deputy, did you come in here looking for a little fun?"

He shook her hands away from his arm and knocked firmly on Rita's door.

"Deputy calling," he called. "Open up, Rita."

Rita opened the door. "Why, Deputy Whitley, what a nice surprise. I didn't think you were a drinking man."

"You know I'm not," he said. "I found Bill Logan in your alley with a bloody knife. You want to show me to the wounded girl or should I find her myself?"

Rita shrugged. "I honestly have no idea what you are talking about. I'll be sure to see that the girls are all well. Thank you for your concern." She tried to close the door, but Joshua caught it and held it open.

"I'm sure you won't mind if I take a look around."

He let the door go and turned toward the stairs. She followed him.

"Surely you won't enter the rooms. We pride ourselves on privacy and anonymity."

He wanted to launch into a sermon about how the families of those men knew exactly what was going on, but instead he started climbing the stairs. "I'll knock."

His boots felt heavy on the soft red carpet runner; his knuckles were white on the polished oak railing. But he made himself keep going. He reached the top and moved down the hallway. He pounded on each door, calling a warning before he opened them. Even so, he saw plenty he wished he hadn't. The images of the past threatened him again as bile rose in his throat.

The last door on the right wouldn't open. He knew it must be the room of the injured girl. He knocked again.

"I want to help," he said. "Open the door and we'll talk about what happened."

He waited with his hand on the knob. He listened for even a whimper that might give him cause to kick down the door, but he didn't hear a thing. He finally sighed and went back down the stairs.

Rita met him at the bottom. "I trust everything is in order?"

"Wasn't anything in order up there," he said. He eyed her. Her smile patronized him and her hands stayed folded in front of her as if she was calming a child. There was no denying Rita Dolsen was a formidable woman. She had a presence that went beyond her tall frame and striking features. Her sultry blend of confidence and mystery managed to capture the attention of men half her age.

Joshua knew as well she was a shrewd businesswoman. The Anti-Saloon League and the Women's Christian Temperance Union, along with the Sheriff and every other decent person in town, had attempted to close down the saloon on many occasions for the past few years. Rita always managed to defend her territory.

"Look, Miss Dolsen, I have plenty of call just by the nature of this place to find any excuse to shut you down. And I will. You ruin lives for the sake of money, and it makes me sick."

She eyed him, her smile unwavering. "Just try to find a reason. I run a clean business."

He scoffed, but she didn't allow him a reply.

"Furthermore, I saved these girls. They would have starved without my benevolence. You call that ruin? I give them a warm place to sleep and food. I protect them and take care of them as if they were my own daughters."

Joshua tried to contain his rage. Tension thickened his voice as he spoke. "What you expect out of them? That hurts them beyond repair. No mother would allow her daughters to be used in such a way."

At the strangled sound of his own voice, he knew it was past time to escape. He turned and made for the door, feeling like he was choking on the atmosphere.

"I'll be back at the first sign of trouble," he promised as he left.

"There will be no trouble." Rita called after him.

Joshua chafed. Dempsey remained at a stalemate with the Iron Horse Saloon and Theater. And it wasn't going to go away without a fight.

Four

Kathleen eased her body onto her bed, trembling with pain. One look at her leg assured her the blood was still flowing. Every noise outside her door made her heart race, thinking Logan had returned to finish the job. She stood again and limped back to the door to wedge a chair under the knob. Spent, she leaned against the door and sank into a sitting position. Her leg throbbed with every beat of her heart.

"What kind of life is this?" she whispered. The thought of ending her life, as Lucy had done, occurred to her. But as tempting as it sounded to be free of Rita and free of the hell she lived in, Kathleen knew she wouldn't kill herself. The thought of hellfire terrified her more than continuing on in her present situation. It was her constant dread – what she would face on her judgment day.

The temperance women were faithful to remind her regularly of her coming punishment. They stood outside the saloon and prayed and wept in loud voices, calling for divine justice.

She knew she deserved God's wrath as much as she feared it. Kathleen was scared she'd end up in this misery forever. And with men like Logan, she assumed her eternity would not be long in finding her. She sat in the dark, panic rising, memories flooding her mind.

Some choices can't be undone. Even if I didn't exactly know what I was getting into.

How many times had she wished it was all a nightmare, and she would wake up, safe in her bed, covered by the patchwork quilt she had made with her sister? Safe in her parents' home on Ash Street in Little Sicily.

If only they had told me the truth, none of this would have happened. But they lied to me. They lied about everything.

Kathleen heard the sound of heavy boots in the hallway. A man pounded on every door, calling a warning before he opened them. She recognized the voice. Deputy Whitley.

The deputy remained nothing short of hero in Dempsey. She could picture his friendly expression, his solid jaw and eyes that crinkled in the corners when he grinned. She often watched him from her window as he played with his nieces and nephews in the street near the jail. She had seen him carry packages for elderly folks and raise the hopes of eligible young women by smiling and opening doors for them.

She found the deputy confusing. He seemed an irony. He was mild, kind and courteous, but also, in no uncertain terms, the very picture of the law. He had a reputation for dealing with lawbreakers in a swift and thorough manner. After all, hadn't he made it his mission to see the saloon doors close for good? Yet here he was, knocking away at hers and asking her to open it.

She wished she could. She laid her palm on the wood, feeling the vibration of his firm knocks. She imagined him touching the other side of the door, opposite her hand. She pretended he really worried about her, and that he could do something to stop the avalanche of destruction she'd pulled down upon herself.

"Please open the door," he said again.

She almost answered, but her voice caught in her throat. What good would it do to tell him the truth? She had nowhere to go, and no proof to provide him. If the Deputy arrested her, what might happen to her? What if she were hung for her crimes? And if he didn't arrest her, and Rita found out she'd spoken to him, she could expect Rita might have her beaten severely. She could die either way.

There were some things that couldn't be fixed, especially not by a lawman. He would probably think she got what she deserved anyway. And wouldn't he be right?

She listened in silence until he walked away. Then she crawled to the window to watch him leave the saloon and get his horse. He headed west toward the Whitley farm. She watched him until the shadows swallowed him, and wished she could run after him.

Pain woke Kathleen early the next morning. She gasped at the throbbing and threw back the sheet to assess the damage.

Her stomach turned when she saw the angry red flesh and the sheets stained with blood. She remembered a similar wound her cousin Harvey had suffered after cutting his leg on a ragged piece of rusted metal when they were playing in the woods by the Spencer place. His injury had quickly become infected, and he would have died without the expert care of their town doctor.

Rita would never call a doctor, and even if she did, Kathleen doubted he would come. Kathleen saw the young man heading to the United Brethren Church on Waterloo and High every Sunday morning. It wasn't hard to imagine his views about saloon girls.

She pulled her long coat over her dress and buttoned it up to the neck. She brushed her hair back and reached for her hat, hesitating a moment to stare at the old Stetson. She'd come across it in her mother's things. It had become her most prized possession.

She fingered the edge of the hat as her eyes fell to the picture of her mother she kept on her nightstand. She'd stolen the photograph and the hat from the Black Eagle Tavern when she'd gone there to find out about her mother. She didn't regret taking the items. If anyone should own the only picture of Clara, it should be her daughter.

Kathleen touched the cheap frame, memorizing every detail of her mother's beautiful face and mysterious smile. Then tendrils of her own hair fell forward and into her view. They were the same light shade of blonde.

She was the very picture of her mother.

She blinked back tears. *I wish you were still here. I wish I could know you.*

She stepped out of her room and closed the door with as little noise as possible. The saloon was silent, as it usually was in the early hours of the morning. No one would rise until mid-morning, and even then it would be quiet until the afternoon when the shows started and the men came from their shifts at the railroad yard.

Kathleen started to descend the stairs until she caught sight of the somber group of women gathering outside the windows of the saloon. She reconsidered her plan to go out.

She turned back and went to the door of one of the older girls, Celeste, who had a reputation for occasional moments of kindness. She knocked softly. A few moments passed before the door opened. When Kathleen saw Celeste's face, she knew this would not be one of those occasional moments. Celeste only opened the door a crack. She had dark circles under her eyes, and Kathleen saw a figure in the bed behind her.

"What?" Celeste yawned and leaned her head against the door. "It's awful early to be bothering a soul without a good reason."

Kathleen gulped. "Logan cut me. I'm afraid it will get infected and I don't have any salve."

Celeste glanced down at Kathleen's leg. Blood had seeped through the cloth she'd used for a bandage. "Go to the store and get some," she said with a shrug.

"The temperance women are here."

Celeste sighed. "So you'll have to hear a sermon and maybe take an ice bath. What do you want me to do? I don't mind helping girls if there's nothing else they can do, but you're wasting my time right now."

Celeste closed the door in her face. Kathleen turned back to the stairway and leaned on the railing overlooking the bar and theater. The growing group of protesters outside the front door had ceased their chattering and gossip and taken up the sober business of pacing and singing woeful hymns, holding their signs high with burdened purpose.

Kathleen chewed on her lip, trying to decide what to do. She considered taking the back door, but she was afraid Logan might be in the alley waiting for her. Her only option was to take the walk of shame through the women. She could die if she didn't, and that was motivation enough to brave the crowd.

She forced her feet to move, cringing with each movement of her injured leg. The moment she opened the door, the women descended on her. One woman stepped in her path and began quoting Scripture about judgment and hell. Another burst into tears and fell to her knees, praying for Kathleen's doomed soul. The rest of the women avoided eye contact with her as she tried to get past them to the street.

"Young woman, you are cursed! Repent of your evil! You deserve hellfire for your sins in this den of wickedness. You should go to your family and beg their forgiveness." The woman she had heard called Mrs. Cooke followed her into the street. Kathleen felt the sting of the words.

"What do you know of my family?" she said, feeling heat spread across her face.

"Perhaps they will show you undeserved mercy." The woman's voice sounded almost gentle for a moment. Kathleen tried to pass by.

"Your husbands don't seem to have a problem with our establishment, and neither do your sons," Kathleen said, hearing the bitterness in her tone and feeling ashamed.

All signs of kindness disappeared from the woman's expression. She leaned into Kathleen's face. Apparently she didn't like to discuss her family any more than Kathleen did. "That is why we are trying to stamp out the stain of this saloon in our town. For the sake of our men who have been caught in your web of degradation."

"Please just let me by." Kathleen gestured to the blood-soaked bandage on her leg, but she didn't expect sympathy. "I need to get some salve."

"If the grocer serves your kind, we will boycott his store," Mrs. Cooke said firmly.

"It's for your own good," another woman said, holding up a sign that read *Lips that touch liquor shall not touch ours.* "We are more concerned for your soul than we are for your health."

Kathleen scoffed. As if any one of those women cared about her at all. They would cheer if the deputy and sheriff came along and strung her up right there on the street for all to see. They would call it a victory for their cause. Another "lady of the night" cast out of her den of sin.

She saw two women running toward her, carrying a large pail of sloshing water. From experience, Kathleen knew it would either be icy cold or scalding, and she had no desire to find out which it was. She pushed through the women and tried to run with her throbbing wound. Taunts followed her.

Your kind shall burn in hellfire.

How could a righteous God ever love a sinner as depraved as you?

You are heaven's outcast.

You will be punished severely for all eternity.

Kathleen pulled her cape over her head and tried not to consider the possibility that they were quite correct on every count.

Five

Autumn's chill swept around Kathleen as she crossed the street, though the wind could not be as cold as the stares she received from the townspeople.

She had heard talk that the town had voted to close the saloon on Sundays. More than that, there had been a strong campaign to close saloons for good and make Dempsey a dry town. Rita refused to cooperate. She knew she held the upper hand because of the large amount of railroad workers that visited the saloon each evening and every Sunday.

She made enough money discreetly keeping the saloon open Sundays that it still made it worth her while to pay the fine each week. The temperance women had insisted the saloon door stay locked, but Rita simply left the back door open. Her business had increased on Sunday, probably because the back door offered men an added degree of privacy.

What else could one sheriff, who spent most of his time in Columbus, and a single deputy, do to enforce the law? The deputy had tried to set up a system of volunteer watchman at the front to report on the men who entered the saloon on the Lord's Day. In turn, Rita sent girls out to "distract" the watchmen.

The battle raged, with no clear winner in sight.

Kathleen knew she was on the wrong side. She deserved the ostracism, and she was resigned to it. But the women, who kept their daily vigil, praying, dowsing and occasionally breaking the windows of the saloon, irked Kathleen. Some of the saloon girls were never given a choice in their destiny. How could they be blamed?

And the men. Church members, husbands, fathers and sons. All of them were quite willing to creep into the saloon under the veil of darkness, shamelessly drinking their whiskey and laughing at the bawdy shows. They appreciated Kathleen's beauty by night, and by day they were repulsed at the sight of her.

She kept her eyes on the ground, trying to avoid their judging, scathing looks, but she felt them just the same. Those men had a choice. They were the reason the saloon had been created. Kathleen might be as rebellious as a young woman could be, but at least she wasn't pretending to be anything else.

She went into the store and hurried to the medicinal products on shelves next to the counter. She scanned the items for salve. She picked up a circular container that promised quick healing of wounds. When she opened the lid and took a whiff of the thin camphor paste, her nose took offense. As she sneezed, she dropped the tin and it clattered to the floor. The reeking substance spilled onto the rough wooden floorboards and between the cracks. Everyone in the long narrow room turned her way. Kathleen bent to clean the mess as the grocer, Mr. Dickinson, headed her way.

He smiled pleasantly, as if he planned to ease an embarrassed customer's discomfort. But then his eyes caught hers and she saw recognition. He knew she came from the saloon, because he had been in there only the night before. She watched the lines of his face harden.

"What are *you* doing in here?" He recoiled. "Making a mess, I see, in my decent place of business. I'll have you arrested!"

"Do you really think your wife is sleeping every night when you slink into *my* place of business?" She mumbled the words, but she could tell he heard her.

His face turned a rare shade of crimson. "I hope you intend to pay for this mess. I can't afford to lose money over the ungraceful intrusion of a *soiled dove*."

A woman standing nearby gasped at his words. Her face went pale as her gaze fell to Kathleen, and she turned quickly and left the store.

Mr. Dickinson fumed, and everyone else in the room looked her way.

"Do we have a problem, Clem?"

Kathleen peeked up to see the deputy leaning against the counter, his ankles crossed and his arms folded across his chest. He wore an uneasy smile on his face bearing marks of tension.

Dickinson subdued himself with obvious effort. His tone was respectful when he spoke. "Deputy, this woman came in from the saloon and began throwing things from the shelves. I hate to say it, but I'll have to press charges."

Kathleen glared at the shopkeeper, but dread stole her breath. She had no right to expect mercy from the law. Joshua Whitley was a decent man, but she knew his opinion of the saloon and its inhabitants. He might see this as his opportunity to make her an example.

She dared a glance at his face, wishing she knew what he thought. His eyes met hers, and an unexpected wave of shame tormented her. He wasn't angry. He seemed troubled.

The moment of indecision ended as he spoke. "Now, Clem, I'm fairly sure the lady sneezed and dropped it by accident. And she appears to be trying to clean it up."

Dickinson frowned and stared at the deputy. He clearly wanted to object. But instead he turned away to distract his other customers from the altercation and left the deputy to deal with Kathleen.

She looked around for a towel or rag she might use to clean the spilled salve, all the time feeling the gaze of the man standing over her. A handkerchief appeared in her face.

She hesitated. Finally she grabbed it and wiped up the mess. She tried to return it to him, but he shook his head, his eyes trapping hers completely.

She saw a guarded distance in his gaze, but behind it she didn't miss the kindness. She tried to get her footing and stand up as he reached over to pick up the tin.

He held out his hand.

Kathleen stared at it in shock. She wasn't alone, for nearby customers had stopped to watch. What could she do? She grasped his hand and allowed him to help her up as he would have done for any decent woman in town.

He studied her, his eyes peering out from beneath the brim of his Stetson. She brushed off her coat as his eyes caught on her own hat, quite similar to his, but he seemed to accept it and instead looked at the red stain that had soaked through her long coat as she kneeled on the floor.

"How bad?" His voice was low. Husky. Her heart seemed to jump inside her chest.

"I'm fine," she said, hearing her voice falter. "I... fell down the stairs."

He raised an eyebrow.

"I'm clumsy. As you can see." Kathleen shrugged and avoided his gaze.

"I should take a look. See if you need a doctor," he said. His words sounded strangled, as if they had been spoken at a cost.

She didn't answer. She was acutely aware that he was a handsome man. The kind of man all the girls in the saloon would vie for the moment he set foot inside the door. Strong arms, thick chest, trim figure and eyes as deeply green as a forest of pine trees. If the outward appearance wasn't enough, his manner and sincerity set off an even brighter light.

"You're Rita's girl. The one who got hurt last night." He sighed. "Why didn't you let me help you?"

Because it would have only caused me more trouble in the end.

"I don't know what you're talking about," she said with a shrug.

He frowned.

Dickinson turned back to them when the customers had left. "Someone has to pay for this."

Kathleen opened her change purse. "How much?"

Dickinson stared at the purse in disgust, as if handling her money would give him a disease. "That tin costs a dollar."

She swallowed hard and dug into her pocketbook. "Let me see," she said, stalling, as she knew she only had a few nickels.

"A dollar seems a little steep for a tin of salve." Deputy Whitley reached into his pocket and pulled out a silver dollar. He flipped it toward the grocer, who caught it with a red face.

"I didn't mean for you to pay it," he grumbled, but he opened the cash register and stowed the money.

The deputy returned his gaze to Kathleen. He nodded toward the door. "Shall we?"

Kathleen followed him out and stood facing him when they reached the street. Neither spoke for a moment.

He cleared his throat. "Let me find you a place to stay."

She almost laughed. Who would put her up, even for a night? "You've done more than most. Thanks for your concern, but I should be getting back."

She tried to turn and walk away, but drew back in surprise when he reached for her arm.

"I'm sorry," he said, his hand falling back to his side. "Miss…?"

"Just Kathleen," she mumbled. The last thing she would do was bring her parents' name into this. If she even knew which name to use.

"Joshua Whitley," he introduced himself, holding out the tin.

She wanted to reach for it. But doing so felt like she was taking something from him she had no right to take, and it had nothing to do with a tin of camphor. She clenched her fists at her side and turned away, quickly crossing the street.

She felt her cheeks go hot. She hoped Rita hadn't seen from the window. Other girls had been punished for less. She'd been talking to the enemy in the middle of town for all to see.

The deputy didn't follow her, but her quick glance back let her know he watched her flee, the tin still in his outstretched hand.

Six

Joshua had never seen such a beautiful girl before. He tried to set the image of her aside, but all his brain wanted to think about were the delicate lines of her face, the way her hair resembled a halo of sunshine framing her face. The haunted depths of her eyes that made him feel like he was swimming in a bottomless, clandestine pool.

She made him want to set aside more than space in his mind to consider her. She made him want to forget about his principles and follow her straight into the saloon and up the stairs to her room.

That it was an option proved an agonizing temptation.

He gulped as he realized what he was considering, and shook his head as if he might shake out the dark thoughts. What was wrong with him? Had he forgotten everything he believed in?

But as his mind cleared, he realized it wasn't just her beauty that caught his attention. Something was buried within the depths of her eyes that compelled him. Was it a cry for help?

He wondered at her story. How did she come to be in that saloon? It had been his experience that people didn't usually forever alter their future without some motivation that at least seemed to force their hand.

Especially saloon girls.

A commotion in front of the grocer's offered a blessed distraction from his thoughts.

"Get out of here, you hooligans, or I'll fix your flint good this time!" Dickinson's voice rose above the gentle noise of morning commerce.

Once again, Dickinson's face and neck were red with irritation. If the man didn't drop dead from a heart attack before he was fifty, the good Lord would be showing him mercy.

Dickinson saw him still standing in the street in front of the store. "One of these days, Deputy…"

"Now, Clem," Joshua said, pulling two mirror-image boys from behind overturned fruit barrels. "I'll take it from here."

Dickinson began to right the barrels and pick up the apples that rolled in every direction. "Just see you do. Between saloon girls and disrespectful boys, I can hardly run a business in this town."

Joshua looked down at the tow-headed, freckled boys possessing equally ornery smiles. "And just what are my nephews up to this morning when they should be in school?"

"It's Saturday," Jeremiah said, scratching his head.

"Boys that cause a ruckus at the store before nine in the morning should be in school, even if it's Saturday." Joshua grabbed them by the ears and pulled them along with him across the street.

"You gonna take us out to the shed and tan our hides?" Jedidiah asked cheerfully.

"Nope."

"Gonna throw us in jail again?" Jeremiah shared a gleeful glance with his twin.

"*No*," Joshua said firmly. That had not been one of his better ideas.

"You gonna tell Ma?"

"Course I am. But that's not your punishment. You were disturbing the peace, and as the deputy, I'm duty-bound to see to your retribution."

"What's reboluting, Uncle Josh?"

"Retribution, Jeremiah. Retribution is you and Jedidiah whitewashing the outhouse behind the jail. Now."

Moans assaulted the peaceful morning air. Joshua smiled in

satisfaction as he gave them a double smack on identical rears in the direction of the assigned outhouse.

"Don't miss any spots. I'll check."

"Hey, Josh," a familiar voice spoke from behind. Joshua turned to see his best friend since childhood, Evan Masters, approaching.

"Morning, Evan. Where are you headed in such a rush?" Joshua smirked. He knew exactly where Evan was headed.

"Don't start, Josh Whitley. I'm helping the reverend." Evan didn't stop walking.

Joshua followed him with his hands in his pockets and a grin on his face. "Well, sure you are. And what is that I hear? Why, is that Miss Beatrice starting her scales on the piano at the church? Warming up to practice for a good hour, I bet. You helping the reverend for an hour, then, Evan?"

Evan shot him a disparaging look as he headed up the path to church. The scales from the piano got higher and louder every step they took.

Evan turned around and huffed at Joshua. "I figure it's as good a time as any to fix that pulpit that's been rocking back and forth and making us all seasick during services."

"Well, you best get to it, then," Joshua gestured toward the church. "But if our pianist ever decides to leave us, I hope our church building doesn't fall to pieces."

Evan scoffed and disappeared into the church. Joshua chuckled as he headed on down the street toward the Sheriff's office.

Once inside the quiet, empty building, Joshua was tempted to think about the saloon girl again. He busied himself by opening mail and answering letters. He went out to hang up a wanted poster and saw his sister, Mary. She was hanging laundry in the side yard of the house she shared with her husband, Isaiah McAllister, and their seven children, ranging in age from thirteen to just a few months.

Watching Mary, with children tugging at her skirts from dawn to dusk, always made Joshua wistful. He hadn't thought it would take him this long to find a wife and start his own family. The day he turned eighteen and inherited his grandfather's farm, as stated in the will, he was determined. He had planned on marching off to the first church social and claiming the sweetest, kindest, prettiest little maiden he could find in the collection of innocent girls ready to marry.

There had been pretty girls sending shy smiles his way. He hadn't minded the thought of bringing one home to the Whitley farm. But he'd been following the Lord long enough to know when he didn't have peace about a decision. And now, at twenty-three, he was still waiting for that peace to show up.

And starting to wonder if it ever would.

Seven

"He's a handsome man. There's no denying it."

Kathleen heard the voice of Celeste at the door and turned, sheepish that she'd been caught watching Joshua Whitley. "Who's that?"

Celeste smirked. She had dressed and combed her pretty auburn hair in a loose bun. She came forward to look out the window beside Kathleen.

"Too bad the good deputy doesn't come around here much. At least not for social reasons." Celeste gave a wistful sigh and directed Kathleen to sit on the bed. She kneeled in front of her and opened a small bag of medical supplies. "Sorry I was touchy this morning. Rough night."

Celeste pulled Kathleen's blood-soaked stocking down and removed the makeshift bandage. Kathleen winced, gritting her teeth against the pain.

Celeste poured water from the pitcher over the wound. "Logan did this?"

Kathleen nodded. "He cornered me in the alley. He'd have done plenty more, but the deputy stopped him."

Celeste was sober. "Logan's a bad egg. Bad as they come. And he's obsessed with you, Kathleen. That ain't good. Especially since you won't give him what he wants."

Kathleen gasped as Celeste applied a sticky paste to her wound and wrapped it with a bandage from knee to ankle. "Are you saying I should?"

Celeste shrugged as she replaced the pitcher and basin on the stand. "I'm not saying anything, Kat. If you were one of the other girls, I'd say give him whatever he asks for and he'll get over you. But you and I both know you don't belong here. I don't want to be the one to tell you to change who you are forever."

"I shouldn't have come here," Kathleen said quietly, looking down.

"Why did you?" Celeste turned back and crossed her arms over her middle. "What happened to make you choose this? Aren't you from a decent family?"

Kathleen gave a humorless laugh. "That depends on which family you mean."

"You got more than one?"

"Not till recently." Kathleen sighed, rubbing her hands over her skirt. "I found out everyone I loved has been lying to me my whole life."

"That's tough," Celeste acknowledged, though she didn't seem surprised.

"My real mother was Clara McCloud." Kathleen pointed to the picture on her nightstand. Celeste picked it up and studied the likeness.

"You mean *the* Clara McCloud? Some of the older men talk about her sometimes. Wasn't she murdered twenty years ago?"

"Seventeen." Kathleen swallowed the familiar lump in her throat.

"So you were a baby." Celeste set down the picture. "And your pa?"

"My real father is the man I knew as my Uncle William. He never told me the truth. He let me believe my aunt and uncle were my parents."

Kathleen expected Celeste to be disgusted, but the other girl only shrugged.

"Did he have a good reason?"

Kathleen felt tightness in her chest, unwilling to consider the possibility that haunted her every waking moment. "They said he was trying to protect me. But he could have told me the truth and taken me home as his daughter when he married Aunt Amelia. I was five. He just left me there and had his own children with her to replace me."

Celeste frowned as she gathered her supplies. "Who knows? Maybe your pa is horse dung. But maybe he was just thinking of you, or of the folks raising you. It all comes down to motivation, don't you think? And you won't know his until you ask him."

Kathleen glared at the floor. She wouldn't do it. She couldn't admit there was a chance her father wasn't trying to hurt her when he abandoned her. It was the same as saying she had no reason to have let herself fall into such a pit. It would mean she was here because of her stubborn nature, not because she had been hurt and could not be mended.

It would be all her fault.

"No," she said, shaking her head. "He knew what he was doing. And I hate him for it."

Celeste opened the door. "I guess you know what you're saying better than I do. But we both know this hellhole ain't worth throwing away your life, even if your parents were trash." Her eyes darted to the window where Kathleen had been watching Joshua Whitley. "You know, your handsome deputy would know all about that."

Kathleen looked up. "What do you mean?"

"He's got his own sad story. But you didn't hear that from me." Celeste started to close the door, but she leaned back into the room. "I'd avoid Logan. But that's only going to hold him off for so long. Eventually, he'll take what he wants. You won't be able to stop him."

If it was possible for one day to be worse than another in a brothel, Kathleen had a bad night. She felt a higher power was assembling a list of all the reasons why she would never again be worthy of favor. As if she needed the reminder.

She was exhausted after dancing three shows and sidestepping Logan for another two hours on Sunday night. When Kathleen finally fell into her bed, her injured leg aching, dawn seemed to come the second she closed her eyes. And dawn always brought the rallying efforts of the temperance society.

She heard the sound of glass smashing. Dutiful voices rose in a somber rendition of *Onward, Christian Soldiers.*

Kathleen stood and pulled a robe over her chemise. When she joined the others at the balcony overlooking the theater, her cheeks flamed when she noticed some hadn't bothered with the robe. Or any other clothes. Kathleen suspected it was an attempt to shock the temperance women enough to make them leave.

On this particular morning they were not to be deterred, not even by wanton nakedness. After demolishing the front windows with a hatchet, Mrs. Cooke stood on a chair and began a vigorous sermon.

"Ladies, I applaud your presence here today. Evil will not be vanquished among the citizens of Dempsey unless we are dedicated to the cause. We follow in the footsteps of our beloved Home Defender, Mrs. Carry Nation. We strike the word *fear* from our vocabulary as we seek to destroy the possessions of the sinful owners of this establishment." She held up the hatchet she had used to smash the window. "This hatchet represents our commitment to starving children, beaten wives and slum conditions brought on by the demons of alcohol, tobacco and prostitution."

Another voice interrupted. "That hatchet is also all the evidence I need to lock you up in the jail, Mrs. Cooke."

Joshua Whitley's voice gave Kathleen's heart an unexpected flutter. She tried to see him from her position at the top of the stairs, but he was hidden behind the group of indignant women.

Mrs. Cooke allowed her adoring followers to help her down from her precarious perch.

"Mr. Whitley, why do you insist on impeding the righteous battle we are waging in the name of the Lord?"

"I'm all for singing and praying for lost souls. I do both on a regular basis. But I can't let you destroy property, and you know it. When you break the law, *you* are impeding the battle," the deputy answered calmly.

"I have the blessing of the sheriff, may I remind you," Mrs. Cooke said with a sniff.

"I can't speak for the sheriff. But I do know when he's gone to Columbus, he trusts my judgment. And I don't intend to let anyone break the law, no matter what they are trying to accomplish."

"We are on the Lord's mission!" Mrs. Cooke's distressed tone rose over the murmuring of the group. "Take up your law with God, if you are righteous enough!"

Joshua sighed. "The Lord and I are pretty close, Mrs. Cooke. And it doesn't have a single thing to do with my own righteousness."

Elizabeth Cooke narrowed her eyes and placed her hands on her hips as she leaned toward him. "You are deceived, sir. What doth Scripture tell us but that 'many shall come to me in that day, saying Lord, Lord, did we not cast out demons in thy name, and did we not heal diseases? And I shall say unto him, depart from me! I never knew you.'"

Kathleen heard Joshua chuckle. "Ma'am, I don't know what you're trying to accuse me of, but I know sure as I'm standing here that by grace I was saved through faith, not of myself, it is the gift of God; not of works, lest me or anyone else try to boast about it."

Mrs. Cooke huffed and started fanning herself with her flyers. She took a quick look back through the broken window and laid eyes on the group gathered at the top of the stairs. She quickly looked away.

"Let us leave this wicked place, fellow soldiers," she called to the group.

"Hold up there," Joshua interrupted. "You all need to understand if you cause any more damage you will spend the night in jail and pay for the repairs. There is a right way and a wrong way to go about fixing what's wrong."

Mrs. Cooke did not answer. Her dismal group followed her in an unlikely parade down Dempsey's Main Street. They were all dressed in black as if part of a funeral march. Eventually someone began to sing and they all joined mournful voices, singing *Am I a Soldier of the Cross?*.

Kathleen saw Joshua clearly with the women gone. She watched his expression. His forehead crinkled in concern as a thought struck her without warning.

He reminded her of Uncle William. Her father.

"Jesus, look after my town," Joshua murmured. His quiet words bounced off the high ceiling and touched her ears.

"I will be pressing charges, Deputy." Rita came out of her office to inspect the mess.

Joshua kept his eyes averted. He must have caught an eyeful earlier. "You won't. Not unless you want me to press the issue of the saloon staying open on Sundays. Get this mess cleaned up before someone gets hurt on the glass."

Kathleen watched Rita for her reaction, but was surprised when the woman said nothing in reply. Joshua shifted, hesitating.

"I need to speak to the girl called Kathleen. I'll meet her in back."

He made his exit, but not before suggestive whistles and laughter filled the air, all directed at Kathleen. She felt her cheeks flush.

"Deputy's got himself a hankering!" One of the girls said and they all laughed.

Kathleen went to her room and dressed in her plainest dress. She pulled a brush through her hair and donned her Stetson before she slipped down the stairs and out the back door, her heart pounding. What could he possibly want with her? He wouldn't ask her to... would he? She had judged him to be decent. But did she really know anything about him?

When she saw him through the door, he was standing a ways off, staring into a small section of wooded area beyond the saloon. Her heart pounded. He would not realize it, but he was in her sanctuary. She hadn't told anyone. It made her breathless to see him standing there in the place where she had spent so much time.

"Someone's got a garden going here," he said, turning as she approached him. He gestured to the small section of earth where a tidy collection of flowers and vegetables had been planted and tended.

"It's mine," Kathleen said quietly. "I love planting things. Reminds me of my...." Her voice faded.

She reached within the plants and picked several ripe strawberries. She offered them to him, but he shook his head with a puzzled expression. His gaze stayed on her face as he watched her eat the fruit.

He cleared his throat. "Rita lets you have a garden?"

"Rita doesn't know."

The corners of his mouth pulled upward. "I see. Well, your secret is safe with me."

Kathleen peeked at him, trying not to smile. The silence became uncomfortable, and she dreaded the question she had to ask. "What do you need, Deputy?"

He pulled out the tin of salve from his pocket and held it out to her. "Wanted to return this. And make sure your wound was tended."

Kathleen glanced down at her leg, where she noticed he was trying not to look. "I'll be okay. One of the other girls helped me."

"And the man who did it? Will he hurt you again?"

First chance he gets.

She shrugged. "I told you. I fell down the stairs."

He frowned, and she mourned the loss of the merry way his eyes crinkled in the corners. His gaze left her face and looked at something behind them. She guessed Rita was watching them.

"I better go," Kathleen said.

"Why don't you let me help you? I could see if I can get word to your family." His voice became earnest and quiet.

When she saw his sincerity, she wished it was possible to accept his help. That it would do any good. Angry tears stung her eyes.

"My family doesn't want me back. There's no saving me now."

His frown lingered. "I don't believe that."

She shrugged again. With great effort, she turned away. She felt like she was turning away from hope. He didn't follow, and disappointment mingled with relief. It didn't make sense to her why a man of the law and of God would try to help her instead of condemn her. She didn't understand his hesitation. He should be confident in his rejection of someone like her.

Nevertheless, when she stole a glance backward, concern was written in subtle shades across the lines of his features.

After Kathleen finished the shows that night, Logan met her by the stage. He grabbed her arm and yanked her forward, causing her leg to throb in protest. She tried to twist free, but he easily pulled her against him and wrapped his other arm around her waist.

"Rita said I can do whatever I want to you," he whispered in her ear.

Kathleen struggled against his iron grip. With a sinking sensation, she realized she had come to the end of her innocence and possibly her life as well. She could blame no one else. It was the inevitable consequence of living in a saloon.

He pulled her across the room and shoved her through Rita's open door. Rita stood up and came to Kathleen, grabbing a fistful of her hair.

"You have tormented that man and made him nearly murderous." Rita's voice was quiet, but lethal. "You're of no use to me dead, and I don't want a mess to clean up or that insufferable deputy poking around again. It's time to give yourself to the life you chose."

Kathleen went limp. She knew Rita was right. There was no turning back now. But when Rita pushed her out and closed the door, and Logan grabbed her arm and dragged her toward the stairs, she panicked. She thought of her family, of the looks on their faces if they could see this degrading scene. Her mama would be devastated. Papa would be so disappointed. Jennifer, her sister, would be repulsed and shocked by the length of her fall. Aunt Amelia would cry for her. She had always thought the best of Kathleen. She had always encouraged her to be her best.

But the face that caused Kathleen the most pain was that of her father. She was proving he should have abandoned her. She was worthless as a daughter.

Logan opened the door of Kathleen's room and pushed her inside. He closed the door behind him and wedged the chair under the knob just as Kathleen had done to keep him out. He turned, and she saw the wild hunger. He was crazed with it.

It's my fault. I did this.

She whimpered as he came closer. She gasped as he grabbed her arms, tightly squeezing them with his calloused fingers.

"You're all mine."

She felt tears wash her cheeks. She would just stay alive. She'd live through the horror and survive, because she couldn't die. She couldn't face God, especially if she would have to do it with a body as defiled as her soul.

But one look into the eyes of her captor, and she suspected she would not survive the night.

Why don't you let me help you?

Had Joshua Whitley really meant it? Had his offer been made after he counted the cost?

She had no choice. She couldn't die. In one terrifying moment of decision, she brought her knee up between Logan's legs with every ounce of power she possessed.

It worked. He doubled over in pain. She did not hesitate. She ran to the window and climbed out, desperately shimmying down the roof over the porch awning and sliding to the ground.

Her dress was torn. Her leg was throbbing. But she was free, if only for a moment. She only had one chance. It was too late to change her mind. Going back into the saloon would mean the end of her life.

She only hesitated a second as she tried to recall the location of the Whitley farm. When she was confident she remembered the right direction, she jumped on the back of a jittery brown stallion tied to the saloon post and convinced the animal to run.

Eight

Joshua hesitated to go home that evening, but he had to milk the cow and take care of the animals. He had a list of chores a mile long he'd been putting off too many weeks. As he walked out of town, he prayed for the saloon girl, Kathleen, asking God to protect her. He knew the Lord could provide a way of escape. He knew it well.

He worked until the sun went down, managing the regular chores and mending the fence in the west field, glad he'd be able to let his horse graze again. She was going crazy locked up in her stall all day. When he lost the light, he gathered his tools and headed back to the barn.

As he started to swing closed the heavy door, a sudden and urgent sensation came over him. He stared into the woods, dark with shadows. He was past sure something wasn't right.

"Show me, Lord," he breathed, moving among the trees, straining to see by the faint lantern light. He heard the sounds of a horse rambling through the brush. The horse stopped and he heard the rider dismount. His fingers fumbled for his gun as something came at him.

Something warm, and quite female.

In the dim light, he saw that he was holding the girl from the saloon, Kathleen. He pulled her out of the woods so he could assess what was wrong in better light. Her clothes were torn and her leg was bleeding again. She was crying.

"Kathleen? What's wrong?" He asked the question even though he could guess the answer. He surveyed the woods behind her, half expecting Logan to follow.

"He's going to kill me," she said, confirming his suspicion.

Joshua sighed, holding up his lantern closer to the woods. "Honestly, I think I'd be out of a job if it weren't for that saloon of yours."

An awkward silence followed. He stared at the path leading into blackness.

"What makes you so sure he's going to kill you?" Joshua asked.

She didn't answer immediately. He assumed she was afraid to offend him with too many details. Little did she know how familiar he was with the details.

"I... I refused him a few times, because he scared me. He became obsessed."

"How did you get away?"

Kathleen looked down, obviously embarrassed. "I kicked him. In the..."

His eyebrows rose, and he had a momentary desire to chuckle, which he stifled.

Rustling of leaves in the distance moved him to action. He grabbed the reins of the horse and ushered both the horse and Kathleen to the barn. He led the stallion into a dark, empty stall next to his own horse. "Go to the back of the stall. Cover yourself with straw in case he comes in."

She did as he said while he closed the barn door and pushed the crossbeam into the slats. He watched Logan approach from the tree line.

"Where is she?" he growled.

"Who'd that be?" Joshua kept his voice even, glancing at Logan only briefly before he returned his attention to the bag of grain he was opening. He shoveled out corn to the flock of chickens standing around him, complaining that they hadn't been seen to until night was beginning to fall.

"Don't play games with me, Whitley. I heard her voice. She belongs to me, fair and square. I paid Rita. You can't have her."

Anger took hold of Joshua so hard his head hurt with the tension. But he stifled his reaction. "Nobody here but me, Logan. And you're on my property. I'm armed and well within my right to protect my interests. You best be on your way."

Logan snarled and stepped closer. "You tell that little adventuress I'll find her. She can't hide forever, and she don't belong to you. I'll have what's due me."

Joshua gritted his teeth together and put his hand on his weapon. "You threatening a woman, Logan? Right here in the presence of the law? I've put men in jail for less and I don't mind taking you back and locking you up right now."

Logan gave a caustic laugh. "A *woman*?"

Joshua didn't flinch. He pulled away the flap and rested his fingers on the handle of his Smith and Wesson, given to him by his grandfather who used it in the Great Rebellion. He'd also taught Joshua how to use it, and use it well.

Logan saw the gesture and understood the meaning, and only hesitated a moment before he turned and slinked back into the brush where his horse waited.

Joshua sighed and tapped absently on his holster. What was he supposed to do with Kathleen now? He really didn't have much of a choice but to march her back to the saloon and throw her back in the lion's den. There was no better option. But it didn't sit well with him. Not at all.

He waited until he was sure Logan was gone before he opened the door. He wasn't so much of a fool that he believed the man wouldn't come back. He'd have a few drinks and return, if he was as obsessed with Kathleen as she had hinted. If she'd been refusing a man like Logan, he was as dangerous as a keg of gunpowder in a bonfire.

He saw her in the dim light from the window. She sat up with an expression of terror. Why had she refused the man in the first place? Had she been teasing him? It didn't make sense for a saloon girl to turn away a paying customer.

"You were right to think he might kill you."

She didn't answer. He went to her and held out a hand to help her up. She stared at it, as if he was crazy to be polite to her. How long had it been since she was treated with respect? He pulled his hand back and reached for the lantern instead, holding it toward her so she could see. She stood up with difficulty. He watched her features, soft in the glow of the low light.

"I don't blame you for not wanting to touch me," she said quietly.

He shifted his stance. "Logan could be hiding in the trees. I'll saddle my horse and get you back to town." But he made no move toward the chestnut mare's stall.

Kathleen's gaze fell to the straw-covered floor. "I don't want to go back."

He felt torn. What was he supposed to do for her? He felt powerless. "You think I want to drop you off in a place like that, knowing that man will most likely be there waiting for you? I can't tell you how many times I've wished that whole place would just go up in flames."

She didn't answer or look at him. He sighed. "Come on, then. I'll see to the horse you stole after I see to you."

He turned abruptly and left the barn. She followed him out, and he closed it behind them. He headed down the path over the bridge and up to the farmhouse. When he stopped and looked back, she stood by the barn, fidgeting as if she didn't know what to do. He motioned her to follow.

Not waiting to see if she did, he headed for the back door of the pretty white farmhouse his grandparents had built nearly fifty years before. He tried not to think of what Grandma Nellie might say about him inviting a girl like Kathleen into her kitchen.

Come to think of it, he wasn't really sure what Gran would say. He knew she'd help her. But would she approve of Joshua getting involved at such personal risk?

"What's going to happen to you for disappearing tonight?" He turned as the screen door slammed, enclosing them both alone in his kitchen. He went back and closed the main door, bolting it for the first time he could remember.

"The usual." Kathleen didn't seem to want to elaborate. He could guess what the "usual" entailed. And, truth be told, her punishment would probably come in the form of Logan, waiting for her in her room. He wished he hadn't asked the question.

He sighed as he lit the lamps in the kitchen from the lantern he was still carrying. A sopping red bandage on her bare leg drew his immediate attention. "You're bleeding."

She looked down at the pool of red on his kitchen floor and gave a small gasp that seemed to resound in the pit of Joshua's stomach.

"Come here," he said, motioning for her. He lifted her onto the large butcher's block in the center of the room. His hands wanted to linger on her waist, and his eyes begged to feast on what the risqué costume revealed, but he forced himself to look away. He went to the drawer and retrieved bandages and iodine. He brought a basin and set it under her leg, and went to the pump outside the back door to get fresh water.

"I can do it," she said meekly when he came back to her.

He shook his head. "Just hold still."

He took off the bandage as gently as he could and pressed a clean towel to the wound to mop away some of the blood. He could see the original wound had been reopened with new injuries. She'd probably got them when she fled from Logan. The wound bled freely. It looked angry and red and felt warm to his touch.

"I think you're going to need stitches."

"I don't think the doctor will see me." She shook her head.

"Who said anything about a doctor?" He went to Grandma's sewing basket on the table in the hallway. He pulled out a needle and thread. After threading the needle and soaking it in iodine, he cleared his throat and brought the needle close to her skin.

"Hold up the light," he instructed. She reached for the lantern, her hands shaking. He tried not to let it bother him when she gasped as the needle met her wounded skin.

She squeezed her eyes shut and her knuckles went white as she held the side of the table. "Do you have any experience doing this?"

He shrugged. "Probably more than you have stitching up yourself."

He worked in silence a few minutes, stealing glances at her face. "I've been in the saloon before when Doc Thomas was stitching folks up. You're the first that hasn't let loose a string of words that would make my grandma faint dead away."

She had bit her lip so hard it was bleeding. "It's not because those words aren't occurring to me."

He reached the worst part of the wound, and she cried out and pushed his hands away. He stuck the needle in the hem of her dress and walked to the pantry. High on the shelf, he found a tumbler and an ancient, half-gone bottle of whiskey Grandma had kept for situations just like this one. He poured a small amount into the glass and handed it to her. He was surprised at the uncertainty in her eyes.

"I've never tried it before," she said with a frown.

He was confused. "You live in a watering trough but you never drank the water?"

She shrugged and shifted. "I don't like the smell. Or how it makes men act like fools."

He shrugged, having no argument. But her simple admission had caught him off guard. He didn't expect her to be perceptive. Smart. It was strange to find such a girl inhabiting a building known for foolish and risky behavior.

"Well, I don't disagree. But in this case, think of it as medicine. It's going to kill the pain a bit if you drink a couple swallows." He handed her the glass and left the bottle within her reach. She was still uncertain, so he resumed his task of stitching. After a long moment when he could feel the depth of her pain by the tension in her body, she grabbed the bottle and took a deep gulp. He smiled as she coughed a groan of repulsion.

"I don't see the draw," she sputtered, setting it down. But he noticed that her eyes dulled a bit and her body relaxed.

"That little needle looks funny with your big old fingers around it," she said, watching him work. He didn't miss how her gaze traveled to his arms and face. He wanted to give her a study as well, starting with the shapely leg he held in his grasp, and even more the uninjured one next to it. He looked away, but his eyes only caught on her revealing neckline and bare arms.

He cleared his throat and made himself focus on the wound. Just the wound.

"I never liked having a man look at me before just now," she said in a quiet, slightly slurred voice. The whiskey was bringing forth truths neither of them needed to hear. He didn't answer, but he did wonder again why she had chosen her profession if she didn't like men looking at her.

"I'm sorry," she whispered.

He shook his head as he stitched. "Sorry for what?"

"That I'm dressed like this."

He chanced a glance at her face. How else would a saloon girl be dressed? His head was starting to spin at the strange conversation. And it only got more peculiar.

Kathleen waited until he glanced at her, and then she held his gaze, her eyes holding him captive while she said what she needed to say. "Deputy, I need you to marry me."

He dropped the needle and almost fell off his stool. He heard himself laugh – not in humor, definitely not in humor – but in disbelief.

Nine

"If you don't marry me, Logan will kill me." Kathleen twisted the fabric of her dress at her sides. She was ashamed of herself, but she couldn't seem to stop talking. "I'm scared enough of dying that I'm not ashamed to make a fool of myself and beg."

He didn't answer. He gave his full attention to stitching, silent for long moments following her request. Finally, he was finished. The wound was bandaged and there was nothing else to keep him from answering her question. He stood up and rubbed his nose in a nervous gesture.

"I don't blame you for being scared to die. And I won't let it happen if I can help it. But I can't just *marry* you. Marriage is for life. God means for us to take it seriously."

She shrugged, sullen. "I'd rather a decent fellow have me than Logan."

She watched him continue to shake his head as he moved around the kitchen. When he finished washing at the sink, he turned around and raked nervous fingers through his hair.

"It's okay." She crossed her arms over her chest, embarrassed. "I don't know what I was thinking. Of course you can't."

She expected it to be the end of the conversation. But he didn't move. He seemed to rally every bit of strength to catch her gaze directly. She tried to imagine what he was thinking the way Aunt Amelia imagined the thoughts of the characters of her novels. Only difference was, Kathleen had no say over how this man felt. She wondered if he saw more than a saloon girl. Did he see who she had been before her world came crashing down around her?

He tore his gaze away and left the kitchen. The back door slammed behind him. A moment later, she heard bits of softly spoken prayer.

"Lord, it goes against everything I've been taught... a woman like her... Not her, Lord. Not this way."

Kathleen's face burned as she had no choice but to listen. She hadn't expected him to take it up with God. She knew what *he* would say.

She eased herself down from the table and crept down the hallway outside the kitchen. It led to a front door. Stairs went up to a landing above. A cozy parlor greeted her from the other side of the staircase, and another door led to the back porch where the deputy still stood, his back to her.

She watched him, affected again by his physique. She was not one to be overly interested in the appearance of men, as some of the saloon girls were, but she could not help noticing Joshua's. His arms were thick and tanned from working in the sun. His chest was broad and his jaw strong. Wistfulness invaded her spirit. What if she had met him under different circumstances – before she threw her life away? If she hadn't reacted so badly to the discovery of the lie she'd been told, maybe she would have been worthy of a man like Joshua Whitley.

Joshua returned a few minutes later and found her sitting on the stairs in the dark.

"We're going back to town," he said simply, not offering an explanation.

She could guess what it meant. "I had a feeling that's how your prayer meeting would end."

He frowned, but said nothing else as he directed her back to the barn.

"The horse you stole is still recovering from the run through the woods. I'll take care of him and return him in the morning. We'll take my horse tonight." Joshua saddled the horse as he explained. He helped her into the saddle, taking care not to jostle her injured leg.

Kathleen reached down and patted the neck of the beautiful horse. Horses made her long for home. They made her think of her father, who had taught her to ride when she was six. When she thought he was her Uncle William.

Joshua swung up in the saddle behind her, causing the leather to creak and the horse to fidget with the added weight. She was overwhelmed by the feeling of his body close to hers, his strong arms encircling her. She breathed in his scent as it surrounded her. He smelled of earth and animals and the faintest hint of old-fashioned cologne.

When Dempsey came into view, she felt his breath close to her ear, which brought a rush of warmth to her middle.

"I'll find a way to save you," he said in a gravelly voice. "I promise."

She tried to smile at his sentiment. But they were in front of the saloon and he was lifting her down. Rita was opening the door. In a few moments, she would belong to no one but Logan, and he would kill her.

"How nice of you to return my wandering lamb," Rita said in a mocking tone. "However can I thank you? Might I offer you a drink?"

"You will make sure no harm comes to Kathleen tonight," he ignored her sarcasm. "I'll check on her in the morning, and there will be consequences if she is so much as touched."

A flicker of unease flashed in Rita's eyes, but she didn't allow it a place. "Go on, Deputy. She's not your concern anymore unless you have the money to pay for her time."

He didn't answer, neither did he back down from his glare until he was astride his horse and she was back inside the saloon. As soon as Kathleen was inside the door, Rita pushed her against the wall, digging her long fingernails into Kathleen's arm.

"How dare you run to the law, you impudent little wretch? After everything I have done for you! If Bill Logan doesn't kill you by morning, I'll do it myself."

Rita spat the words and pushed Kathleen in the direction of the stairs.

Tears flooded Kathleen's vision as she limped to the top of the stairs. She closed her door and sat down on the bed, wishing she had any right to pray for help.

She was about to meet God anyway, one way or another, and she was more than deserving of eternal punishment.

Ten

Joshua sat on the bench outside his sister's home for an hour. All the while he tried to convince himself Rita wouldn't call his bluff. Surely she would protect Kathleen, if only for one night. Just one night, so he could figure out what to do with her.

It wasn't a surprise when he saw Logan saunter through the swinging doors.

Joshua sighed and headed back to the saloon. Rita met him at the door as if she'd been waiting for him. "Unless you're drinking or buying time, you'll have to leave."

"I saw him come in here, Rita. Let me through, or I'll call the judge and reinforcements from Columbus first thing in the morning and this place will be shut down. If Kathleen is hurt when I get up there, I'll put you in a jail cell tonight and say whatever I have to say to make sure you are locked away for good."

He wasn't sure who was more startled by his threats – Rita or himself. But she stepped aside and let him pass without comment.

Joshua took the stairs two at a time and went to the furthest door. It wouldn't open. He heard Kathleen's cries, and a surprising panic came over him. He stood back and kicked the door open.

Logan stood over Kathleen. Her clothes were more torn than they had been before, and her cheek had a nasty red mark. Blood dripped from her mouth.

Logan sneered at Joshua, reaching for his gun with one hand as the other held Kathleen's hands together behind her back.

"You can have what's left when I'm done with her. Get out, lawman."

Joshua knew his case would be shaky if he tried to arrest Logan. If he was going to arrest one saloon patron for disorderly conduct, he'd have to arrest them all, and they wouldn't fit in Dempsey's small holding cell. But without Logan actually killing her, Joshua couldn't arrest him for murder. He tried to think, but the sight of Kathleen, hurt, brought a rush of unwanted memories.

"Deputy, I insist you leave," Rita said from behind him.

Joshua ignored her and stared hard at Kathleen. "You can press charges. Obviously, he's hurt you, and I can at least put him in jail overnight for that. You have to say so, though, Kathleen, or I can't lawfully do anything."

"Kathleen," Rita said, and the hardness of her expression told Joshua all the things she didn't say aloud. If Kathleen said anything, she would pay the price, and would only prolong the inevitable. She was powerless. Her only option was to try to stay alive while Logan assaulted her.

Joshua's mind grasped for a solution. He crossed the room and grabbed Kathleen's chin, pretending to examine the cut on her lip. She stared at him with uncertainty.

"Hit me," he whispered as Logan began to complain to Rita behind them. "Hit me as hard as you can, and make it convincing."

She shook her head and stared at him like she was afraid of him, too.

"Do it. Trust me." He willed her to do it. It was the only way.

As Kathleen contemplated his strange request, Logan returned to the bedside. She saw him. It was only seconds before she brought her fist back and slammed it forward into Joshua's jaw.

He drew back with a yell. "Of all the fool things to do when someone's trying to help you!" He saw her fear intensify at his outburst. "Now I'll have to arrest you for assaulting an officer of the law."

She understood then. He saw the light go on in her expression.

She even put up a fight for show as he attempted to handcuff her. Rita threatened every sort of retaliation in her arsenal while Logan roared at the violation of his rights. But Joshua managed to get Kathleen down the stairs and out the door.

Once they were in the jail, Joshua took off his coat and put it over her shoulders. He gave her a handkerchief for her split lip and ushered her into the cell. He went to the closet and got her a pillow and blanket. He handed them to her and closed the door, locking it with a loud clanking that seemed more a sound of security than of punishment.

"I know this is only a temporary solution," he said. "I'll figure something out."

She stared at the armful of comforts and covering he'd given her, confusion in her expression.

"Why do you care what happens to me?"

He shrugged and didn't look her in the eye. "I just believe in hope, that's all."

He wondered if she could read the untold story in his words. He fastened the keys to his belt and took his rifle from the weapons cabinet behind the desk before he went to sit on the bench outside.

He contemplated the hole he'd just dug for himself, and the longer he did so, the more confused he became. By the time dawn started playing with the corners of the horizon, he was past ready for some sound guidance. He locked the outer door of the jail securely and made the short walk to the parsonage beside the church.

Pastor Thomas Merchant opened the door after Joshua knocked. Though bleary-eyed from sleep, he still gave Joshua a welcoming smile. "Joshua. Please come in."

Joshua stepped over the threshold, rubbing his hands together in a nervous gesture. "Sorry to wake you up so early, but I need your advice something fierce."

"Of course. That's why I'm here." The pastor motioned for

Joshua to sit in the parlor and went to the kitchen to put the kettle on for coffee. When he returned, he sat down across from Joshua with an expression of concern.

"What happened?"

Joshua took a deep breath and blew it out, leaning forward and resting his elbows on his knees. He had no idea where to start. "The truth is... I've got a woman sleeping in the cell at the jail. She's from Rita's."

A silence followed, and in those moments the two men shared a conversation deeper than spoken words. So deep it dug a hole to the past.

"How are you involved, son?"

Joshua shook his head. "This girl has a monster after her, Pastor. I don't have a solitary doubt in my mind he'll kill her if I don't do something. But I have no earthly idea what to do."

Pastor Merchant was thoughtful. Troubled. "What does the girl say?"

"I don't know. She's scared to say anything because Rita's threatening her. I do know she's scared of dying. Enough that she asked for my help."

The pastor sighed. He leaned back in his armchair and tapped his fingers in contemplation. "I understand why you can't walk away. I'm not going to try to stop you from intervening."

Joshua gave a quick nod, thankful for the understanding.

"You arrested her to get her out of the reach of this man?"

"I did," Joshua said. "But I can't hold her. Rita will be back in an hour or two demanding that her *property* be returned, and there's no question that devil will be waiting for this girl. He's fixated on her."

"I see your problem. And it reminds me of a verse in Proverbs. *"Hold back those stumbling to the slaughter."*

"The thing is... I know this will sound crazy, but she asked me..." Joshua hesitated, loathe to say it aloud. "She asked me to marry her. She said she was willing to beg, she was so scared of dying."

The pastor raised an eyebrow, but did not comment. He went to get the coffee. When he returned, he sat for a moment in thought. "I suppose that would solve the problem. Although I doubt it would completely deter her pursuer, if he is as persistent as you believe he is. Still, she would have your protection."

Joshua took a big gulp of coffee, burning the roof of his mouth. "So what do I do?"

"I guess you have two choices. Marry her and be willing to make her problem your problem, too, or take her back and pray for her safety."

Joshua tossed his hat on the other side of the couch and ran a hand through his short hair. "I was kind of hoping you'd know a third option."

Pastor Merchant watched him. "You could try to find her family or someone who would be willing to take her in –"

"I tried. She's either scared of them or too ashamed, but she refuses to try to contact them. Maybe they're no better than Logan."

Pastor stood and came to him, putting a hand on his shoulder. A kind smile touched his face. "Then your choice is simple."

Joshua breathed a nervous laugh. "All due respect, Pastor, this ain't simple at all. Her being what she is, well, how's a man supposed to overlook that? In the Old Testament the people of Israel were told to execute harlots."

Pastor Merchant nodded. "And God also told Hosea to marry one."

Joshua was overwhelmed. He stood up and paced the length of the room.

"I'm not trying to tell you what to do, Joshua. I don't think there's a right or wrong answer here. You're choosing justice or love. Much of the choices we make in our lives boil down to those two pursuits."

Joshua stopped pacing. "I never said I loved her. I don't even know her. How could I choose love?"

Pastor Merchant smiled. "You wouldn't be so torn up over this if she hadn't affected you in some way. But even if you had known nothing about her, love would still be a choice. I know it's hard to believe when you're young. You have a picture in your mind of a girl who is innocent and sweet and beautiful – everything in one person. If it helps, you aren't going to find that girl if you spend your whole life looking. But the good news is that love doesn't have much to do with those things, anyway."

Joshua fought the gentle admonishment. He *would* find the perfect girl. They *would* share a perfect life. It was his non-negotiable plan. He had been under the impression God agreed.

"Gran and Grandpa were perfect for each other," Joshua argued.

The pastor sat back down and took a sip of coffee. He had a nostalgic smile on his face. "Son, when you lived with your grandparents, they were living out their last years. They'd already made the mistakes. You know that. Love takes a lifetime for God to patiently sculpt away all the rough material he has to work with. What you end up with is never what you started with."

Joshua rubbed his chin and exhaled loudly.

"God is giving you one of those rare opportunities in life to learn what *his* love is like. You can take it or leave it. But be sure you're willing to live the rest of your life with the decision you make."

"How could you even suggest it? Knowing what you know?" Joshua stared at Pastor Merchant.

"I didn't suggest it, Joshua. It seems God wants you to make this choice."

"But why would he do that? After everything? How can I even be sure she'd stick to a marriage covenant? How –"

"How do you know she won't betray you?"

Joshua clamped his mouth shut. He pushed away the memories. He didn't need them clouding his judgment like a thick fog.

"I know it's hard to take a leap of faith," the pastor continued calmly. Compassionately. "But you can be sure you'll find he's able to see you through, whatever you decide."

Joshua turned away. "This is too much."

"God's ideas can seem a little strange to us when we don't have the whole picture."

The moment came when Joshua let go. He released his plan with another long and deep exhale. Long minutes followed. Joshua collapsed on the settee with resignation and fingered Mrs. Merchant's crocheted doily covering the armrest.

Did Kathleen know how to crochet or sew? Did she have any idea how to run a household? Would she be a good mother?

A *mother*? He could hardly believe he was considering the motherly capabilities of a saloon girl.

She was beautiful. She was the most beautiful girl he'd ever laid eyes on. But could he ever bring himself to touch a woman that had given herself to other men? It went against everything he believed.

"I know one thing for sure," Joshua said. "I can't let her go back. I'll die before I let it happen. I keep thinking of all the reasons I shouldn't marry her, but the truth is, if I'm going to love in some fashion of the way Jesus loves... well, that's why I'm here, right?"

The pastor's eyes were glassy with tears. His voice was soft when he spoke. *"Love as I have loved you and gave myself up for you."*

Joshua nodded. He nodded with all the hesitation and certainty he felt.

"Would you like to pray together?" Pastor Merchant offered.

Joshua took one more deep breath. "I think that's a good idea, considering afterward I'm going to ask you out to my farm to perform an early-morning wedding."

Eleven

Turning points in life made a soul notice the tiniest details.

Kathleen stared at the worn leather covering the reverend's Bible. She memorized the dips and fanciful turns of the shapes scrolling the carpet under her feet in Joshua Whitley's parlor, thinking of how they matched the churning of her insides. She noticed her feet, clad in garish satin slippers. His, in weathered work boots.

The lantern light cast disproportionate shadows on the ceiling, to remind them it was barely light outside, and weddings shouldn't happen under a veil of darkness.

"Join hands," the pastor instructed. There was a pause, heavy and lingering as Kathleen felt Joshua struggle within himself. Finally, he grabbed hold of her hand. He held so tightly it made her fingers ache.

She didn't blame him for his hesitation. She had her own rushing tide of uncertainty. She felt like she was drowning in it. What was she doing except heaping more wrong choices upon bad decisions, piling them higher in some peculiar effort to end her life with the biggest pile of grief a girl could garner?

"Do you, Kathleen Able, take this man to be your lawfully wedded husband? Do you promise to love, honor and obey Joshua for better, for worse, for richer, for poorer, in sickness and health, for as long as you both shall live?"

"Yes," she said before she could consider the impossible nature of the things she was promising. "I do."

"Do you, Joshua James Whitley, take this woman to be your lawfully wedded wife? To love and cherish her, protect her and keep her, no matter what, as long as you both shall live?"

Joshua took a ragged breath and his eyes searched the ceiling as if he might find the answer there. Kathleen almost told him not to think about the words. She wouldn't hold him to the promises. It wasn't as if she could live up to her side of the agreement, anyway.

"I do," he said, quickly and softly.

"Then in the name of Jesus Christ and according to the laws of the state of Ohio, I pronounce that you are man and wife. Joshua, you may kiss your bride."

The reverend cleared his throat, as if he hadn't meant to say the last part but it slipped out as a matter of habit. Joshua pulled at his shirt collar, but when he glanced at his friend, Evan, who had come to be their witness along with the pastor's wife, the two men seemed to share a silent exchange. Evan's expression held an amused challenge. Joshua glared at him, then turned and leaned to kiss her on the cheek.

Very quickly.

"Amen," Evan said with a grin.

"Thank you, Pastor," Joshua said, letting go of Kathleen's hand. "I appreciate your help today."

"Of course. Don't hesitate to ask if you need anything else," the pastor replied.

Joshua nodded in response, but everyone heard the words he didn't say.

There's nothing you can do to get me out of this now.

"I guess we better get out of your hair." Evan poked Joshua in the ribs with his elbow. "So you two can get to know each other."

Joshua didn't smile. He saw them out, and when he returned to the parlor, Kathleen felt the charged tension in the room. She stared down at her folded hands and waited for him to say something.

He took the lantern from the side table, though light was beginning to shine dimly through the curtains.

"I'll show you to your room. I think we could both use some rest."

He started up the staircase. If Kathleen had been able to find any words, she would have thanked him. But it seemed peculiar to thank a man for marrying her against every last bit of his better judgment.

When they reached the top of the stairs, he opened the first door on the right.

"You should be comfortable in here. Help yourself to whatever you need."

She nodded, her face burning. She heard the implication. They would not be sharing a room or a bed.

"We'll talk more about this arrangement later today," he continued, and she heard weariness in his tone. "Just try to get some sleep."

Joshua went to his room, which used to be his grandparents' bedroom. He closed the door behind him, staring with renewed grief at his deceased grandparents' things left behind, as if to taunt him. Grandpa's spectacles stayed on the bedside stand right where he left them the night he died. Gran's homespun dresses still hung in the wardrobe. But there would be no fatherly advice. No maternal comfort. He was on his own.

"Why, Lord?" The words fell on the quiet air as if one too many emotions had been shelved in his mind and they were toppling.

He'd been thinking about courting Audrey O'Malley. She was nice. Pretty. He could have married her, or one of the other girls in town. It would have been a good life. They'd have had kids. Joshua always wanted lots of kids.

Now he was tethered by an inseparable bond to a girl who had, no doubt, given herself to more men than she could count. He didn't know how he'd ever overcome the disgust.

He went to the window and looked out over his farm. *Why would you send me back to this place? You know the worst details. You saw me as a boy, cowering in the corner while men did unspeakable things. Why would you bring me back to all that pain? I just wanted to forget.*

He leaned his head against the cold windowpane. "What now?" he whispered. "Will we be stuck here for the rest of our lives? I know you say all things are possible, but I don't see a way through this."

He thought of the girl across the hall, and the weight of what he'd done hit him like a load of bricks. His lungs struggled for air. His fingers burned as he grasped Gran's curtains in his trembling hands.

He'd made her safe, at least for this night. But at what cost?

Twelve

It took Kathleen a long time to fall asleep that first morning in her new home. She wasn't used to absolute silence. The only thing she could hear was Joshua's voice – mumbling prayers.

The sun was high in the sky when she woke. She stretched, reveling in the peace. Her stomach rumbled, indicating it was well past time to eat. She sat up. Her dress was folded across the chair where she'd left it that morning, dirt-stained and ripped across the front. Her blood-soaked stocking was beyond repair, and she couldn't very well wear one without the other.

She wondered what to do as she looked down at her bloomers and camisole. She'd left Joshua's coat downstairs when they had gone to bed. She couldn't wear a coat around the house, anyway.

She went to the basin to wash, her attention catching on the embroidered hand towel decorated with a carefully sewn rooster. A smile pulled at the corners of her mouth. It looked like something Mama would make.

Oh, to go back and make different choices.

She went downstairs, feeling a tremor of nerves when she heard Joshua moving around in the kitchen. He stood at the sink, downing the last swallow of a cup of coffee. He looked her way until he noticed she was not dressed. His gaze quickly went back to the window, to the tangle of trees beyond revealing a bright red spot of color. She assumed it was the barn beyond the creek.

"Folks living on a farm can't sleep the day away," he said. "Get to the chores before I get back. I'll be home at five."

"Where are you going?" Kathleen moved to the pot of coffee, wondering where the cups were. He took one from a peg on the cupboard and set it in front of her without looking at her.

"I need to go to town and check on things at the saloon. I want you to feed the chickens and milk the cow."

He took his hat from the stand by the door and quickly made his exit.

Kathleen ran after him, feeling the crisp cool of the morning through her thin undergarments. She wrapped her arms around her chest and called after him. "I've never fed chickens or milked a cow! I grew up in town! And what am I supposed to eat?"

He sighed, rubbing his chin. "Plenty of eggs."

"Where?"

"I usually look under a chicken."

Kathleen wanted to run after him and shake him. She had no idea where anything was. She had *no clothes*. She understood he resented her being there, and she knew he'd given up everything to keep her sorry life safe, but there was still so much they hadn't discussed.

"What if Logan finds me here?"

"If you hear anyone coming, find a place to hide. I'll make sure I know where he is in town and I'll keep a lookout on the road leading out here."

"So I'm here for slave labor?" She wanted to take it back as soon as she said it. He didn't turn back. He shook his head and walked faster in the direction of the barn. She sighed and went back into the kitchen. If this was the way it would be, she'd just have to figure out how to take care of herself.

And he could look after his own wretched chickens.

Her first item of business was to look for something to wear. In Joshua's room, of all places, she found a grandmotherly pink robe.

She donned it and set out. Instead of trying to wrestle eggs from their owners, Kathleen took her cup of coffee and gave herself a tour of the farm. Outside the kitchen she found a cozy porch with a mismatched rocker and chair. She passed through the bricked courtyard with the water pump and woodshed until she found a large washtub and clothes wringer. She eyed them with uncertainty. Mama had always sent the laundry out, and in the saloon someone else was responsible for washing clothes. The thought of scrubbing her new husband's long johns and hanging them out to dry caused her face to heat.

A summer kitchen was attached to the woodshed. She opened the door and found the small room filled with canning supplies and dried herbs hanging from the ceiling. She stepped inside and breathed in the robust scent.

To her delight, when she came back out of the summer kitchen she was facing an immense, gated garden. It occupied the south field. She stopped at the gate and took in the sight of the wild, untended plants that wound around each other in a chaotic dance of vegetation. A supply shed just inside the gate held as many tools, seeds and other necessities as a gardener could possibly need or want.

"Oh, Mama," she whispered. "Wouldn't you love to see this?"

Most of the garden was neglected. Weeds were rampant. But she thought she spotted beans, peas, carrots and lettuce at first glance. She would have to sort through them to find what was hidden beneath the tangle of overgrowth.

Beyond the garden she found an orchard of apple trees and grapevines which were kept company by a few sheep. She took an apple from the ground, wiped it on the robe and bit into the juicy, tart flesh. So many apples were on the ground, rotting. It was a shame to see so much go to waste.

Kathleen surveyed the rolling fields nestled within stretches of forest. This farm had been built to sustain a family. To build a legacy. She wondered why Joshua had waited so long to start his own family. There was so much potential here.

She wandered through the pumpkin patch where pumpkins

waited, whole and perfect, for someone to tend them. Further down the path she found a smokehouse and a root cellar. Several old jars of canned goods remained from the last woman who had cultivated and harvested the bounty. Was it his grandmother? When had she died? She could guess when she saw the empty shelves covered with dried leaves and spider webs.

The smokehouse was empty as well. What did this man eat? How did he expect to make it through winter?

She crossed the bridge and climbed the short hill to the barn. A picturesque pond flowed from the creek. Ducks and geese waddled by as a cow stood munching, swinging her tail back and forth with a look of abiding disinterest.

Kathleen was followed into the barn by chickens that strutted around her and clucked loudly. She had seen the long henhouse in the south field by the garden, so the birds had traveled a ways. She supposed they were hungry.

"I don't know what you're supposed to eat," she said, shrugging at them as if they could understand her. They did not give up their loud protest, so she looked around until she found a sack of dried corn against the door. The chickens seemed interested, so she opened it and spread some on the ground.

They didn't seem very grateful.

She looked in the horse stalls, but they were empty, so she assumed Joshua had taken both the horses with him to town.

Unable to avoid her chore any longer, she armed herself with a stool and bucket she found just inside the barn. She walked around and pushed open the gate that led to the enclosure where the cow stood.

Cow and human eyed each other with equal distrust for some time until Kathleen set her stool down and placed the bucket under the cow. She reached for an udder and made a face as she pulled. Was that how it was done?

The cow glanced at her as it chewed and swished its tail. Kathleen might have imagined it, but was the cow mocking her? She sighed as she continued to pull the udders with no luck.

The cow stamped, impatient.

"Well, where is it?" Kathleen demanded. She pulled harder. The cow stepped back and knocked over the bucket. Kathleen had to set it right before she could try again. Finally, a thin stream of milk flowed. She squeezed and pulled until her arms burned, but barely managed to cover the bottom of the pail with milk.

"Blasted cow," she muttered. The cow must have been offended, because it shifted just enough to knock over the pail again. The little bit of milk she had collected ran into the grass and disappeared into the dirt.

Kathleen stood up and kicked the bucket. She was tempted to kick the cow as well. "Fine. It will be your fault when *Master Whitley* doesn't have his cup of milk at supper."

She spent the rest of the afternoon trying to think of something to make for dinner. She pulled a few carrots from the garden and gathered two cans of ancient beans from the root cellar. She might have found more but she heard slithering under the shelves and decided to give the occupant some space. She braved a flurry of feathers and squawking to gather eggs. She ended up with a pecked hand and two eggs for her fifteen-minute battle.

When she arrived at the porch to the kitchen, the door was opened. Had she left it that way?

She heard a creak on the floorboard inside and glanced up at the position of the sun. Joshua had said he would return at five, which was still nearly an hour away.

Maybe he's early.

But Joshua would go to the barn first to care for the horse.

Her heart pounded.

Thirteen

The girl standing at the stove may have been more startled by Kathleen than she was of the girl.

"What are you doing here?" Kathleen said breathlessly, her arms filled with meager supplies. She dumped them on the butcher's block. An egg fell off the side and broke on the floor.

The egg went unnoticed by the girl, whose entire attention was taken up by Kathleen's lack of clothing. The girl's hands fluttered to the collar of her shirtwaist, as if the gesture might somehow cover Kathleen's indecency.

"Sorry," Kathleen said, feeling exposed as she hastily reached for the sides of the robe and pulled them together. "I don't have anything else to wear. Are you supposed to be here?"

The girl gulped. "I'm... I'm Annie. I make dinner for Uncle Josh and tidy up."

"Does he pay you?" Kathleen pulled a rag from the sideboard to clean up the egg.

"Yes," Annie answered. She turned back to the stove and stirred whatever was steaming in the pot. Her hands were shaking.

"I'm guessing it's going to be my job from now on," Kathleen said. "Though I won't be getting paid."

Annie looked back at her, confused. "Who are you?"

"I'm Kathleen. Your uncle and I got married this morning."

Annie's face went from pale to ghostly. Kathleen hoped she

didn't faint. She helped her sit and grabbed the newspaper from the table to fan her. "You okay?"

"Uncle Josh is *married*?" Annie said in shock.

"It was a last minute decision," Kathleen tried to explain. Without really explaining.

"Oh." Annie pressed her hand to her temple. "I had no idea. I even said hello to him in town this morning on my way to school. Why wouldn't he say anything? And why don't you have any clothes?"

Kathleen didn't see a way around the truth. If Annie was Joshua's niece, she was going to find out, anyway. "I was working at the saloon. The costume I was wearing was torn when I escaped. Your uncle married me to save me from a bad man who would have hurt me. Maybe killed me."

Annie's eyes grew wider.

Kathleen cleared her throat and gestured to the stove. "Where you did you find food? I've been looking all over trying to find something to feed him. The shelves are bare and the garden has been abandoned."

Annie nodded. "Uncle Josh has been so busy in town he didn't get to the womanly chores. We've been saying forever that he needs to get himself a wife, but no one is ever good enough for him…" She stopped.

Kathleen decided to spare her further discomfort. "Well, if I'm going to have any earthly idea how to take care of this farm, I'm going to need a little advice. I grew up in a town, and I've never done farm chores before today. Can you help me?"

Annie seemed worried at the request. "I better check with Ma first."

Kathleen nodded, feeling ashamed. She'd almost been able to forget she was a stain on society. She shouldn't even be talking to a young girl.

Kathleen was headed to the water pump with a bucket when she heard voices. Twin boys cackled as they wrapped a little girl in the hammock by the woodshed, apparently against her will. She wailed.

"Joshua James Whitley!" A woman's voice matched the sound of the girl's squawking. "What kind of man gets married without telling his only sister?"

So Joshua *was* home. She heard him mumble something and then go silent as his sister lectured him. They were standing on the brick path between the back porch and the summer kitchen.

One of the twins lost interest in terrorizing the girl and left the other to the task. He ran up to stand beside the woman and proceeded to parrot everything she said.

"Of all the things you've done, Joshua, this takes the cake!"

"Uncle Josh, you get a cake."

"You *married* her?" The woman continued as if the boy wasn't there. "Did you consider simply putting the man in jail? Or shooting him? Isn't that what a deputy does?"

"You really shoulda shot him, Uncle Josh." The twin nodded with enthusiasm.

"Honestly, Joshua, sometimes I don't know what's going on in that head of yours. How could you throw away the rest of your life for one sticky situation with a stranger?"

"Sticky." The boy made a face. "Like syrup."

Kathleen peeked around the corner and saw Joshua, hands buried in his pockets and his eyes on the ground. "I know, Mary. I don't need the reminder. I'm the one that has to live with it."

"Ha!" Mary stomped her foot. "You are *not* the only one. We're a family. Now *my* children have a s-a-l-o-o-n g-i-r-l for an aunt. Are *you* going to explain that to them?"

"Mama, what's a sa-loony-girl?" Another young girl appeared from behind the summer kitchen with a bouquet of dandelions.

"Heavens, child, who taught you to spell? You're not even seven!"

"My teacher," she said with a prim smile.

"Get inside, all of you." Mary herded them toward the back

porch. Kathleen jumped back and went inside where Annie gave her a curious look. She'd probably heard every word of the conversation outside.

The kitchen seemed to shrink as everyone entered. Mary set down the baby and helped the toddler, who'd been freed from the hammock, to find the box of toys in the hall. Everyone stood awkwardly as Mary laid eyes on Kathleen's state of undress.

"My lands," Mary held a hand to her mouth as she took her first glimpse of her sister-in-law.

Joshua gave Kathleen a sullen expression. "Mary, do you think you could sew her a decent dress?"

Mary narrowed her eyes and glared at him. "You got a whole heap of nerve, Joshua James."

"A whole heap," the twin repeated with a shake of his fist.

"Is that a yes?" Joshua leaned back against the table where he tore off a piece of Annie's freshly baked bread. He stuffed it in his mouth and chewed as the children began to clamber for some. He tore more pieces and passed them out with all the patience in the world.

Kathleen glanced at Joshua and found he was almost smiling at Mary. When she looked back at Mary, she saw the sister was also trying not to smile.

"Of course I'll sew her some clothes," Mary said and punched him lightly in the arm. He feigned injury.

Mary turned to Kathleen. "Forgive me my outburst. I'll send Annie back tonight with a few of my old dresses to use until we get some made."

Kathleen was speechless at the woman's generosity, especially since she had assumed the woman highly disapproved of her. "I can't take your clothes."

Joshua stuffed another piece of bread into his mouth. "Will Grandma's dresses fit her?"

Mary gave him a disdainful look. "She can't wear Grandma's clothes. Goodness, Joshua, they're twenty years old and made for a woman much shorter and wider. She'd look ridiculous."

"And she doesn't now?" Joshua gestured to Kathleen's bloomers peeking out from under the robe.

Mary flicked him on the forehead before she looked back at Kathleen. "You're welcome to mine. After seven babies they don't fit anymore, and they never will again."

Joshua snickered. The boys followed suit until they all receive a look of reprimand from Mary.

"I could sew," Kathleen said, though she wasn't certain it was true. "Maybe. If I had a pattern to follow."

Mary scoffed. "You'll have plenty to do around here, especially since my brother is one step away from completely helpless. Annie and I love to sew. Don't we, Annie-girl?"

"We'll make you some really pretty things," Annie promised. She must have been bolstered by her mother's giving attitude.

"Not pretty. Functional." Joshua had a dark expression. "She's had enough pretty for a lifetime."

Mary sniffed as she gathered her little ones. "No woman ever has enough pretty. You leave the dressmaking to me and take care of your wife." She pulled one of the twins down from where he was standing on the butcher's block. "We need to go. I have supper on the stove and Isaiah will be home."

Mary gave Kathleen a quick introduction to the younger children before they left. The seven-year-old was Sally. The twins, Jeremiah and Jedidiah, were five. The toddler, Louisa, was two, and Baby Frank was six months. Mary said she had a twelve-year-old son at home, named for his uncle.

Kathleen watched them file out, suddenly envious of their family. The family she would never have.

Joshua moved to the stove where Annie's supper waited. A perfect beef stew simmered.

Joshua went past Kathleen to wash at the basin. Their arms brushed in the small space. "Supper smells good."

Kathleen stirred the stew and ladled it into the bowls Annie had set out. "Did you think you wouldn't have supper?"

He shrugged as he accepted a bowl. "I know Annie's capable."

The words stung.

Joshua waited until she sat down across from him and then he bowed his head. "Thank you for the food you provide in your goodness. Help us walk in your ways."

They ate in silence. Kathleen enjoyed the stew. The food at the saloon had been greasy and overcooked. It was usually cold by the time she was able to eat. This meal reminded Kathleen of home. Of Mama standing by the stove while her sister chopped onions and Kathleen washed lettuce. Her heart gave an unexpected lurch. All the treasured moments of her childhood, and now they were all poisoned by lies. Kathleen pushed the plate away, rejecting the food that had caused the painful recollection.

When she looked up, she found Joshua was watching her. He leaned forward and rested his chin on his folded hands. "We need to talk about our arrangement."

"I thought it was called marriage."

"I think we both know that's not what this is." He stood and took his bowl to the sink. He turned around and folded his arms across his chest.

She didn't answer. He was right, but it didn't keep the lump from burning in her throat. She didn't want things this way. How was it any better to be safe from unwanted advances of men only to exchange it for the loneliness of rejection?

Joshua shook his head. "Did you expect something else? I have to walk down the street in town now, wondering how many of the men I pass have shared your bed."

She heard the resentment in his voice. She wanted to make him understand the truth, but it wouldn't do any good to explain. He wouldn't believe her.

"How can I ever trust that a woman like you would be faithful?"

Kathleen glared at her uneaten supper. "You don't know me."

"Ain't that the point?" He sighed. "All I see when I look at you, as lovely as you are, is a…"

"Go ahead. Say it. It's not as if I've never heard those words before."

He shook his head. "I don't know what I was going to say. But the first rule in this house is that we don't speak of that life. Ever. You will cook, clean, do some of the farm chores, care for the garden and the laundry. You will dress as a decent woman would dress. I'll ride out and get Mary's dress."

She swallowed back tears of humiliation. "Anything else, *Master*?"

He stepped forward, irritation in his expression. "Don't take that tone with me. It's not my fault you're here. I expect you to earn your keep around here." He turned away from her and headed to the back door.

"Shall I earn my keep in your bed as well?"

He stopped with his hand on the screen door. He didn't turn back as he answered. "I'd prefer we keep to our own rooms."

Fourteen

Kathleen noticed Joshua stayed in the barn when he came back from town. Maybe he was hoping she'd go to bed so he didn't have to see her or speak to her. She didn't hear the door until it was late and she'd already headed to her room. She'd washed the dishes and banked the fire in the stove, hoping to avoid giving him further reason to wish she wasn't there.

She heard him climb the stairs. He paused at the top. She heard the crackling of paper as he set something against the door.

When she heard his door close, she opened the door and retrieved the parcel. She opened it on her bed and unfolded two serviceable dresses. She eyed the necklines and the well-used corset. They reminded her of the past. Of a life before the saloon.

It hurt to consider.

In the morning she tried to concentrate on making the banked fire in the stove ready to prepare breakfast. As she fiddled with the handles, she pulled at the tight collar of her dress. She had forgotten the work it took to maintain a household, and the farm was even more of a challenge. She felt like an inexperienced bride, but as she noticed the dark expression on Joshua's face as he came in from the barn, she knew she lacked the adoring and forgiving new husband.

She continued to poke at the fire until she realized he was watching her. She turned to get eggs from the bowl on the butcher's block. He gave the plate a critical eye when she set it in front of him, but he didn't comment.

He prayed instead. "Lord, we thank you for this day to work and to honor you. Thank you for food to give us the strength. In Jesus name, Amen."

Without looking at her, he pulled down an old Bible from the shelf above the table. He opened it to the bookmarked page and began to read.

"*For, brethren, ye have been called unto liberty; only use not liberty for an occasion to the flesh, but by love serve one another. For all the law is fulfilled in one word, even in this: Thou shalt love thy neighbor as thyself. But if ye bite and devour one another, take heed that ye be not consumed of one another. This I say, then, walk in the spirit, and ye shall not fulfill the lust of the flesh. For the flesh lusteth against the Spirit and the Spirit against the flesh and these are contrary the one to the other, so that ye cannot do the things that ye would.*"

Her mind wandered as he read. She watched his mouth move without really hearing the words he said.

"*But the fruit of the Spirit is love, joy, peace, longsuffering, gentleness, goodness, faith, meekness, temperance: against such there is no law. And they that are Christ's have crucified the flesh with the affections and lusts. If we live by the Spirit, let us also walk in the Spirit.* Galatians, chapter five."

He looked angrier having read the verses. She'd heard the word "lust" quite a few times. Maybe the passage reminded him of her having lived in a saloon.

"Dress fits, then?" He gestured.

She shrugged. "For the most part."

"Is there some reason you're still wearing your hair down?"

Irritation flooded her. She felt as scalded as she had when she was doused by the temperance woman.

"I'm your makeshift wife. You said yourself this isn't a

marriage. You have no right to dictate how I wear my hair."

He seemed equally annoyed. "I have every right. You are living in my house. It is for your own safety that you dress the right way. I expect you to wear your hair in a way that doesn't offend or draw attention to yourself."

"Don't make it sound like you're concerned for me," she scoffed. "You're worried I will make you look bad."

He set his fork down – hard – on the table and brushed past her to the hallway. "Put your hair up."

She saw him stomp off toward the fields instead of the barn. She assumed he was not going into town.

She kept her eye on the field all day. When she saw him approaching the house that evening for supper, her hair was down, and she had unbuttoned the collar of her uncomfortable shirtwaist.

She had also made sure the beans were overcooked.

He eyed the plate she put in front of him. "You know how to make anything but eggs and beans?"

"Didn't do a lot of cooking in the saloon," she replied with an indifferent shrug.

He made no further comment. Instead he prayed over the food and began to eat. When she came from the stove with the bread and tried to pull out the chair across from him, he hooked his boot heel on the bottom rung and pulled it tight against the table.

"You want to sit at this table, you button your shirt and put your hair up."

She stared at him, speechless. How could she have believed Joshua Whitley was kind? She didn't want to be in the same house he was. She turned and headed for the door.

"Tonight is mid-week prayer service at church. You will come with me. You will wear your hair up and you won't wear the hat."

Kathleen pushed open the screen door, suppressing a scream of frustration. Not only did her husband speak to her as if she was an ornery toddler, but he would make her go to church. Had he considered the uproar she would cause?

"I'm not going." She tried to speak without tears, but her voice wavered.

"Fine," he said. "I expect you to be out of my house within the hour."

She trudged down the path to the barn, where she saw Joshua's horse, Sundi, standing within the yard enclosure adjoining the barn. Kathleen opened the gate and swung up onto the horse's back. She grabbed fistfuls of Sundi's mane.

"Ride, Sundi!" she said, and the horse seemed to understand. They flew out of the yard and into the wide expanse of the overgrown north field.

Tears stung her eyes, but they only served to make her angrier. How could he command her to go to church and sit in the pew as if she belonged there? Couldn't he see that he would be shamed right alongside her?

She doubted he would change his mind. He was a stubborn man. Since the only alternative she could think of was to go home and face her family, she would have to endure his church for tonight.

But she would find a way out of this unreasonable marriage.

He was waiting with the wagon and hitch when she got back from her ride. He didn't look at her as he helped her down.

"Get freshened up and I'll pick you up in front of the house in ten minutes."

She glared at him, but he didn't look her way as he busied himself with harnessing and hitching Sundi to the wagon.

Kathleen fingered the ends of her blonde hair, staring into the mirror. She had already buttoned the collar of her ill-fitting dress and slipped on the sensible, nearly-new work boots that had belonged to Joshua's grandmother. The only task that remained was to pin up her hair.

Kathleen had been too proud to tell Joshua the reason she didn't put up her hair. She sighed and pulled her thick locks together and started to shape the "schoolmarm bun," as Aunt Amelia used to say.

When she came downstairs, Joshua was standing by the wagon in front of the house. He was dressed in his good trousers and coat. Her heart betrayed her and starting pounding.

As mean and selfish as he was, Joshua was a handsome man.

His features softened when he saw she had complied with all of his wishes, but he did not say anything as he lifted her up to the wagon seat.

They drove in silence for a few awkward minutes. Finally, Joshua cleared his throat. "I'm sorry. I was harsh."

Kathleen didn't answer, but Joshua was pretty sure he felt her relax.

"Thanks for doing what I asked with your hair," he said. She didn't answer. In fact, she looked away so he couldn't see her face. Was she having the same fight with pride he was?

He was ashamed of the witness he'd been showing her. But it would take God changing his heart for him to do any better in the future. The ache was strong. It continually reminded him of all he was losing in the arrangement and how unfair it was.

"You sound as if you are trying to praise me as you would your horse," Kathleen said. Her voice was sullen, but resigned.

He felt the hint of a smile on his face. "You definitely ain't a horse, Kathleen. I'll give you that."

His grin widened as she fought a smile. It occurred to him she was probably afraid to go to church with him, and he didn't blame her.

"It won't be easy – you going to church. I realize that. But I'm not going to leave your side."

She looked up in surprise, but made no reply. Joshua wished she would say something. Had he imagined the bit of hope that seemed to dawn in her expression?

Joshua stepped inside the foyer of the United Brethren Church he'd been attending since he was nine years old. It was the first time he'd ever felt uncomfortable entering his church. He felt Kathleen's hand on his arm stiffen. Her face was pale. She stared up at the reaches of the spire as they walked through the door, which was old and stern and surrounded by a pointed arch that made a person feel small.

"Josh," Evan met him in the doorway and clapped him on the back. "How's married life?"

Joshua didn't miss the mocking tone, though he doubted Kathleen would pick up on it. "Careful, Evan. What goes around tends to come back around."

They walked forward into the spacious sanctuary that smelled of aged wood and lemon oil. The people met in quiet conversation under a canopy of peaceful sounds from the brand new organ on the right side of the platform. When no one approached them immediately, Kathleen's grip on Joshua's arm relaxed.

"Did you hear about the train explosion?" Evan asked, though his eyes were steadfastly fixed on the woman who was briskly setting forth to take possession of the piano.

"What train explosion?"

"Boiler overheated last night and exploded at the train yard. Quite a few injured. Four killed." Evan tore his eyes away from the woman and looked at Joshua. "I was over at the clinic most of the night helping Doc Luke."

"And you still showed up for church?" Joshua said in mock surprise.

Evan smirked. "You of all people should know that I *never* miss church."

Joshua chuckled as Kathleen eyed him. He nodded toward the dark-haired, solemn faced pianist whose fingers flew across the keyboard as she played an opening selection of hymns.

"Beatrice Walsh, our piano player. Evan here hasn't missed a

Sunday service, prayer meeting or revival since she moved to town," Joshua explained.

Kathleen smiled.

"I'm going to stay after tonight and climb up to work on that pane of glass way up there by the ceiling," Evan said, pointing.

"Something wrong with it?" Joshua played along, sending Kathleen a forbearing glance.

"Probably not, but you never know when one of those panes will just break off and come crashing down on some poor soul's head."

Joshua patted Evan on the back. "Something tells me when Miss Walsh is finished practicing your interest in everyone's safety will mysteriously disappear."

Evan slapped a hand over his heart. "You wound me."

"You should have come get me last night, though. I could have helped, too," Joshua said, his smile fading.

"I would have, but we didn't have a spare moment."

They moved to take a seat in the back of the room where prying eyes were less likely to find them during the service. Evan sat forward and rested his arms on the back of the pew in front of them, continuing to watch Miss Walsh.

"So how's married life? Really? Don't spare the details." Evan kept his voice low so Kathleen wouldn't hear them.

Joshua shifted. "This is church, Evan."

"It's in the Bible," Evan protested.

"I'm telling Miss Walsh to run for her life."

Evan cackled in a most unrighteous manner as Pastor Merchant made his way down the aisle to the platform. The sound caused many to turn around and look at the three of them.

When people caught sight of Kathleen, the whispering started.

Fifteen

Joshua followed Kathleen down the aisle to greet the pastor when the service was over. He shook hands with the older man, who gave Kathleen a kind smile.

"Good evening, Joshua. Mrs. Whitley, I'm glad you're here." The pastor gave Joshua a surmising glance. "Is anything the matter?"

Joshua tried to relax. He knew he should put on a cheerful face for the sake of appearances. "I'm just concerned about the train explosion. Figures it would happen the one day I don't come in. What can I do to help?"

"It was a long night," the pastor said, nodding. "I ache for those poor families, losing their loved ones so violently. But I think the doctor has it under control for now. The more seriously injured were taken to Columbus. I should let you know, Joshua, Bill Logan was one of the men sent to Columbus."

Joshua exchanged a look with Kathleen. "Well, I can't say I'm altogether sorry to hear that," he replied. "Won't have to keep a constant eye on him for a time."

Pastor Merchant nodded in understanding.

"Well, I'll stop by and talk to the doc anyway, just in case." Joshua was going to move on, but Pastor Merchant's hand on his shoulder stopped him. Kathleen moved toward the door without him.

"How are things, really?" Pastor said so quietly only Joshua would hear.

"I don't know what to tell you," Joshua said. Because he didn't. "Things are... as you might expect."

"I can imagine what that means. But it will get easier, Joshua."

Joshua shrugged and looked down at his boots.

"Whatever the past has done for us, there's always hope for a new start." Pastor Merchant waited until Joshua looked at him. "Give her a chance. Don't blame her for the sins of someone else."

"She's got plenty on her own count," Joshua said.

"The same can be said of any of us. If you hold in all that bitterness you carry from your past, you'll regret the burden. I'm here if you need me."

"Thanks." Joshua nodded and moved on to join Kathleen. He stopped when he heard a familiar shrill voice.

"I simply must protest, Reverend Merchant. We have *children* in our midst. *She* shouldn't be allowed to come into our *church*, of all places!"

Joshua turned and stared at Elizabeth Cooke with an even expression. "You want to discuss my wife, you discuss it with me."

Mrs. Cooke gave him a quick, disparaging glance.

"Now, Mrs. Cooke," the pastor spoke. "I beg you to have understanding. Mrs. Whitley is no longer employed by the saloon and she is married to one of our deacons."

"The Good Book warns us not even to eat with such a person! I am alarmed you would not only perform their wedding ceremony, but welcome her into our congregation! I'm afraid my family and I will be unable to continue our worship here if she returns."

The murmuring around Mrs. Cooke began. Joshua glared.

Pastor didn't raise his voice. Joshua was amazed at the older man's knack for gentleness. "The Bible warns us not to eat with people who say they are believers in God's way, yet continue in open rebellion. Mrs. Whitley has left her old life, just as you urged her to do many times in front of the saloon. If the point of your mission is to help women like Mrs. Whitley, why would you desire to keep her away when she has been the first courageous soul to heed your advice?"

As the pastor's wise words silenced the naysayers, Joshua felt the uncomfortable edge of guilt.

Kathleen looked up in surprise at the pastor's words.

She knew condemnation. She understood that sin brought destruction. But she had never heard any of the temperance women speak to her about the possibility of hope for her soul.

What did the pastor mean? Surely he was too kind. Surely it was too good to be true. He spoke as if it wasn't too late for Kathleen.

Mrs. Cooke was the first to recover from the admonishment. "We know someone like that doesn't really change. She's still the same person that did things we would never dare consider. Her sins will cause a stain on the decent folks of this church if you allow her to stay. I will not be corrupted."

Kathleen looked down at the floor, feeling her cheeks heat. She knew the woman was right. She was ugly. She was a mark on Joshua's good name.

Joshua cleared his throat to get the attention of all the church members listening and whispering to one another. "Listen up! Kathleen is my wife. I don't intend to leave my church. I don't intend to let you speak ill of her. You keep your comments to yourself and leave it be, or you can go somewhere else. Your choice."

He left the building before anyone could respond. Kathleen followed him to the wagon without speaking.

Mary and her husband were waiting outside with their family. Well, some of them were waiting. The twins were halfway up in an old oak tree in the yard, shouting and laughing. The two little girls were running across the yard until they tripped over each other and the toddler started crying.

"Hello, Kathleen," Mary said brightly, as if she couldn't hear the children. "We're glad you came. This is my husband, Isaiah." Mary heaved her baby to her other hip and nodded toward a tall man who seemed kind and quiet. He offered Kathleen a quick nod before he had to move to catch one of the twins who had evidently decided to test his capacity for flying.

Mary continued to smile, as if her son's brush with death was commonplace and quite dull. "I've got some clothes ready for you at the house. Would you two care to join us for supper?"

Kathleen figured by the way Mary grabbed her arm with her free hand and pulled her along the street toward their small home that it hadn't been a request. She didn't tell Mary they had already eaten. She was hungry enough, anyway. Her own meager supper hadn't been substantial, and she was sure Joshua felt the same.

Minutes later, Kathleen was staring at a crisply ironed selection of beautiful new clothes spread across Mary's bed. "They're lovely!"

"You should have seen the dreadful fabric Joshua bought," Mary scoffed, waving her hand in the air. "I marched right back to the store and exchanged it for these. No sense wearing ugly, scratchy dresses if nobody's up and died. And you can tell Joshua I said it."

Kathleen couldn't help the small giggle that escaped.

"I made you two everyday skirts, two blouses, a nice green calico for Sunday best and some underthings. You let me know if there's anything else you think you might need. Annie and I can make it up in no time. Or you can join us and we'll make it together. That would be fun, wouldn't it?" Mary folded the clothes, wrapped them in paper and tied them with twine. She set the package in Kathleen's arms and went to the kitchen.

"I put plenty of room in the necklines. I noticed the latest McCalls patterns aren't so drawn up to the chin, if you know what I mean. They look so comfortable I might even make one for myself if I can find the time."

"I don't know how to thank you," Kathleen said, following Mary across the small parlor into the kitchen. She was humbled by the woman's generosity.

Mary shrugged, as if the gift was nothing.

"I do know how to sew," Kathleen continued as she watched Mary stir the gravy and pull a beautifully roasted chicken from the warmer in the stove. "I'm just not very good at it."

Mary was thoughtful as she worked. She seemed to hesitate before she responded. "I admit, Kathleen, I was nervous when I found out Joshua had married up with you. But I've been thinking over it, and I am sure God is going to make this all come out right. And I'll be praying for you. Marriage isn't easy when you go into it lovey-dovey, so it's bound to be a chore when you start from necessity."

Kathleen found comfort in her words. She felt herself relax, even if just a little. She wondered if Mary knew of her brother's resentment toward Kathleen.

"What is it? Best just to spill the beans." Mary winked.

"It's just that Joshua seems... angry. He doesn't want to be near me. I was surprised when he spoke up in my defense at church." It was a relief to say the words.

Mary nodded, glancing out the window where Joshua was playing baseball with Isaiah and the other boys. Her gaze held affection mingled with wistfulness. "There's a whole lot you don't know yet. Joshua had his heart broken, and he's awful slow to trust. Give him time. If you do him good, he'll come around. He's a good man and he fears God above all. You may even come to appreciate these struggles someday."

Mary gave her a conspiratorial smile. "But brace yourself tonight. He isn't going to be happy that I went against him in the matter of your clothes."

Sixteen

Mary was right about Joshua's reaction to the colorful fabrics. He asked to see the clothes when he came inside. When they were unwrapped, Kathleen watched in discomfort as the siblings exchanged a few heated words. Joshua seemed to let it go when he caught a glimpse of the lacy underthings and told Kathleen to wrap it up. Mary winked at Kathleen behind his back.

The children finished their meal in record time and began scurrying around the house like mice – rather noisy mice – until their parents sent them outside to play, even with the autumn sun giving up its last threads of light to the day.

Mary sighed. "Sometimes I believe the whole town is judging me for letting my children be wild. But I fear I'd be nigh to exhausted every moment of the day trying to rein them in."

Isaiah put a hand on his wife's back. "I never saw the point in forcing young ones to be still. Goes against nature."

"What did your parents believe?" Kathleen asked. She regretted it when the room went silent. Joshua's hazel-green eyes looked stormy before he looked away.

Mary watched him as she answered Kathleen. "Our grandparents tried to get us to be still." She smiled. "They were fighting a losing battle with your husband. Joshua couldn't sit for more than a minute. Must be where my young'uns get it."

Kathleen smiled, but her attention was on Joshua. "I'm sorry."

He shrugged. "No harm done."

"What about you?" Mary stood to start cleaning up. "How did your folks handle children *being seen and not heard*?"

Heat flooded Kathleen's face. "My... father was away on business often. When he was home he wanted us to sit quietly and read or play a game. It was just my older sister and I, and we didn't mind."

Another silence followed, as if everyone in the room recognized Kathleen's answer had been as evasive as Mary's.

Joshua stood. "We should go. It's getting late."

Mary piled the wrapped clothes and two helpings of cherry pie in Kathleen's arms as they left. "You come back soon, you hear me?"

As they walked to their wagon, still at the church, a chorus of goodbyes followed them from every corner of the porch and yard.

It was a quiet ride home. Joshua seemed to be brooding, and Kathleen had no interest in talking. She was too caught up in memories that had returned without her permission – of treasured times with the people she had called her family. When she was living the beautiful lie.

She pulled her bonnet from her head and rubbed her temples, trying to dispel the ache settling over her head.

"What were you leaving out of your story, Kathleen?" Joshua said suddenly, pulling her out of her thoughts.

She swallowed. "I could ask the same of you."

He didn't speak again. When they arrived at the farm, he dropped her off in front of the house before he went to the barn to take care of Sundi and the other animals.

She closed the front door behind her and quickly pulled the pins from her hair, feeling the tell-tale ache all over her head and knowing the damage had already been done. She sat down on the stairs and rested her elbows on her knees, cradling her head in her hands.

The pain was so intense by the time Joshua returned that she didn't hear him come in.

"Kathleen?"

She moaned at the sound of his voice. He kneeled in front of her and grasped her arms.

"What's wrong? Are you hurt?"

She pushed her fingers into her temple, willing the pressure and pain away.

"My head," she managed.

Suddenly she was in his arms and he was climbing the stairs. Joshua nudged open the door of her room and set her down on the bed. He went to the water basin and soaked the towel in the water, wrung it out and brought it to her. She held it to her forehead, thankful for the marginal relief of the coolness.

"Do you know what's wrong?" Joshua asked again. She heard the concern in his voice.

"It's just a headache," she whispered.

"I've had headaches, Kathleen. This is worse."

"It's a bad one," she admitted. Her stomach lurched and she hoped she wouldn't lose her dinner in front of him.

He took the cloth and rinsed it before he handed it back to her. "What caused it?"

She felt his strong fingers on the inside of the collar of her shirt, kneading the back of her neck in a gentle motion. The gesture relaxed her stressed body, though her middle warmed with a new sort of tension.

"It… It happens when the weather changes or I'm in bright sunshine too long." She fumbled for the words as he continued to massage her neck.

"Neither happened today." Joshua's voice was gruff.

She hesitated before she admitted the truth. "It also happens sometimes when I put my hair up."

The room was quiet for an endless moment. He stopped rubbing her neck and frowned. "I did this?"

She shook her head. "I didn't say that."

He gripped the edge of the dresser with a severe expression. Was he angry at her for telling him the truth?

"Why in the world would you not tell me?"

Kathleen shrugged. "You were right. I can't be walking around town with my hair down. It's not decent, especially for me."

She tried to pretend he wasn't glaring at her. She closed her eyes and put the cloth on the back of her neck.

"You have to be honest with me, Kathleen. If I had known it would do this, I wouldn't have made you put your hair up."

She was skeptical, but she didn't say it. Joshua would have thought she was making excuses or being obstinate if she had told him the truth.

"I don't feel up to arguing," she said.

"I'm going for the doctor." Joshua moved toward the door.

"Don't go to any trouble. It will pass. I just need to sleep."

He was still for a moment before he disappeared from the room. She got up and paced the room. He came back a few minutes later carrying a glass with a small amount of white liquid.

He held it out to her. "It's laudanum. Gran had some in the sideboard for Grandpa's rheumatism."

Kathleen took the medicine and drank it quickly. Within several minutes she began to relax. She sat down on the bed and lay back on the pillow.

He watched her for a long moment, still frowning, but not in a way that made Kathleen think he was angry. He seemed genuinely concerned.

"Call me if you need anything else," he said in a gravelly voice before he left and closed the door behind him.

She didn't tell him what she really needed. She wanted to lay her head in his lap and have his hand massage her neck again. She wanted his quiet voice, reassuring her, like Mama had always done.

But she knew she had no right to ask for it.

Seventeen

Lightning flashed, illuminating the room as bright as noonday for a moment. Joshua thrashed in his bed, sweat beading on his forehead. A soft moan caught in his throat as he hovered on the edge of the dream.

Rain poured outside the house, down the window pane in swirling rivulets. He grasped the sheet in an attempt to escape the images that beckoned to him from the place in his nightmare.

With each fracturing rumble of thunder, images flashed in his brain he could not control. Could not stop.

He was a young boy. He cowered in the dark room, facing the wall, as if he might push through and flee the scene.

The acrid smell of whiskey was strong. He held his hands over his ears, trying to block the sound of the cruel laughter. Each flash of lightning and desperate glance revealed what was happening behind him. His conscience warned him it was dangerous. Wrong. He closed his eyes tightly as tears squeezed free and fell down his cheeks.

A fearful cry of a familiar voice made him sob. Another angry splinter of thunder. Another flash. The crazed expression of the drunken man sneering at him –

"Joshua?"

He sat up straight in bed, inhaling sharply as another crack of thunder sounded overhead. Kathleen was standing in the doorway.

"What's wrong?" Joshua asked. He was breathless as he tried to shake off the remnants of the dream.

"Were you having a nightmare?" she asked quietly.

He rubbed his eyes and put bare feet to the cold floor. "Yes."

"Do you want to talk about it?" Kathleen sounded hesitant, but curious.

"I hate it when I go back to that place," he said before he could stop himself.

"What place?"

He looked at her, noticing the pretty white nightgown Mary had made her. He dragged his eyes back to her face and cleared his throat. "Your head feeling better?"

Kathleen nodded. "The medicine helped. I was just going for a cup of tea when I heard you."

He reached for his nightshirt, realizing he was only wearing his pajama pants. "I'll get the tea. Go back to bed."

"I don't want you waiting on me," she said. "I'll be fine."

"It's my fault you're sick. I'm getting the tea."

He buttoned his shirt as he went down the stairs. She followed him. He noticed she didn't get a robe to cover her nightgown as she was moving around the house. Grandma had always worn a robe. Maybe Kathleen had lived in the saloon so long she didn't remember.

He put the kettle on and leaned over the butcher's block, still haunted by the impression the dream had left behind.

"I used to have terrors in the night," she said suddenly, surprising him.

He turned and looked at her. "Why?"

She tried to answer and only succeeded in stuttering.

Joshua nodded. "I take it they weren't random."

She shook her head and looked down. For several moments she seemed to wrestle with her thoughts and memories. She winced as if they caused her pain.

"She's always in my dreams, but her face is just out of view. Her arms are always out of my reach."

"Whose arms?"

She looked at him in surprise, as if she didn't realize she'd spoken aloud. "My – my mother's."

The water boiled and he poured the tea through the strainer. He handed her one of the mugs and went back to his place at the table. He supposed he owed her an explanation. "I saw things. As a boy. Things no one should ever see. Sometimes I dream about it. Especially during storms, for whatever reason." He looked up at the ceiling, where they could hear the steady patter of rain against the roof.

She frowned. "But… your grandparents seemed so good."

"My grandparents were the best people you could ever know," Joshua answered immediately. "They were the ones that saved me from that life."

He clamped his mouth shut. She wouldn't understand. She'd lived in a saloon – she couldn't appreciate the scar left on his soul.

"Like you saved me." Her voice was soft and she avoided his gaze. "But it was too late for me."

They were quiet as they finished their tea. Joshua turned down the lantern and the room returned to darkness except for the lingering flashes of light outside. They walked back up the stairs in the dark. As Kathleen went into her room, Joshua put a hand on her door to keep it from closing.

"You're wrong, you know," he said. "If you're alive, it's not too late."

Eighteen

As the days of September passed, Kathleen found a sort of routine.

Life on a farm was not as unpleasant as she had supposed. As her body adjusted, she began to rise earlier, until she started having breakfast ready before Joshua came in from chores and before he left for town. While he was gone, she had plenty of work and was usually surprised when it was time to make supper.

She was determined to prove she wasn't worthless. She knew Joshua was wrong to suggest there might be hope for her, but she still felt compelled to try to convince whatever powers might be watching that she was willing to redeem herself. Even if she only convinced Joshua, at least then she could continue in the peaceful existence she was learning to love.

She kept the house in order, mastered the old country stove and harvested the garden and orchard until she ran out of room to store the produce in the summer kitchen.

She worked in the soil, breathing deeply of the rich scent of earth. She saw the tangible evidence of her labor in her hands, and thought of Mama's garden.

Her mama seemed to have magic fingers that caused beauty and sustenance to spring to life where before there was nothing. It was in the garden she sang to Kathleen and her sister Jennifer. In the garden she told them Bible stories and drilled them on their schoolwork.

Kathleen paused one day in the middle of her weeding. She sat crouched in the middle of the big farm garden, seeing the changes she had made. There came a fleeting longing to show it to Mama. Kathleen could see her, flushed and pretty in the late afternoon sunshine, her mild manner the only thing keeping her from exclaiming with joy at the sight of what Kathleen had accomplished in only several weeks' time.

Kathleen didn't brush away the tears that fell. Her chest ached at the thought of her beautiful, quiet Mama. How could she let those memories go? How could she fathom the truth that Mama was not really her mother?

As dearly as she wanted to hold on to the lie, she felt an undeniable desire to consider the truth. To understand the mother who had given her birth. The information Kathleen had already learned in Indianapolis told her of a beautiful and graceful woman who stole the heart of her true father. But something didn't add up. Clara had been a saloon girl, and yet Kathleen had the impression her mother had been... good.

She paused in her work and lifted her Stetson from her head. She stared at it. It was old and worn, but it was a connection. Wearing it, she almost felt like she was Clara McCloud. Trying to make a different life.

Trying to be worthy.

Kathleen noticed the sun had started sinking in the western sky, so she put away her tools and washed at the pump before walking down to the barn.

She had developed a relationship with the ornery cow, which she called Esmerelda after one of the characters in Aunt Amelia's novels. The chickens had also learned to trust her and came when she called. But her favorite duty by far was taking care of Sundi.

Her affection for horses went back to her earliest memories. Though she had lived in town and her family did not own horses, she frequented the livery and came to know all the animals. Her uncle – father – had noticed her interest and taught her how to ride his horse, a gray named Becky. Becky had a talent for hearing the whispers of a young girl's secrets. She never told.

Kathleen had plenty of time for thinking while she milked. Not wanting to return to her memories, her thoughts went to Joshua.

She hadn't seen him much lately. He left after breakfast, speaking only to wish her a good day or to give her instructions about her duties. Sometimes he would drill her on what she should do if she saw any sign of Logan. When he came home for supper, he gave her the town news, read the Bible aloud and prayed. After supper he went to care for evening chores before he sat in the parlor and read, his eyes so glued to the pages that Kathleen felt she could not interrupt. When the clock struck nine he would retire to his room, shutting the door with an unambiguous click. She heard no more from him until sunup.

She wouldn't admit it to Joshua, but she had started to linger when she cleaned in his room. He had trinkets that covered a shelf, almost as a shrine. The most beautiful item was his grandfather's elegant gold pocket watch with the inscription *J. Whitley*. She studied the photograph of Joshua with Mary and their grandparents. The pose was somber and staged, but John and Nellie Whitley wore kindness and intelligence in their expressions. They held their grandchildren close. Kathleen wished she had known them.

One afternoon she came across Joshua's grandmother's recipe book in the pantry. She made dinner that night from one of the recipes. Though Joshua didn't comment, he ate three helpings of the pot roast and mashed potatoes. She could tell he appreciated the effort.

As she washed dishes afterward, he saw the basketful of apples she had brought in that afternoon from the orchard. Without a word, he went to the butcher's block and sliced several of the apples. He arranged them on a plate and sprinkled them with cinnamon and salt, and then doused them with lemon juice from a bottle he found in the pantry.

"What was that for?" she asked, curious.

He sat down and reached for one of the apple slices. "I used to watch Gran do the same thing. Keeps the apples from turning brown."

She didn't comment as she ate the portion he offered her.

"What do you have on your head there?" Joshua gestured.

Kathleen reached for her head and remembered she had stolen one of Joshua's handkerchiefs from his dresser when she was putting clothes away. She'd tied it around her hair to keep it out of her face while she was working on the laundry.

"I... I should have asked," she said, embarrassed. He gave her a small smile.

"It's cute."

She felt her cheeks go hot and felt the need to change the subject. "I found a dead mouse in the pantry this morning."

He shrugged. "Did you now?"

She frowned at his lack of concern. "Aren't you afraid the creatures will multiply and start biting us in our sleep?"

He grinned. "Never thought about it. Do you worry about that, Kathleen?"

She heaved a dramatic sigh and waved him off as she moved to clean up the kitchen.

But the next morning, Kathleen woke to find a kitten with yellow and white stripes and white paws curled up next to her on the bed.

Kathleen had stopped dreading church by the end of September. It wasn't so much that she enjoyed it, but she was at peace with it. The second week she had shown up at Sunday morning service beside Joshua, Mrs. Cooke, her family and several other families had made a show of standing up and walking out of the building. Kathleen had been mortified, but the reverend's kindness and the tolerance shown by the other members of the congregation made her feel a little more at ease.

The fourth Sunday she was in attendance, she started listening to what the reverend had to say. She couldn't deny her curiosity. On the ride home, Kathleen took a deep breath and broke the usual code of silence she and Joshua had adopted.

"I've been wondering… about Jesus."

Joshua immediately looked at her. She saw the hint of a smile. "What were you wondering about?"

She eyed him. "Seems that bringing up the Bible makes Deputy Whitley find his tongue."

He shrugged. "How do you feel when you talk about your mother?"

Kathleen looked away. "You mean my real mother or my aunt who played the role of my mother?"

He watched her. "I mean the one who raised you."

"I love her," Kathleen said, though it made her sad to consider how much she really did love Mama. "I think of all the wonderful times we've spent together and everything she patiently taught me."

"Well, that's kind of what I feel like when you mention Jesus."

"Why?" She shook her head. "You've never actually met him. He lived so long ago. How can you be as close to him as family?"

"Because that's what he is." A grin possessed Joshua's face, causing the merry crinkles around his eyes that seemed to make them shine.

"But how?" Kathleen couldn't help her smile. She was a little uncomfortable with the subject, but she found she was relieved he was talking to her.

"What do you know about Jesus, Kathleen?"

She tried to remember her Sunday school lessons, which had all but faded from her memory. "He was born in a stable. He grew up to be a great teacher. Men followed him everywhere. One of them betrayed him and they killed him on a cross."

"All true." Joshua gave her an emphatic nod.

She frowned. She was missing something he obviously understood. Her parents, her aunt and uncle, her sister – they had all known that same something Kathleen had never been able to grasp.

She felt Joshua's eyes on her. When she met them, she realized she could see a measure of acceptance and affection she didn't expect. Almost as if he was a different person. He was more than the semi-cordial stranger she had been sharing a home with.

Joshua spoke. "What happened after he died on the cross?"

She tried to remember the story. "He rose from the dead. But I always assumed that was a myth. No one can come back to life."

If they could, I would know my mother.

"Sure they can. Jesus is the one that proved it once and for all. But he ain't like us, Kathleen. He's the Son of God. All God, all man. His power was proven when he conquered death."

She shifted uncomfortably in the seat. "How can you believe that, Joshua? It sounds crazy. You weren't there to see it happen."

He looked back at the road and flicked the reins, mulling over his answer though he didn't appear troubled by her doubts. "There are evidences. But that's not how I know. I believe it because of faith."

"So you just *hope* it's true," she said.

"Not hope. Know."

"But how?" She lifted her hands in frustration.

He was quiet for a time. He looked up at the trees that were showing the first signs of their brilliant fall colors.

"Kathleen, there are things you don't know about me. I'll just say I wouldn't be the man I am if not for the grace of God. And for the love of Jesus."

She didn't answer. She wasn't sure what Joshua meant, and she was afraid to press him further. Whatever he believed about Jesus had made an impact on him. She almost wished the same could happen for her. What would it be like to have no fear of death? No dread of the punishment she deserved?

It would be everything. It would change everything. If only she could believe it was true.

Nineteen

Kathleen trudged up the path from the barn, pulling her sweater around her shoulders as icy wind and rain bit her skin. It would snow any day. Joshua said if the Farmer's Almanac was right, it would be a snowy, cold winter for Ohio.

She imagined being snowed in with Joshua, and it wasn't an entirely undesirable prospect.

She shivered through the milking and stayed close to Esmerelda's warmth. When she was done, she put the full pail of milk by the bridge and went to the barn to feed the chickens, who for some reason had a long-standing tradition of being fed in the barn, far away from their pens.

A distressed whinny came from Sundi's stall. She stopped short as hens clucked around her feet.

"Sundi-girl," she called to the horse. Sundi was usually waiting at the front of her stall for Kathleen's attention and treats.

"Something's wrong," Joshua said behind her, causing her to jump.

"Heavens, Joshua!" She put a hand to her chest and felt her heart racing. "I thought you already left for town!"

He didn't acknowledge her surprise. He went to the stall and opened the gate, motioning her over. "When I came in here this morning she was lying down. Horses don't generally lie down this long unless they're sick."

Kathleen felt a jolt of fear as she moved next to him and saw Sundi's lethargic form. She pushed open the stall door and went to the horse's side. She tried to recall all the sicknesses Becky and the other horses at the livery had experienced through the years of her childhood as she helped care for them. She checked for a puncture wound or broken bone, but felt neither. Sundi wasn't feverish; her belly wasn't distended as it would be with colic. Kathleen inspected the hooves for stones, and noticed that the front two were hot to the touch.

"What?" Joshua knelt next to her. "Do you know what's wrong?"

"The fields aren't overgrown this time of year." Kathleen murmured.

"No. Why?"

She didn't answer. Instead, she went to open the bin where the feed grain was kept. A few of the bags were split open.

"Did you leave this open yesterday?"

Joshua shook his head. "I don't think so."

"Maybe she got it open herself. Naughty horse!" She came back to the stall, wagging her finger at the horse. Sundi whinnied another complaint.

"What is it, Kathleen?" Joshua said in an exasperated tone.

"I think she broke into the bin and ate too much grain. She's got founder," Kathleen answered.

"How do you know?" He watched her incredulously.

Would he ever trust Kathleen's judgment? "My uncle's - a horse I spent time with got it when she was out to pasture too long. The veterinary doctor in Columbus called it 'laminitis.' We have to get Sundi up on her feet, and she's not going to like it."

"Great," Joshua said, making a face. They both pulled and pushed and chided until Sundi finally heaved herself up. She stood awkwardly, her hind feet pushed up under her body in an effort to take pressure off her front legs.

"We need cold water from the pump. In a couple deep buckets," Kathleen said, trying to soothe the horse. "I'll keep her on her feet."

Joshua nodded and went to grab the buckets. "She'll be okay?"

Kathleen smiled and rubbed Sundi's neck. "In a week or two. We'll have to keep her on her feet and keep the hooves cold to get the blood moving. She'll be in pain for a couple days, but as long as we keep her from overeating again, she'll be fine."

"I'll move the feed out to the shed."

Kathleen nodded, expecting him to leave to get the water, but he lingered. She felt his gaze. Finally, she peeked at him.

"Just when I thought I had you figured out," he said with his eyebrow raised.

"Joshua, I did live a normal life before. I know other things besides the saloon." Her voice was soft.

He nodded quickly and turned abruptly to leave.

As Joshua filled the buckets at the pump, he splashed his face as well, gasping at the chilly temperature of the water. He was glad for the distraction. The image of Kathleen standing in the horse stall, capable and beautiful as she cared for his creature, proved a tempting one.

He felt nervous as he made his way back to the barn, and he knew why. Suddenly, all he could think about was stealing a kiss. And why shouldn't he? She was his wife, after all. Perhaps, in all his teasing over the matter, Evan had a point.

He wondered how to go about such a task. He was embarrassed he'd never tried it before, even when Audrey O'Malley had practically given him an engraved invitation. They were seventeen and had been stranded just outside of town during a rainstorm. He'd been a coward. He was afraid she might misunderstand and expect him to propose immediately following, so he'd only held her hand. He could tell she was disappointed.

Now, as then, logic reasoned he would risk too much by giving in. He could lose his head. He could allow things to get out of control and find himself deeper in this mess than he already was.

But it was just a kiss.

He was thoroughly confused by the time he got back to the barn. He could hear her speaking to the horse in sweet, soothing tones. He cleared his throat and brought the buckets into the stall as Kathleen held it open.

"Good," she said, giving him a shy smile as his heart hammered away. "Let's get her hooves in the buckets. She will fight it, so be prepared to make another trip to the pump."

While Kathleen held the bucket steady, Joshua carefully lifted the sore hoof into the water. Sundi tried to pull away, but he kept a sturdy hold and the hoof slid to the bottom of the pail. They did the same with the other one. Sundi gentled as she realized the water helped the pain.

With no other task to keep his attention, Joshua was left standing behind Kathleen, inhaling her flowery smell and trying to keep his wits about him.

He gave in.

He grabbed either side of her narrow waist and whirled her around. She was surprised. Surprised, but not afraid or unsure. Her cheeks were rosy, creating an appeal that nearly stole his breath away. Did saloon girls blush?

This one did.

"Kathleen," he said, leaning as close to her face as he could without actually making contact.

It was time for Joshua to decide. But there was no decision to be made. He pulled on the back of his hat to keep it from colliding with her forehead, and used his hold on either side of her waist as well as his own body to push her back against the post of the stall.

She watched him. She didn't encourage his kiss, but her eyes rested on his mouth. He was pretty sure she wanted him to kiss her. He pushed away the worry that she would laugh at his first attempt, and leaned in to give it his best shot.

At first, the touch caused him pleasure so distracting he could do nothing but remain there for a few moments. Then a desire took the helm and directed him in the happy task of giving and receiving the kind of comfort a kiss was meant to provide. He noticed that she responded, but with hesitation he might expect from a girl who was just as inexperienced as he was.

How did she do that? How in the world did she manage to give him the impression she'd never done this before? Was that just part of the charm of a saloon girl?

A shout outside the barn ended the experiment. He jumped back and her hands nervously reached to smooth her hair.

"Joshua James!"

It was Mary. And a passel of young ones, judging by the other voices. He glanced out of the barn, hoping his sister hadn't seen anything. He could see Evan getting down from the buckboard of the wagon. Joshua scratched the back of his neck and pushed his hat back in place, clearing his throat again.

"Should we do anything else?" He asked Kathleen without looking at her. When she didn't answer and he glanced at her red face, he thought about what he'd asked. "For Sundi, I mean?"

Kathleen was as pink as a perfect sunset. "She... she should have a thick bed of hay to stand on. I'll do it; you see to your sister."

"No sense in that." He looked upward where he could hear scuffling in the loft above them. "Boys, get down here and pitch some hay into Sundi's stall. And if either of you touch my saws again, I'll tan your hides. Don't think I won't."

He gave Kathleen one last, lingering look before he turned and made a quick exit.

Joshua met Evan following Mary's brood into the farmyard.

Evan stopped and gave him a curious look. "What's wrong with you?"

"What? I didn't say anything." Joshua shrugged and buried his hands deep in the pockets of his overalls. "Why are you here?"

"I came to tell you that the sheriff rode in from Columbus this afternoon. He's staying through tomorrow, so you don't need to come in if you got farm chores."

Joshua nodded and sniffed, pushing up the rim of his hat.

Evan grinned. "You kissed her."

Joshua curled his lip with a sputtering huff. "You don't know a thing."

"I know you kissed her."

"How could you know that, you enormous fool?" Joshua sneered.

"You mean, besides the fact that you're blushing like a little girl?"

That was that. It was clear Joshua's best friend was set on getting a good punch in the nose.

But Evan wasn't done talking. "Now are we talking an *actual* kiss, or another one like that sorry excuse at your wedding?"

Joshua shot him a warning look. "It was as real as they get," he growled.

"Okay," Evan shrugged. He stuck his thumbs in his belt loops. "I wasn't sure you knew the difference."

"You're looking to get walloped right now."

Evan smirked. "Tell me what happened."

"Are we a couple of girls who have to sit here gossiping about kissing? It was a kiss. I put my mouth on hers and everyone seemed satisfied with the result." Joshua turned on his heel and walked out into the cow pasture by the pond. He picked up a pitchfork and started baling hay off the wagon and spreading it over the mud. He suddenly felt the need to be about a man's work.

"I just asked," Evan shrugged innocently. "If you're embarrassed about your romantic skills, I'll understand if you don't want to talk about it."

Joshua shot Evan a glare he hoped would garner a little respect. "Alright. I wanted to do a whole heap more than kiss her, if that's what you're asking. I've never been so tempted in my life. Besides you interrupting, only one thing stopped me."

Evan nodded with a look of forbearance. "That you had no idea what you were doing?"

Twenty

The children pulled Kathleen toward the house, telling her of packages Mary had brought. Kathleen saw movement and looked over to see Joshua tackle Evan. They started wrestling in the tall grass by the pond.

No, now they were wrestling *in* the pond. Muscular arms flailed in the muddy water.

"Come on!" The twins pulled her across the bridge. She stopped to pick up the toddler, Louisa, who was having trouble keeping pace, and they made their way up the hill and down the brick path to the back porch. The boys promptly lost interest in their quest to bring Kathleen to their mother when they saw the water pump.

"Kathleen," Mary greeted her with a cheerful smile when Kathleen opened the screen door to the kitchen. Mary was unloading a parcel wrapped in brown paper and tied with string, along with a covered dish, at the same time she held on to her baby with the crook of her elbow. Kathleen set Louisa down and moved to take the baby.

"Thanks. We brought coffeecake. I didn't stop to think how I was going to carry it."

"How nice of you," Kathleen said. The boys' shouting at the pump caught her attention. "Uh, do you want them getting wet?"

Mary sighed and went to the door. "If you two get drenched, you will be traveling home that way, and there will be not a word of complaining, do you understand me?"

As she yelled, little Lou tried to slip out the door. Mary caught her and pulled her back in, eliciting a loud squeal of protest. Her mother hauled her across the room and set her in front of the toys, which successfully distracted her.

"Grandpa made these for Joshua when he was a boy," Mary said, fingering the wooden blocks. "Seems like yesterday."

Mary stood up. "Where in the world are Joshua and Evan?"

"Last I saw, they were wrestling in the pond," Kathleen answered. She thought Mary would think it as strange as she had, but Mary just shrugged.

"And who is this?" Mary picked up the yellow and white cat Joshua had left on Kathleen's bed as the antidote for the mice problem.

"Ginger." Kathleen stroked the kitten that was growing fast into the expert mouser they had hoped. "Joshua gave her to me to take care of the mice."

"She's a pretty thing." Mary set the kitten down and it bounded under the table to hide from the toddler who had caught sight of it.

Since Kathleen had the baby in her arms, Mary unfolded the brown wrap on the butcher's block to reveal a beautiful wool coat. "Courtesy of Annie."

"Oh!" Kathleen reached a hand to finger the fabric. "She did a beautiful job! And how thoughtful of her to realize I needed a winter coat."

Mary smiled. "That's my Annie. She may talk a mile a minute, but she pays attention. Loves to bless others."

The back door opened and Joshua and Evan entered, wet and muddy.

"Joshua James Whitley! What are you thinking – coming into a woman's kitchen in such a state? You two are no better than the twins, and there's no denying it."

They were sheepish as Josh handed Evan a towel from under the sink and excused himself to go upstairs to change.

"Honestly, Kathleen, boys are boys no matter their age. Don't let them tell you any differently." Mary narrowed her eyes at Evan as he went to the sink to try to wipe off some of the mud.

When Joshua returned in a fresh shirt and overalls, he took Baby Frank from Kathleen as if it were the most natural thing in the world for a man to hold a baby. "Try on your new coat."

She pulled it on and reveled in the warmth of the sturdy material. Annie had sewn a soft cotton material to the inside to keep it from being scratchy. It was the nicest coat Kathleen had ever seen, let alone owned.

"Sure looks pretty," Joshua said, surveying her form. She met his gaze with a smile.

"Hmm," Mary mused. She wore a secretive grin as she started cutting the cake.

They sat down, quiet for a few moments as they ate the delicious treat. Joshua occupied himself by staring at Frank's face as he slept. Kathleen observed Joshua watching the baby, surprised at how comfortable he seemed to be. He didn't hold the baby away from himself as men often did when they held infants. Joshua snuggled the little one right up to his chest.

An image came to her mind without her permission. She saw Uncle Will, her father, holding his first son, Harvey, in nearly the same way. As Harvey grew, he rarely left his father's side. He worked in the carpenter's shop from the time he was old enough to pick up a hammer.

Had her father held *her* that way when she was a baby? She swallowed hard and closed her eyes in an effort to shut out the memory of his face.

Mary continued to look from Joshua's face to Kathleen's, but she didn't comment.

Joshua eventually picked up on the fact that Kathleen, and then Mary, and then Evan, were all watching him. He stood up.

"Frankie and I are going to go make sure those boys aren't flooding my entire yard."

Evan returned his attention to his cake. Mary eyed Kathleen suspiciously.

"So what's going on?"

"I don't know what you mean," Kathleen said in a high-pitched voice.

"Sure you do. Have you and Joshua…"

Kathleen clearly heard the suggestion in her words and felt her cheeks go hot.

Evan stuffed the rest of his cake in his mouth and stood up. "Uh, I'm going to… go help Josh." He quickly left.

"Well, have you?" Mary prodded.

"Of course not!" Kathleen protested.

Mary laughed. "You *are* married, Kathleen."

"Well, not in the traditional sense," Kathleen sputtered, avoiding the question.

"Something's going on. I can feel it. It's written all over both your faces. Just tell me," Mary said. "I can be very persuasive if I need to be."

"And I can be very stubborn," Kathleen replied.

Mary raised an eyebrow in challenge. "I suppose I could just ask Joshua." She stood and took an exaggerated step toward the door.

Kathleen panicked. "No, wait! Fine." She took a deep breath. "What do you want to know?"

"I want to know why my brother's staring at you like you're a big old piece of chocolate cake and you're looking back like he's the icing on top."

"I beg your pardon," Kathleen squeaked.

Mary was not deterred in her quest for the truth. "Has he kissed you?"

"I just don't see how –"

"Oh, Joshua," Mary called in a sing-song voice.

"Okay! Yes. He has." Kathleen took a long sip of her coffee and burned her mouth.

"Nothing else?"

"For heaven's sake, Mary!"

"Try the green dress," Mary said as she took another bite of cake. "I made it especially for Joshua. It's his favorite color. And he likes the smell of lavender – there's a bush out in front by the path."

"Maybe if I was trying to ensnare him," Kathleen huffed in disbelief.

"Not ensnare. Woo."

"I thought the man was supposed to do that." Kathleen frowned at her dessert.

"Oh, the man decides when and where, but the woman is the one who makes him want to in the first place."

Kathleen looked up in confusion.

Mary eyed her with curiosity. "You really don't know what I'm talking about?"

Kathleen shrugged. "I've never tried to 'woo' a man before."

"But you were a saloon girl," Mary reminded her. "Isn't that what they do?"

Kathleen looked down in embarrassment. "I danced, I sang, I took men their drinks. I was not interested in attracting any of them."

Mary stared at her for a long moment, her eyes widening in surprise. "Kathleen, are you saying you never..."

Kathleen shook her head with vehemence. "No. Almost – at the end. But no."

"Kathleen, does Joshua know?" Mary gripped Kathleen's arm across the table. Her voice was excited. Kathleen pulled her arm back and frowned.

"You have to tell him," Mary insisted.

"Why does it matter?" Kathleen slipped her arms across her chest. "He's the one that assumed otherwise. He wouldn't believe me if I told him the truth."

"This is Joshua we are talking about," Mary said in a serious tone. "It matters."

"I'm not trying to make him love me. I just need his protection. Anyway, if he did care for me, it wouldn't matter what I've done." Kathleen stared at her cake, suddenly dismal.

"But what if it's the only thing holding him back?" Mary's voice was pleading.

"Then he doesn't love me all that much."

Mary shook her head. "You're making a mistake, Kathleen."

"Not if I don't care either way."

Mary scoffed. "I think we both know better than that."

Kathleen kept quiet. Mary watched her for a long moment and then gave a soft "humph."

Joshua came back inside, two soaked little boys in tow.

"Oh, goodness gracious," Mary said, sighing loudly. "You two go sit by the stove and dry out. And don't touch the stove or you'll get burned."

Joshua must have felt the tension in the room because he shifted uneasily from one foot to the other and stared at the door until Evan returned.

"Any more news about the train yard explosion?" Joshua asked him quickly, like he was hoping to avoid whatever subject was being discussed by the women.

Evan shrugged. "People have been donating food and clothing. But there's no telling how they're going to get through winter if we have a bad one, which folks are predicting."

"What's the word on the wounded that were sent to Columbus?"

Evan shrugged. "If you're asking about Logan, I'm not sure. But he hasn't been back to work at the train yard and I haven't seen him around town. Either he died or he's still laid up."

"Well, at least he's out of our hair for the time being." Joshua glanced at Kathleen. She nodded. She couldn't describe the feeling of freedom that came in knowing Logan wasn't a threat.

They were quiet. Kathleen thought about the families that had been changed forever by the explosion. She knew how it felt to have everything one day and nothing the next. She wished there was something she could do to help those scrambling to find a way to survive the winter.

She sat up. "Mary, have you ever canned?"

Mary nodded. "Sure. But since I live in town, I don't get much from my small garden."

Kathleen smiled at Joshua, excited. He eyed her thoughtfully, and Kathleen remembered the intimate moment they had shared in the barn. Heat spread up the back of her neck when she recognized his expression was the same now as it had been before he kissed her.

Mary smirked.

"Are you talking about the garden?" Joshua said to Kathleen, ignoring Mary.

"And the orchard! There is so much fruit on those trees we could feed a small army for a season. We have more than we'll ever use, even with it all growing wild and the late start on gathering it."

"What about supplies?" Mary mused, tapping a finger against her chin.

"Your grandmother has a monstrous supply in the summer kitchen," Kathleen answered immediately, gesturing in the direction of the small building.

"And whatever you're missing I can get from the store," Joshua said, still watching her with the same expression.

Mary nodded in agreement. "Mrs. O'Malley cans every last pea in her garden, so Dickinson should have plenty of glass jars and sealing wax in the store. Even if he doesn't, he could easily order it from Columbus. Come to think of it, Mrs. O'Malley would love to help us. She learned from her grandmother."

"How much produce do we have, Kathleen?" Joshua shrugged. "Enough to make a difference?"

She couldn't hold back the excited chuckle that escaped from her throat. She grabbed his hand and pulled him toward the door. "Come!"

She led him across the back porch and the brick path to the summer kitchen door. They were followed by a procession of children and several chickens.

She threw open the door and pulled him inside. The room was filled with stacked baskets and large tin buckets of apples, grapes, squash, pumpkins, peppers, beans, peas, carrots and many burlap sacks of potatoes and onions. Joshua, Mary and Evan stared, speechless. The twins whooped and grabbed a few potatoes to try their hand at juggling.

"All this came from my garden and orchard?" Joshua surveyed the bounty. It covered the floor and was stacked as high as his head in places.

"I didn't steal it from someone else's," she teased.

Joshua still held her hand, and he squeezed it. "I had no idea we had so much. I knew Annie planted a few things in the spring, but since Grandma died a couple years ago, I haven't paid her gardens any mind. To think – all the food I've wasted."

He turned to her, admiration making his eyes shine. "You've been busy, young lady."

She felt herself blush. "There's plenty more to be harvested," she said softly. "The more I pick, the more seems to pop up in its place."

"We could do some pickling, too," Mary said, lifting baskets and peeking at all the stock. Evan grabbed a peach for each of the children and sat outside on the step, letting them climb all over him as they dribbled juice.

Kathleen couldn't remember the last time she had felt so content. So motivated. She looked up at Joshua again and caught him smiling at her like he was tempted to stage a repeat of their moment in the barn. She was surprised by the satisfaction of being wanted.

"Sundi!" She suddenly remembered the horse, letting go of Joshua's hand and reaching for the door. "I better check on her."

"Kathleen," Joshua said gently as he caught her hand. "Thank you."

Twenty-One

Joshua watched Kathleen jog down the path. He realized he was holding his breath. When had she become so beautiful?

"Joshua James," Mary said. "You listen up. I want you to hear me loud and clear."

"That depends on what you're going to say." He met her gaze and narrowed his eyes.

She ignored him. "You haven't given that girl enough credit. She's not the same person as Mercy. Not even close."

"Mind your business, Mary." Joshua turned toward the door with thoughts of escape.

She grabbed his arm so hard her fingernails dug into his skin in only the way an older sister could manage. "You're letting yourself be blinded by your insufferable opinions. See her through God's eyes. You'll be surprised at what you find."

He shook off her fingers. Suddenly all the affection he'd been feeling for Kathleen dissipated as he remembered the obstacle that remained between them. How could he have forgotten and allowed things to get out of hand? He shrugged in a helpless gesture. "She was a harlot. I can't change it. Even if I tried to overlook it, it's there, like a big old boulder, sitting in the way of whatever might happen otherwise."

She crossed her arms over her chest and stared at him with a severe expression.

"Mary, I know you know the truth," he said quietly, and saw her features soften. "I'm drawn to her. I admit it. But how do I get past everything in the way?"

"You'll miss *so much* if you don't. I think you're beginning to realize that yourself, little brother. And it will be your own fault. Your thinking has nothing to do with the facts, Joshua. Hear me on this."

He didn't understand what she was trying to say. His sister's womanly sentimental views couldn't overcome the chill of reality. Kathleen had given herself to other men. There was no undoing it. He hadn't been given a choice in the matter, and he couldn't escape the unfairness of it, or the fear that Kathleen would go back to her old ways again in the future.

It wasn't fair, and he wasn't about to act like it was.

Joshua took the wagon to town the following Monday morning so he could bring home the supplies Mary and Kathleen needed for the canning bee they were planning at the end of the week.

He watched Sundi pull the wagon, obviously having regained the usual spring in her step. She had been proclaimed healthy by his resident horse expert.

He'd been watching Kathleen. She was industrious and full of ideas for the farm. He could already see the difference her care was making. His house was starting to feel like home again, in every way, from washed and ironed curtains in his bedroom to neatly arranged sunflowers and marigolds on the kitchen table.

He wouldn't admit it to Mary or Kathleen, but he loved the sight of Kathleen in the cheerful clothes his sister had made. Kathleen had taken to using his handkerchiefs to tie back her hair, and it made his heart hammer away in his chest to see her like that, humming as she scrubbed and stacked and swept and cooked. He'd noticed her meals were starting to remind him of Gran's, and he suspected she'd found Gran's recipes.

It was like his dream was coming true. He had a hard-working, beautiful wife to help him with the farm. If only...

He sat up straighter on the buckboard, clearing his throat. Kathleen wasn't everything she seemed to be. If only that shadow of her past didn't hover over them, spoiling the notion he kept having that he'd sure like to make the whole arrangement a more permanent understanding.

In the evenings, when he pretended to be reading in the parlor, he pondered their future. What should he do with this girl he'd so quickly made his wife? Was it possible in the eyes of God and law for him to annul the marriage when he was sure she was out of danger?

I have loved you with an everlasting love.

He flicked the reins and chafed. He couldn't send her away. He couldn't keep her. So what in the world was he supposed to do?

Joshua found Evan at the clinic helping the young doctor, Luke Thomas, carry crates of medical supplies.

"Aren't you supposed to be at work?" Joshua couldn't remember the last time he'd actually seen Evan headed toward the railroad yard where he was the foreman of the maintenance workers.

"I *was* at work," Evan said in defense. "Doc ordered extra supplies for the injured men from the explosion and needed help unloading and tending the wounds."

"No surprise he needed help. I don't even think the guy went to school. Not old enough."

Evan snickered and Luke made a face at Joshua.

"How are they doing?" Joshua asked as he picked up a crate.

"Better," Luke said. "The two or three I sent to Columbus may not make it, but I believe all the men that are in the clinic will survive."

Joshua sighed. "Such a shame. Did you lose any of your men, Evan?"

"No one from my team, thankfully. But all those men belong to somebody."

Joshua nodded and clapped him on the back. "Let me know what

I can do to help. How have things been at the saloon?"

Evan shook his head. "The same. Isaiah and I had to break up a brawl in the street outside the saloon last night."

"I appreciate you helping me out, Evan," Joshua said. "Are the temperance women behaving?"

"Here they come now." Evan nodded toward the group heading toward the jail.

"Oh, joy. Looks like I've got visitors." Joshua headed for the jail and sheriff's office.

"Deputy, we demand to speak to Sheriff Stacy." Mrs. Cooke sniffed at him as if she was only speaking to him because it was necessary. He was well-aware his good name was in question because of Kathleen.

"You planning another uprising again today, Mrs. Cooke?" Joshua said the words before he thought better of them. Her petty view of the world was irritating in light of what some people were dealing with.

"Where is Sheriff Stacy?" The woman's face looked as red as a beet.

Joshua raised an eyebrow as he moved to unlock the door. "You know where he is. He works most days in Columbus now. I have the authority when he's not here."

"You can't help us," she said in an overly dramatic tone. Some of the women hung their heads and wiped tears from their eyes. Mrs. Cooke continued. "You have been deceived by the demon of prostitution."

"Whoa now, hold up there, lady." He held up a hand of warning. "I ain't been fooled by any demon, leastwise that one. You best mind your words and be on your way."

"I think you protest too strongly, Mr. Whitley," she said, more to the group of women than to him, "which only proves my assertion has merit."

I'll show you an assertion that will put the color right back in your hair, you cranky old busybody...

Joshua checked his attitude with a few measured breaths. "Last chance, ladies. You tell me what you need or you get out from underfoot."

Mrs. Cooke continued to speak on their behalf. "The woman at the saloon told us we couldn't stand in front of the saloon on the veranda. She said she would have us physically removed by her bartender if we did. We want the permission of the law to stand wherever we feel the Lord is calling us to stand."

He squelched the desire to roll his eyes. "It won't make any difference whether you stand in front of the veranda or on it. For your safety, I think you *should* stay on the street. Now leave me be."

Mrs. Cooke sniveled and turned, followed by a dozen others as they marched dutifully back in the direction of the saloon.

"Give me patience, Lord," he said under his breath as he watched them go.

Twenty-Two

Restless energy was as irritating to Kathleen as an ill-fitting shoe on a long walk uphill.

The canning bee was Saturday. Until then, she had nothing to do but chores. She spent every moment she could in the garden, hoeing and pulling every stray vegetable or herb she could find before she prepared the soil for winter by covering it with a blanket of dry leaves.

We'll tuck it in for a good long sleep, Mama used to say as they spread the leaves from the stately oak trees that hung bare over the garden. Kathleen felt the sting of tears and tried to think of something else. Anything else.

She went to the pump to wash the dirt from her hands and face, noticing the bucket of scraps sitting on the edge of the porch. Joshua must have forgotten to take it to the pigs. She hadn't cared for the pigs yet, but she figured it wasn't any harder than her other chores. After she washed, she grabbed the pails and headed for the field beyond the barn where the pig dwelling stood.

The smell hit her before she was near the long red house with five long pens and doors. She wrinkled her nose. She was glad Joshua hadn't made her do this job every day. Animals that spent their days wallowing in muddy slop and eating garbage weren't animals she wished to spend any great amount of time with.

She tried not to breathe through her nose as she stepped up on the platform that ran along the outer edge of the pens. Each long enclosure led inside to a dry bed of hay. She could see a mother in the first pen, trying to nap as a herd of piglets crawled over her.

"Mary could relate to you, poor old girl," Kathleen murmured with a smile.

She poured the slops in the muddy troughs as snorting pigs announced their joy at her arrival. They pushed each other out of the way for a chance to root through the reeking mess. She watched them with disgusted fascination.

"Always reminded me of the Prodigal Son."

Joshua stepped on the platform beside her. She put a hand to her chest, wondering if her heart was suddenly beating so fast because he had startled her or if it was because he was standing so near.

"You scared me," she said, narrowing her eyes.

"Sorry." He didn't seem very sorry as the corner of his mouth pulled up in a teasing smile. He winked at her, and she immediately decided to forgive him.

She leaned on the side of the fence. "The Prodigal Son. I remember some of it, but tell me the story."

"Well, Jesus told this tale of two sons. The younger asked the father for his portion of the inheritance. Maybe he thought he could handle his father's money better. Maybe he just had things he wanted to buy. But the father gave him what he wanted."

"Why would the father do that?"

Joshua shook his head. "I don't know. Maybe this son was the kind of person that only learns lessons the hard way."

A person like me. She swallowed back the lump in her throat.

"Anyway, the younger son went far away and soon spent all the money. He lost all his friends. When a famine came he was homeless and hungry. He went to a pig farmer and asked if he could feed the pigs and live off their food."

Kathleen scrunched up her nose and grimaced at the thought of eating the leftovers of pigs.

"When he saw the low place he'd come to, he asked himself how many of his father's servants had ever gone hungry. He knew they were living much better than he was. He decided to go home and admit to his father he'd sinned and ask to work for him as a servant."

Kathleen remembered the story, but she couldn't recall how it ended. She held her breath while she waited for Joshua to finish the story in his familiar, gruff voice.

"When he was a long way off," Joshua said softly, "his father saw him and started running. He grabbed him. Hugged and kissed him. The son tried to start his speech about being a sinner and him being willing to work as a servant, but his father was too busy having a feast prepared and clothes brought that he didn't pay any attention.

"When the older brother questioned his father's actions, the father said he was happy because his son had been dead, but was alive again; he was lost, but then found."

Kathleen thought about his words, but she couldn't make sense of them. "What does it mean?"

Her soft question brought his inquisitive gaze. He didn't answer for a time.

He looked back at the pigs. "It means God doesn't care where we've been or how bad we've messed up. He only cares that we come home. When we do, we find his mercy in the form of a father, running to us, embracing us, and celebrating our homecoming."

That beautiful sentiment doesn't apply to me. I'm past all hope.

She stepped down from the platform and walked back to the house without saying another word. He didn't follow her.

Kathleen found it a little trying to her soul that the kitchen she'd come to think of as her own was filled to the brim with other women. They were undertaking the massive canning project, and they weren't being very quiet about it.

She didn't like the chaos, with children running everywhere a body could walk, babies crying, and women she didn't know gossiping about other women she didn't know. She felt even more uneasy when she recognized a few familiar faces from the temperance women's group.

Finally, Mrs. O'Malley stood up and called for everyone's attention. "Ladies, thank you for helping today on behalf of the families who suffered loss due to the recent explosion at the train yard. We are indebted to Deputy Whitley and to his sister, Mary, for their selfless work and donations to meet the needs of our community."

Mary glanced at Kathleen with apology, but Kathleen just shrugged. It didn't surprise her that she was excluded. She wasn't doing it for the praise anyway.

At least not for praise from the women.

"You are probably all adept at the art of pickling. The task today will be more complicated, and it is important we do it correctly to prevent illness in these families that have already lost so much. We will follow a precise formula, and I will oversee the sealing of every jar to ensure success.

"The majority of you will focus on washing, peeling and slicing. I will select a few to assist me with boiling and sealing the wax. Now let us ask God to bless our efforts."

They all bowed their heads for prayer. After, an orderly commotion made the room buzz with energy. Mary was whisked away to help with the delicate sealing process, and Mrs. O'Malley's daughter, Audrey, was left in charge of the group preparing the produce. She looked to be in her early twenties, with pink cheeks and golden-brown hair that seemed to be perfectly tamed in the Gibson girl style. Her simple flowered dress and white apron were as elegant as a ball gown the way they flowed around her curves. Kathleen noticed Audrey didn't wear a ring and assumed she was unmarried.

Kathleen was assigned a place at the table shelling peas. She set to work, determined to keep up with the other women at the table. They shelled, sliced, peeled and cut with practiced dexterity. Kathleen noticed that Audrey, who had sat next to her, was watching Kathleen as she worked.

"Am I doing something wrong?" Kathleen finally asked her,

trying to sound cheerful. Audrey's cheeks went even redder.

"No. You're doing fine."

"Why are you watching me?" Kathleen realized it was probably because Audrey was uncomfortable sitting next to a former saloon girl. She regretted asking the question.

Audrey squirmed, peering nervously around the table as the other women tried to pretend they weren't listening to their conversation. Audrey focused on the carrot she was peeling and blinked as if she had something in her eye.

"You can't blame the poor dear," an older woman at the head of the table said.

"Not at all," another woman said and clicked her tongue. "After all, we all expected this to be *her* home."

Kathleen glanced back at Audrey in surprise. The girl's face had gone purple with embarrassment.

"Did you and Joshua have an understanding?" Kathleen asked quietly, but it was pointless to try to keep the conversation private. Everyone at the table had gone quiet to hear them.

"Of course not… Mrs. Whitley," Audrey said quickly, her tone mortified. Kathleen recognized the lie.

"I hadn't considered until now that what Joshua agreed to do for me would affect anyone but the two of us," Kathleen admitted, feeling contrite.

Audrey shrugged and tried valiantly to paste a smile on her face. "God knows the plans he has for us. Joshua and I had no understanding. I had only hoped." She chuckled uneasily. "It was silly of me, really. No matter."

The women around glanced at each other.

Kathleen leaned closer to Audrey and whispered. "Did Joshua share the hope, Miss O'Malley?"

Audrey didn't look her in the eye. "I honestly don't know, Mrs. Whitley."

"Please call me Kathleen."

Audrey opened her mouth to speak but quickly shut it again, returning her attention to her task.

Kathleen stayed quiet after that. She felt guilt like a chain around her ankle, keeping her away from the decent women. She would never be one of them. She would always be Kathleen the Saloon Girl, responsible for tearing homes apart and stealing poor Audrey O'Malley's sweetheart right out from under her nose.

Kathleen gulped back the shame. "It should have been you," she mumbled. She stood up and left the overcrowded kitchen and wandered down the path to the barn. She ended up in Sundi's stall, stroking the sides of the horse with the dandy brush.

"Why was I ever born?" Kathleen spoke into Sundi's inquisitive ear. "They'd all be better off if I'd never existed."

Twenty-Three

"What a blessing," Pastor Merchant said. "What a blessing."

Joshua stood next to him as they surveyed the hundreds of jars stacked in boxes in the back of his wagon.

"Thank you, Joshua." The pastor turned to him and put his hand on Joshua's shoulder.

Mary huffed. "Don't thank him. This was all Kathleen's idea. And the Ladies' Aid Society did all the work." She winked at Joshua. He made a face at her.

"I do thank you, ladies. From the bottom of my heart." Pastor turned to Mary and Kathleen with a genuine smile.

"Now we just need to get them to the folks in need," Joshua said. "If you give me a list of the families I can deliver them."

"I wrote them out in order of need." Pastor Merchant handed the list to Joshua. As he did, he gave him a thoughtful look. "I think you should take Kathleen with you."

Joshua frowned, and an uncomfortable silence followed. Was Pastor serious? Surely he could understand why taking Kathleen wasn't a good idea. Finally, he spoke. 'It's not that I don't want to, but…" He shifted and stuck his hands deep into his pockets.

"But I'm a saloon girl," Kathleen finished for him. "And seeing me with him might make them turn down supplies they need."

Joshua gave a short nod to the pastor before he directed Kathleen to Sundi. "We'll both ride on the horse. No sense in taking the wagon further than necessary with all those glass jars."

It was a quiet ride home. Joshua tried to think of the delivering he needed to do that evening, but all he could seem to think about was Kathleen's arms around his waist. When Sundi hit a bumpy stretch of path, Kathleen's chin bounced against his shoulder and her loose hair trailed down his arm.

He cleared his throat. "I'm going to be out delivering for a few hours. I'll make a cold sandwich when I get back. No need to fret over supper."

He stopped in front of the house and she slid down easily, reminding him how adept a rider she was. And, ah, but she was easy on the eyes.

It was almost enough to make him forget where he'd found her.

He tried to pull the reins back in, literally and figuratively. He started to turn Sundi to head back to town, but he found he couldn't take his eyes from her form.

Kathleen had accepted his decision to leave her behind without an argument. She was headed toward the garden, he assumed to see if she could gather any more produce before the frost that was sure to arrive soon.

The garden. She'd single-handedly used that garden to feed a community, and by no other means than the sweat of her brow. Did he have a right to tell her she didn't deserve to deliver the food? And what if there was no easy way out of this marriage? At some point, people would have to accept her. He might as well start working on that goal now.

"Wait."

Kathleen turned, pushing back wisps of golden hair that sparkled in the sunlight. She waited for him to continue as if she expected him to bark out some demand.

He felt shame over the way he'd been treating her. "I think I want you to come."

She frowned and crossed her arms in a pose that told him she wasn't at all sure she agreed. "You think?"

"I know," he said. "You should come."

She still seemed troubled, but she nodded. She looked down at her work dress and apron. "Can I change?"

"You look fine." He was understating things. She was breathtaking, and he imagined she'd be the same in a potato sack.

"Please?"

He gestured toward the house. "Hurry up, then."

If watching her walk the path in her work clothes was distracting, having her all primped up and smelling like soap and flowers and hanging on to his waist atop the horse was downright problematic. Joshua tried holding his breath, humming, thinking about jail time figures for the past year of criminals he'd locked up – anything but the agonizing temptation of being so close to her. He eyed the green fabric of her dress and inhaled the comforting scent of lavender. His favorite. How could it not be his favorite? It reminded him of Gran. She had planted the bush by the door.

She must have noticed him looking at what he could see of her. "You like the dress? Mary said you like green."

"Sure, it's alright, I guess," he said. He tried to sound indifferent. Like he wasn't mighty beholding to Mary for her infernal interfering.

He was relieved when they got back to the wagon and they could sit on the buckboard instead of so close together on the horse. Maybe he could get control of his senses. He gave her a perusal as they set off and noticed her hair was pinned up.

"Get those pins out of your hair. I'll not have you sick."

She touched her hair but didn't take out the pins. "It'd be best if I wear my hair up, Joshua."

He shook his head, adamant. "No, ma'am. I said no more pinning your hair up and that's what I meant. If you want to wear something on your head, you take my handkerchief. You can tie it up real nice like you do when you're working."

She pulled out the pins and used his handkerchief to tie back her hair. He nodded in approval.

"It isn't the style," she said. "Folks will think it odd. But maybe it will be a distraction."

He shrugged. "Could be. But no sense worrying over what folks think."

Joshua glanced at Kathleen. "So, you ever going to tell me where you're from?"

Immediately her gaze went down to her hands in her lap. Her eyebrows drew together in a troubled expression. She peered out into the forest that sheltered them, watching the stream rush along at the bottom of the ravine below the road.

"Do you come from around here?" He was undaunted by her reaction. It was high time he knew more about this wife of his, even if it was hard for her to answer. And eventually, she did.

"From up north."

"So you're going to make me guess? Because I know Ohio towns pretty well." He tried to make his voice lighter to ease the tension, but he watched her to let her know he was serious about her answering.

Her voice was low and hoarse when she spoke. "Little Sicily."

Joshua nodded. He'd heard the name, though he'd never been there. He leaned back against the seat and stretched a foot out to the front board as he let the reins hang loosely over his knee. "You grew up there?"

She nodded, her gaze trained on her tightly folded hands. "I wasn't quite two when I went there to live."

"Where were you before that?"

He noticed she hesitated for a long moment. Eventually she spoke again. "Indianapolis."

"How'd you end up in the saloon?"

Her voice went even softer. "Rita found me. At the Black Eagle Tavern. She convinced me to sing in her *opera house* here in Dempsey."

He nodded slowly, several questions occurring to him as she spoke. She seemed to be waiting for them, resigned to the painful conversation.

"Why'd you leave your family, Kathleen?" He turned to look at her face.

Her eyes were shiny with tears and she didn't speak for a long moment. "Because I found out they weren't really my family."

He was curious. "So you've said. Tell me what happened."

"My father brought me to Little Sicily and gave me to my Aunt Amy, his sister, to raise. They never told me the truth."

He shrugged slightly, and noticed that she glared at him as he did. "Well, you were with family, Kathleen."

A dark expression clouded her face. "He abandoned me. He let me believe he was only an uncle, even after he married Aunt Amelia and they had a family together. I belonged with them!"

Joshua scratched his nose, feeling perplexed over her response. It was clear that it was a tender subject and her feelings went deep. He warned himself to tread carefully, knowing full well he had his own touchy subjects. "You think maybe he was trying not to upset your life or the people who loved you as their own?"

She had tears in her eyes, and she looked away, quiet.

"What about your real mother? Where was she in all of this?"

"Dead," Kathleen said the word as a sigh.

Joshua regretted he'd brought it up. "I'm sorry, Kathleen."

She pursed her lips. "She was a saloon girl, too."

The words sounded like a dare.

"So you went to the tavern in Indianapolis when you found out the truth about her? Because you wanted to be a saloon girl like she was?" He didn't understand her reasoning. Was he missing something? "I can appreciate you'd want to know about her. But to jump into the same life with your eyes wide open? Throw away your innocence and your good name? Seems like a mighty high cost."

He tried to speak gently. But he wanted to know why she'd done it. By the grim set of her mouth, he wasn't reaching her.

"What about you?" she said, her voice full of challenge. "Were you born on the farm?"

He hesitated, watching her. She had to know he wasn't born on that farm. But she had a point. If he was going to press her for her secrets, he had to be willing to share his own.

"Grandpa built the farm when the railroad asked him to move from Michigan to help build the Traction Line Car." He'd left out a huge chunk of his story, and he was aware she knew it.

"You mean the one that travels between Dempsey and Columbus a few times a day?"

"That's the one. Just opened last year. Grandpa died before he got to see it."

"I'm sorry."

He shrugged. "Gran always wanted a farm in Michigan, but Grandpa said the weather wasn't right for crops."

"Did you live with them in Michigan?"

Joshua's glare got darker. "Nope. We started living with them on the farm when I was nine and Mary was fifteen. She met Isaiah when he started as Grandpa's assistant in the railroad office. He was the son of an Irish immigrant working in the train yard mending machines. Grandpa saw how bright he was and hired him even though other folks didn't like his nationality. It didn't take Mary long to catch his eye after that. They got married pretty young."

Kathleen didn't ask him why he'd started his story at the age of nine, but he saw the question lingering in her eyes.

He found he wasn't ready to discuss it with her. Not yet. Maybe not ever.

Twenty-Four

"This is the Patrick homestead."

Kathleen heard the strain in Joshua's voice. He pulled the wagon up to a small, run-down farmhouse outside town. He read the paper Pastor Merchant had given him and then surveyed the house. "Joe Patrick was killed in the blast. Left behind Ellen and their five small children."

"I can't imagine the heartache," Kathleen said. She peeked at Joshua and wished she could ask more about his story. But it was obvious he didn't want to talk about it.

Joshua hopped down and came to her side, reaching up to lift her down. She felt her face flush as he gently set her on the ground, his hands lingering at her waist and his eyes darting to her lips for just a moment.

A young woman with a screaming baby on her hip answered the door. She gave them a polite smile, but her red-rimmed eyes revealed extreme exhaustion.

"Good day, Mrs. Patrick. I'm Deputy Whitley and this is Kathleen, my wife. We are sorry for what's happened, ma'am. We've come with supplies to help you through the winter."

The woman said nothing, but she covered her mouth with her hand as she tried to still a sob. The baby's frantic crying increased as the movement jolted him.

Kathleen stepped forward. "May I hold your little one while you decide what you can use?"

The woman handed Kathleen the baby and allowed Joshua to lead her to the wagon. Kathleen could see inside the house where two little boys fidgeted on the settee. A little girl maybe the same age as Mary's Lou stood near the door, wailing. Another girl swept the floor with a broom too big for her, her face sorrowful and pale. Kathleen's throat constricted as she hugged the baby's head to her chest and bounced him until his cries diminished.

When Joshua had filled the family's kitchen with crates of supplies, Mrs. Patrick came to Kathleen to take the baby back.

"I'm so sorry," Kathleen said as she passed her the infant, now relaxed, with only an occasional sniff or hiccup.

"I appreciate it," Mrs. Patrick said in a brave tone before she turned and went inside.

Joshua didn't speak again until they arrived at the next house, a clapboard home on the edge of town. "Glenn O'Neil lost his leg and part of his hand. The wife is Constance and they have twins, a boy and girl, who are sixteen."

The boy answered the door and held it open so Joshua could bring in the first crate. "Deputy's here, Ma," he called.

The boy disappeared and a stony-faced woman came from the back room carrying bloody bandages and a basin of water. She stopped short and glared at Kathleen.

"We brought supplies to help you through the winter," Joshua said as he set the crate down beside the stove in the small kitchen.

"We do not take charity." Mrs. O'Neil narrowed her eyes, still watching Kathleen.

"We're visiting all the folks affected by the explosion. The town wants to help."

"We didn't ask for help," she snapped. "Who is this woman you've brought into my house?"

Joshua hesitated, but his voice was even and sure as he spoke. "My wife, Kathleen."

"How do you do?" Kathleen said, trying to keep her voice steady.

The woman scoffed. "She's no wife. She's unclean, and I don't want her in my house."

Joshua stepped back and put his hand on Kathleen's back. She saw his jaw constrict. "Let's go."

Mrs. O'Neil followed them outside to the wagon. "Men who cavort with women like her fall under judgment of the Almighty," she called after them. Joshua helped Kathleen up to the seat.

"You don't know the first thing about her. We came here to help. You don't want help, that's fine, but I won't allow you to –"

He stopped abruptly. Kathleen watched him climb into the wagon. He forcefully pushed the brake forward and snapped the reins. The wagon jerked as the startled horse stopped munching grass and started moving.

Kathleen stared at the back of the horse as Joshua took deep breaths through his nose. She felt tension in his arm brushing against hers.

He finally spoke, causing her to jump. "Don't listen to her. She takes her pleasure tearing folks down. You aren't the first."

Kathleen looked at him with curiosity. "You don't agree with her?"

He looked at her with a dark expression. "What are you trying to say?"

She kept her voice low. "You've said the same things."

"I never said anything like that!" He raised his voice. She didn't answer, afraid of his temper. She didn't know him well enough to be sure he wouldn't take out his anger on her, and she'd seen enough male outbursts in the saloon to know she didn't want to encourage one.

Kathleen watched the sun slowly fade into the western horizon, saying goodnight to the late September day. There was a brisk coolness to the air. A whispered reminder that winter would soon be upon them.

"I want to know what I said to make you think I believe the sort of drivel that came from her mouth." Joshua's voice was quiet. More controlled. But far from pleasant.

"Words aren't the only way to say something," she replied.

"I've provided everything you needed. Everything you asked of me."

Kathleen chewed on her bottom lip as she considered her answer. "You married me, but you didn't. You said the words, but you hold yourself back. I don't fault you for it, but I can't smile and say it feels good to be despised by the man who keeps introducing me as his wife."

"I didn't have a choice but to marry you," he said, irritation evident in his tone. "There's a difference between that woman preaching her hate sermon and me being honest. She assumed. I know. As your husband, I deserve an opinion."

Kathleen dared to look at him. "You're a hypocrite. You feel the same way she does. You just don't want to see it in yourself." She braced for his reaction.

"I don't need *you*, of all people, calling me a hypocrite," he snapped. "You've been in that saloon having men pay you to say and do what they want. You never felt a thing for any of them, but you gave them what didn't belong to them. What didn't belong to you, for that matter. You can't get more hypocritical than that, Kathleen Able."

She flinched. His words felt like a slap across the face.

Joshua watched her cower as his words fell on her like a hailstorm. She was bracing for the blows. He was sorry, but he was too proud to admit it.

As if he'd ever hit her.

"You don't know me at all," she mumbled. She spoke so quietly he barely made out the words.

"I know enough."

Joshua had plenty of time to think the rest of the evening. It started pouring rain when they arrived at the farm, so he sat in the parlor pretending to read his book as he inwardly chafed. He hadn't asked for this. Any of it.

All things work together for good.

"How can this possibly work out for good?" he whispered. He heard the pouting in his tone and felt ashamed for doubting. But how could God ask him to believe in this? This marriage. This woman.

It was impossible.

Kathleen didn't go to town other than to church. Joshua was careful to whisk her straight from the doors to the wagon afterward. She hadn't seen or had contact with anyone from the saloon in weeks. Her life at the saloon and the threat of Rita and Logan had become like a bad dream – one she was happy to forget.

But the reality of the danger returned when Joshua brought her to a harvest social in town near the end of October. The women were receiving a commendation from the mayor for their work canning and distributing supplies. Mary had badgered Joshua until he agreed to bring Kathleen.

Kathleen wasn't all that sure she wanted to be there, but it was nice to do something away from the farm. She contented herself to stand by the back wall of town hall and watch the socializing from a distance. She had no desire to be a part of it. She knew the people eyeing her with distrust felt the same way about her presence.

While Joshua was busy talking to Evan and a group of other men from church, Kathleen slipped outside. She wandered down by the creek and sat on a log, listening to the sounds of the town in the evening. They had once been familiar. Now, she found she preferred the total silence of the farm.

Her thoughts wandered to the other girls in the saloon. How many of them couldn't even imagine the kind of life Kathleen had been living at the Whitley farm? Even with the frustration of trying to get along with Joshua, Kathleen knew there wasn't a girl in the saloon who wouldn't trade places with her the instant they were given the opportunity. The thought caused her guilt. Some of them deserved a second chance far more than she did.

"I don't know if it's a good idea for you to be down here by yourself."

She heard Evan's voice and stood up quickly, startled by his presence. In the dim shadows of evening, his large frame was intimidating, even though she knew he was harmless.

"I was just getting some air," she explained, climbing back up the hill toward him.

"I know it's been some time, and you feel safe with Joshua," Evan continued, fingering his hat in his hands. "And I don't like worrying Joshua any more than he already is. But I've been keeping my eye out for Logan, and he showed up at work today for the first time since the explosion. His leg is still healing, but he hasn't forgotten about you, ma'am."

"Please call me Kathleen." She avoided thinking about what he was saying to her.

Evan nodded. "Kathleen. Bill Logan likes to boast about his questionable appetites. He says quite a bit about the feisty little saloon girl who keeps getting away from him. I told him in no uncertain terms you are a married woman now, but he's promising everyone he's going to get to you somehow, and he doesn't care what Josh thinks about it."

Kathleen nodded and looked away. "Thank you for telling me the truth, Evan."

"I'll let Joshua know Logan's back." Evan replaced his hat and motioned for her to follow him back into the church. "But I think you are owed a fair warning as well, and I'm not sure your husband would tell you anything."

"I appreciate your honesty. I'll not wander away alone again."

"That's for the best, Kathleen. I don't want anything to happen to you. Joshua cares a lot about you."

Kathleen couldn't help the ironic chuckle that escaped. "Joshua tolerates me because he made a promise and he's honorable. But I wouldn't be surprised if there was a part of him that would be relieved to be free of me."

Evan frowned. "That's just not true. You don't know Joshua like I do. I don't mind telling you I've never seen him so flustered before. You've made quite an impression. Kind of like Miss Walsh has made on me."

Kathleen smiled politely at his mention of the piano player he was sweet on, but she didn't agree with his assessment of Joshua. Maybe Evan didn't know him as well as he thought he did.

"I hope you're right." She followed him back into the town hall, stopping once to look behind her. For a moment she felt sure someone was close. Watching her.

Twenty-Five

The snows came early that year, in biting sheets of frozen rain followed by a foot of snow on the first day of November.

Joshua went to town every day he could manage it, but after the third day of wind and snow, the trail was too much for Sundi. He stayed home and hoped the sheriff had the sense to stay in Dempsey or that, at the very least, the criminals were also snowed in.

He didn't talk to Kathleen much. He wasn't angry with her, but he couldn't think of anything to say other than to discuss that conversation they'd had when they were delivering the supplies over a month before. He had no desire to pick it up again. His opinions hadn't changed, and he doubted hers had, either.

They did the few necessary chores in the morning and spent the afternoons in the parlor, trying to amuse themselves without conversation. He re-read his favorite books from his grandparents' library. Kathleen played with her kitten on the carpet and made a few little pillows from Grandma's leftover supply of fabric and thread. Joshua played hymns on his guitar.

To his surprise, she hummed along as she stitched. She might not have even realized she was doing it. Where had she learned the songs? Why hadn't she responded to the message contained within them?

After the fourth straight day of snow, Joshua was starting to go stir-crazy. He suspected Kathleen was as well. She had nothing left to clean. She tried to play the pianoforte, but gave up after a few minutes. She couldn't find anything to read, judging by the way she perused the books over and over again and always came back empty-handed.

"What kind of books do you like?" He watched her search the shelves a third day in a row, as if she was hoping something new might appear if she kept checking every day.

"Stories," she said, narrowing her eyes at the book spines.

"Sorry. My grandparents were the commentary and encyclopedia type of folks."

"My aunt is an author," she said, giving up and settling in the chair across from his.

"You don't say? What does she write?" Joshua looked at her over his book.

Kathleen surveyed the thick volume in his hands and gave him a doubtful expression. "Different things. Romance, mostly. Her latest was about a time-traveling machine. It was featured in a magazine."

Joshua chuckled. "Huh. Sounds interesting."

"What are you reading?" Kathleen slouched on the chair and stared across the room at him.

"It's called *The Higher Christian Life* by W.E. Boardman. Brand new – just got it from Dickinson the day before the storm hit."

"Sounds dull," she said, wrinkling her nose.

He shrugged. "I think it's interesting. Shall I read some to you?"

She sighed. "Why not?"

He tried to find the right selection to share with her.

"The Soul alone, like a neglected harp
Grows out of tune, and needs that Hand divine
Dwell thou within it, tune and touch the chord,
Till every note and string shall answer thine.

"Abide in me: there have been moments pure,
When I have seen thy face and felt thy power;

Then evil lost its grasp, and passion hushed,
Owned the divine enchantment of the hour.

"These were but seasons beautiful and rare;
Abide in me, and they shall ever be;
I pray thee now fulfill my earnest prayer.
Come and abide in me; and I in thee."

When Joshua looked up, he was surprised. Kathleen's eyebrows were drawn together in a troubled frown. He hadn't expected her to be affected at all by the words that resonated like a clear note of music in his own thirsty soul.

She didn't speak. After watching her for a moment, unsure of what to do, he set down the book and crossed the parlor. He sat down on the edge of the settee next to her, leaning forward and folding his hands over his knees.

"You know you're like that harp, Kathleen. So am I," he said quietly after a pause. "God can make anybody's song end up beautiful. Even the stained or broken ones."

She twisted her hands in her lap. "I don't think those nice words are meant for someone like me. God knows I'm past hope."

He stared at the faded red carpet his grandma had loved, trying to decide what to say. He turned abruptly and caught her chin with the tip of his finger, making her look at him. "Without him, we're all beyond hope. But when Jesus shed blood on that cross, he was making sure no soul ever went without hope."

She was breathless as she stared into his eyes. He hoped it was because she was feeling the love of Christ, and not just the pleasant tension of their closeness.

Because he definitely hadn't missed that.

"It's a beautiful thought, Joshua," she said softly. He was struck by the fact that he couldn't remember her ever calling him by his first name before. He wished she didn't look so sad as she continued. "I'm glad you believe them for yourself. And I'm glad for Mary and Pastor Merchant and my family. But they aren't for me."

142

He shook his head, frustrated, and resumed his study of the carpet. "It doesn't have to be that way."

She smoothed her dress. "God's given me up to my sin. There's nothing you can say that will make me believe any differently. But thanks for trying, anyway."

He stood up and walked to the window to stare out into the whiteness. Pure white sky and land as far as his eyes could see. "Kathleen, I'm not sure what went wrong in your life. But I'm telling you, sure as I'm standing here, there ain't a person breathing that can't be washed clean by the blood of Jesus." He turned around and considered her. "This idea you have, that you're somehow the only exception to his grace – it's nothing but pride. The very notion comes right out of hell. Wouldn't you rather trust what God says?"

It was clear she was offended. "Do you want me to lie and say I believe it? I'm just telling you the truth. I can't see a way for God to forgive me, or make any good out of the mess I've made of my life."

"Then you have a rotten view of God," he said quickly. "Not to mention, you're dead wrong."

She didn't answer. He felt the chill of her beliefs more than the one coming from the snow-laden window. He turned around and leaned against the pane, feeling the cold contend with the warmth of his back.

"Can't you see he's already started his work in you, Kathleen? Can't you feel him chasing after you?"

As he watched her fight the truth, he understood just how helpless a body could feel watching someone reject God's love. He couldn't convince her. He couldn't make her understand. It was true, what the Bible said. Kathleen was dead in her sins. How could Joshua make a dead person come out of her grave? What could he say to raise her up?

It is not your work. It's mine.

"What can I do, Lord? What can I say?"

Joshua saw Kathleen turn his way and watch him and realized he'd said the words aloud.

Love as I loved you.

143

"I'm trying here."

"Are you?" Kathleen answered the words he'd meant for the Lord. Her sharp eyes the shade of olives watched him carefully. "You say all the right things, but the way you act speaks louder."

Joshua tried not to show his surprise. He knew she'd tried to say as much before, but suddenly he could see the truth like all the grime had been polished away from the glass.

She was waiting for him to be like Jesus. To prove what he said was true.

"Please, Kathleen, don't put Jesus and me in the same category." He heard the urgency in his voice and hoped she did as well. "I'm just a man. I have a past, too, and God still has plenty of work to do in me. I am not capable of loving you the way you're hoping I will."

She looked down. "That seems convenient."

He closed his eyes tightly and exhaled. How could he make her understand where he'd been? "I used to be in a very bad place, Kathleen. I told you as much before. I guess I'm still trying to let go of it."

She met his gaze. "What happened?"

He had expected the question, but he couldn't form the answer. After a long pause, he gave up. "I can't. I can't talk about it. Especially not to you."

She shrugged and looked away. "I don't expect it of you."

She stood and left the room, brushing past him so that he could smell her lavender scent and be reminded how soft and feminine she was. He wanted to punch something. He couldn't ignore the feelings he was starting to have for her. And he definitely couldn't let her go on believing that God had given up on her.

But to do anything about it, to change her mind, he would have to tell her his story. He'd have to be willing to let God do a work to change his heart as well.

Again, he met the impasse.

Twenty-Six

"I'm about ready to move all the animals into the house," Joshua joked as he bundled up, preparing to head to the barn in the late December snowstorm.

Kathleen smiled half-heartedly from her place at the stove. Long November days had turned into long December days as the frequent snowstorms continued. As the snow piled higher, it became quite an undertaking to care for the animals. Joshua spent much of his time trying to keep the path clear between the house and the barn.

When he returned several hours later, he was dragging something behind him. She opened the door for him and he entered, maneuvering a six-foot tall pine.

"A Christmas tree!" Kathleen could not help her childish delight. She clapped in excitement.

Joshua smiled. "A reaction like that makes all the effort of digging this thing out of the snow and chopping it down worth every second. Anyway, it's Christmas Eve and we won't make it into town, so I figured we'd need a bit of our own Christmas."

She was surprised. The days ran together so much she didn't realize the holiday was upon them. She helped him take off his snowy boots and coat and sent him to the stove to dry off and warm up. He eyed the cup of steaming coffee she had poured when she saw him coming down the path.

"Thank you," he said as he picked up the cup with reddened

hands.

He took a few sips as she hung his coat and other things on the line near the fire she'd hung for that purpose. When she was done, she went to him, taking the cup and setting it on the counter. She took his chilled hands between her warm ones and gently rubbed them.

"That feels nice," he said, watching her.

"I could pop some corn and string it for the tree," she said, hoping her voice sounded cheerful and didn't betray her breathlessness.

"I think Gran has some ornaments somewhere. I'll check up in the extra bedroom over the kitchen."

She felt tears and tried to brush them away. She didn't want him to think she was unhappy about his gestures.

"What?" Joshua reclaimed his coffee cup and waited for her explanation.

"Christmas makes me think of home."

He nodded, taking a long sip. "You could write them. Let them know you're okay."

She shook her head and turned back to the stew simmering on the stove. "It would just cause them pain. It's best they forget me."

"They seem like decent folk, Kathleen. No decent parents would ever forget you."

Kathleen listened to Joshua rummage around in the room above the kitchen for the next half-hour. He came down the narrow stairs with a box full of pretty handmade ornaments and a tin star. They trimmed the tree after supper.

Kathleen stood back to admire their work as Joshua pinned the star to the highest bough.

"Thank you," she said softly. "This means more than you know."

He nodded and stepped back from the tree to stand beside her. "I haven't had a tree since Gran died. It's nice... having someone to share it with again."

The silence that followed held an element of purity as they stood in front of the tree. It felt almost reverent. The snow fell in a soft blanket over the earth, causing a soft glow through the window. The sky gave up the last of the daylight, and the lit candles on the mantle became the only illumination.

"My aunt used to play Christmas hymns on the piano for Christmas Eve. We sang along as we decorated the tree. My favorite was the one about angels bending near the earth." Kathleen smiled at the memory.

"No reason we can't keep that tradition alive," Joshua picked up his guitar in the corner and tuned it. He came back to her and began to sing in a strong and clear voice.

> *It came upon the midnight clear,*
> *That glorious song of old,*
> *From angels bending near the earth,*
> *To touch their harps of gold.*

She sang along, noticing his surprise. Her voice trailed off when he began to sing verses she didn't know. She couldn't help but consider the words as he continued to sing.

> *And ye, beneath life's crushing load,*
> *Whose forms are bending low,*
> *Who toil along the climbing way*
> *With painful steps and slow.*

> *Look now! For glad and golden hours*
> *Come swiftly on the wing,*
> *O rest beside the weary road*
> *And hear the angels sing!*

He stopped playing and looked up at her. "You have a lovely voice."

She shrugged. "My mother could sing. And my aunt. You have a nice voice, too."

He stepped closer to her. "You're wearing the green dress. I sure do like that one."

She flushed and looked down at her dress. They stood together for a long moment, and it was awkward in a sense, but it was not in another. Kathleen wanted to capture the beauty and stillness of the evening and remember it forever. She closed her eyes and hoped she might hold on to the recollection when she was suffering eternal punishment. She prayed she might take this one moment with her.

She was surprised when she felt his hands on either side of her face. He gently lifted her gaze to meet his.

"I wish I could tell you how beautiful you look." His lopsided grin made her heart beat faster. His voice was so quiet she had to be still to hear him. "Your cheeks are pink and your eyes are shining..." His words faded away.

Kathleen could predict what was about to happen. A part of her protested, as much as she longed for it. What good could come of them getting closer? It would only cloud their judgment; make everything more complicated. And as much as she wanted to believe it would be based on his loving commitment to her, she knew better. He was only thinking of his desire in the moment.

In her experience, desire only led to pain.

She saw the eagerness in his expression. Besides the brief moment they had shared in the barn, had Joshua ever been this close to a woman? Was he trying to pretend she was what he wanted in a wife? Pure, whole, devoted? He seemed determined to have this moment and whatever might follow.

His lips searched for hers and found them. He took his time, reveling. And as determined as her objections remained, she could do nothing but respond to his gesture. All the passion they had been denying and suppressing for nearly four months came to the surface like water starting to boil. She felt the force of it, knowing it could smother them as easily as an avalanche of snow coming down a mountain.

Though she had little personal experience, she could sense a fire building in Joshua by the way he pulled her nearer, by the way he took charge of their exchange. It reminded her of things she'd seen in the saloon.

If she allowed him to continue, she knew the outcome.

Kathleen wanted to be his. She was surprised how much she wanted it. But she couldn't let it be. He was only offering his body, not his heart.

She realized in that moment, she wanted his heart. His whole heart.

"No," she said, trying to pull back. He moved with her, refusing to release her. She put her hands on his chest and pushed him away.

"What's wrong?" His voice was thick and unsteady, as if their kisses had been wine, slurring his speech and slowing his thoughts.

"You aren't kissing me, Joshua," she said in a whisper.

"I ain't kissing anyone else," he said with a shrug and tried to pull her back to him.

"You're trying to pretend I'm her."

"Her who?"

"The woman you wish I was."

He retreated. He cleared his throat and stepped back like he'd been doused with a bucket of cold water. He shoved his hands in his pockets and looked back at the Christmas tree, clearly embarrassed. He turned away and abruptly went to the stairs. A moment later his door clicked shut.

She imagined his heart making the same sound.

Twenty-Seven

Joshua had barely spoken a word since Christmas. She suspected he was angrier with himself than with her, but it didn't make living with him any easier.

The snow melted New Year's Day. Kathleen knew Ohio well enough to know the warm-up wouldn't last, but she stepped out on the back porch and breathed in the warmer air. She watched with satisfaction as the sun turned the snow to liquid.

The first morning of the new year of 1906, Joshua sat down at the table as she set his plate in front of him. He didn't look at her when he spoke. "You need to pack your things."

She gulped in terror. "You're sending me back to the saloon?"

He looked at her then, and his features softened. "Of course not. You'll be staying with Mary and the family for the rest of the winter."

She went back to the stove, swallowing back a lump of disappointment. "So you are removing the evil temptation from your house?"

"It's safer in town during winter. I'd stay in town myself if it weren't for the animals." His voice remained even and he didn't look up from his plate.

She scoffed, setting the skillet in the sink with a loud clank. "How is it safer? There is plenty of danger in town for me. Have you forgotten about Logan? What danger is here other than the possibility you'll make a mistake you'll regret?"

He sighed. "You'll be under Isaiah's protection. And Evan will keep an eye on you. You'll be safe enough. Between Logan's injury and the snow, I don't think he'll be bothering you. Rita, either."

"I wish you'd be honest about why you're doing this."

"I'm not the one who called it off at Christmas," he reminded her.

"You *were*, Joshua." She tried to ignore him and do her work, but she couldn't resist saying more. "If you were thinking clearly, you would have. I was just saying what you couldn't say. You are the one that holds back. Don't try to say it's me when it's not true, Joshua Whitley."

He apparently had no argument. She felt foolish for speaking such a vulnerable thought. Joshua ate quickly and gulped down his coffee. As he left the kitchen, he spoke without looking at her. "I'll let you know when the snow melts enough for us to get to town."

Two days later, Kathleen was sitting on the wagon seat with her bundle of clothes on her lap. As the town came into view, she sat up rigidly and clenched her jaw to hold back her angry tears.

Joshua remained aloof. It didn't seem to affect him at all to drop her off in town and leave her behind.

When they arrived at the McAllister's small home, Kathleen climbed down before he could come around to help her. She walked to the door, turning only once to speak to him.

"So much for all your talk of forgiveness."

He didn't look at her, and he didn't answer right away. She thought he might drive off without a word. But he finally spoke. "I'm just a man."

"A handy excuse," she replied as she lifted her hand to knock.

Mary opened the door before she could do so. Her welcoming smile faded as she met Kathleen's expression, and then Joshua's.

"What's going on?" Mary directed the question to Joshua.

151

"I need you to keep Kathleen here until the weather turns," Joshua said. "Thanks, Mary."

Mary shared a long look with Joshua before she directed Kathleen inside.

Kathleen's face burned as she followed a slightly bewildered Mary into the house. She felt like a burden. An intruder, no matter where she went.

She'd always been an intruder. Her own father had rejected her. It was simply the story of her life.

But Mary didn't seem upset over the imposition. "We're glad to have you anytime, Kathleen. The children will be thrilled to have time to get to know their aunt."

Mary said the words in a loud voice, before she shut the door. Kathleen assumed Joshua had been meant to hear. When the door was closed, Mary gestured to a chair. "Tell me everything."

"There's nothing much to tell," Kathleen said with a sigh. "He doesn't want me."

Mary surprised her by smiling. "What makes you think he doesn't want you?"

Kathleen was speechless for a moment. "Well, he dropped me off here. It seems rather obvious."

Mary motioned her back to the kitchen where she put on the teakettle. Little ones pulled on her skirts. The twins rushed back and forth in the small space, tackling one another and bursting into frequent bouts of giggles. It made Kathleen remember with longing the peace and quiet of her farm kitchen. Mary, on the other hand, didn't seem to notice her children at all. She continued the conversation as if there were no distractions.

"You're taking Joshua's actions the wrong way," Mary said in a matter-of-fact tone. She sat down and cut slices of bread to spread with butter before she handed them out to the children. Lou climbed up her back and the baby pulled on her skirt and fussed from his nearly helpless position on the floor. She looked back at Kathleen with a smile. "He brought you here because he wants you quite badly."

Kathleen blushed and tried to hide her smile. "Well, I realize that much."

Mary chuckled and waited for her to continue.

"But it's all wrong, Mary. We got close on Christmas Eve, but I stopped him. It felt like he was pretending I was someone else."

Mary reached for the boiling teakettle and poured through a strainer into two mismatched coffee cups. "That's when he decided to bring you here?"

Kathleen shrugged. "I suppose so."

"Why didn't you want to be close?" Mary asked, though her tone suggested she already knew the answer. "You and Joshua are married. It wouldn't have been wrong. Maybe it would have helped you both come to an understanding."

"It wouldn't be the same as it was for you, Mary," Kathleen answered. "That part was easy for you."

"And how do you know that?" Mary raised an eyebrow.

"Joshua said Isaiah saw you at the railroad office and fell in love with you immediately."

Mary laughed loudly, inspiring the twins to join her. "Ha! Shows you how deeply a boy considers these things. Isaiah and I fought for a solid six months about whether he would leave the railroad. I knew train engines were in the habit of blowing up and I'd heard of another foreman who had died in an explosion. He works with a rough crowd besides. I just knew he was going to be killed and I'd be left to raise a family on my own. I outright refused to marry him until he agreed to leave his position. In the end, I had to decide whether I was willing to accept his job or live without him, because he wouldn't budge on the subject."

"But how could you know he really loved you if he was unwilling to change?" Kathleen fingered her cup.

"I considered that," Mary said with a nod. She grabbed the baby as he scooted by. She wiped his nose with a handkerchief before releasing him to continue his journey across the kitchen floor. "Isaiah told me it was because he loved me that he wouldn't leave his job. He had to provide for us, and it was the only thing he knew how to do."

Kathleen sipped her tea. She could see Isaiah's reasoning. "I don't know what to tell you, Mary. I don't understand why Joshua is so angry, but I'm not in a place to demand his love."

Mary went silent. Little Lou climbed into Kathleen's lap and snuggled against her, sucking her thumb and closing her eyes.

"I was hoping you'd be able to love him past it." Mary sighed and sipped her tea.

"What?"

"If he hasn't told you, I have to respect his wishes. It's something you should hear from him."

Kathleen shook her head, confused. "My guess is that your parents died. But why did it affect him so much and not you?"

Mary wore a sorrowful expression. "It *has* affected me," she said softly. "It hurts every time I think on it. Which is why I hardly ever do."

Kathleen had never heard Mary's voice take on such a tone. Haunted. Wounded. Helpless in the face of some giant of old that tormented her still.

Just like Joshua.

Mary continued. "Joshua's different than me. He holds on to things. Thinks about them until he can figure out what went wrong and fix it. I let go of things that cut too deeply. I put them away and forget as best I can. Besides that, I was older. I could see things for what they were, as sad as it was. He was just a child."

"I wish I knew what you were talking about."

"I do, too," Mary said with a shrug. "I promise you, if it weren't for the fact he has obviously chosen to keep you in the dark, I would tell you myself."

"Thank you," Kathleen leaned back and put her chin on the sleeping toddler's head.

Mary jumped up and clapped her hands so loudly Lou woke and started crying. "We are going to have so much *fun!*"

❄

154

They did have fun. Kathleen enjoyed the energy of being in a town again. She worried about Logan, but Mary said he wouldn't think she was there anyway. If he was going to find her, he would head to the farm. It gave Kathleen a measure of peace.

There was always something to clean, discuss or play with in the busy household. Kathleen had brought her kitten, which delighted the children. Kathleen reveled in the simplicity of going to the store with Mary or sitting in church, even if the stares and whispers didn't stop. Joshua still sat beside her and offered his arm up and down the aisle, but he barely spoke a word to her. When he joined them for dinner, he talked almost exclusively with Isaiah or the kids and left as soon as he finished eating.

Kathleen sat up with Mary in the evening and talked while they sewed or quilted. Mary told her about Joshua's childhood antics, like the time he got himself stuck in the outhouse when he was ten and the way he climbed the apple trees and hid in the high branches when Gran came out of the house yelling at him for something he'd done.

"Eventually he figured out the punishment was always worse the longer he stayed up there," Mary chuckled.

"I'm surprised he's not still sitting up there for how stubborn he is," Kathleen said as she bounced the baby on her knee.

"He is stubborn," Mary said, her eyes twinkling. "But not as stubborn as Gran was. That woman had a will of iron."

It was an adjustment to sleep in the same room as Annie and Sally. Annie stayed up late most nights whispering to Kathleen about boys and fretting over her relationships with her classmates. Kathleen had no idea why Annie thought she had the answers.

"Why aren't you living with Uncle Josh?" Sally interrupted Annie's lamenting one night, after Kathleen had thought the girl was asleep. "Did you have a fight?"

"Not exactly," Kathleen whispered back.

"Did you forget to bank the stove or feed the chickens?" Annie asked. "Uncle Josh has a temper, but he gets over it. If you went home, he'd probably forgive you."

"As far as I know, he's not mad."

"Oh. Well, he likes things done a certain way. Maybe you made him mad without realizing it." Annie paused. "Kathleen, what's it like to kiss a boy?"

"Annie McAllister, you are too young to be thinking about kissing, and Sally doesn't need to hear about such things, either. Why don't you go to sleep?"

Annie sighed loudly and turned over. "You sound like Mama."

A minute later, the girl giggled again. "What's it like to kiss Uncle Josh? Now there's a funny thought!"

"Mama!" Sally yelled. "Annie's talking 'bout kissing!"

"Go to sleep, Annie," came Mary's muted call. Kathleen could guess by her tone that it was a common reminder.

Kathleen smiled into the darkness. She definitely hadn't forgotten either kiss with Joshua, though she wasn't about to tell Annie and Sally about them. All she knew was he had taken her breath away. She hadn't realized such a sweet expression of affection could exist.

She fell asleep reliving those two favorite memories.

Twenty-Eight

Logan and Rita remained absent, as Joshua had said they would. Kathleen felt like she was always looking over her shoulder, like she could feel the hate from across town, but she saw no sign of either of them. Evan came as often as the snow would allow and let her know what he'd seen. Logan was always at work, but he was still in pain from his injury. Evan said Logan had gone silent on the matter of Kathleen, but he didn't expect Logan had forgotten any of his threats. It made Kathleen nervous to be so close to the saloon and to Logan. She was tempted on many occasions to be bitter toward her husband for leaving her there without his protection.

Influenza came to Dempsey, and to the McAllister household. Lou was the first to show signs of illness, followed quickly by the oldest son, Josh, and the twins. Kathleen helped Mary nurse them back to health. Mary worried that Kathleen would catch it, but Kathleen could hardly stand by and not assist. Mary was exhausted, and Kathleen was afraid it would make the weary wife and mother more likely to catch the illness.

"Kathleen, I'll send you home with Isaiah. You shouldn't be here."

"It's too late for that," Kathleen answered as she sponged Jeremiah's feverish brow. "I think if I'm meant to get it, at this point, I'll get it no matter where I am. Besides, it's been snowing for two days and it doesn't look like it will be stopping soon. We can hardly get across the street."

"You're right, of course," Mary sighed as she helped Lou take a few sips of water. "I just worry. People die of the grippe all the time."

"Not young, healthy people," Kathleen said.

The sickness did pass quickly in the children. Before long, Lou had resumed her ear-piercing howls, and the twins were back to full strength in their destruction and arguing, though they never really stopped, even in the worst of their fever.

Just when Mary was starting to voice her hope that the sickness had left the house, Kathleen began to feel achy and cold.

"You don't look so good," Mary said with a sigh. She felt Kathleen's forehead and ushered her to bed.

The second night of fever, Kathleen knew she would die.

She tried to escape the chill, but it seemed to crawl into her bones and turn them to ice. She wanted to sleep, but a fear that she might never wake up clung to her soul and kept her awake and miserable.

In the dead of night, as she shook with chills and tossed and turned in pain, she heard a slithering on the floor. She couldn't see anything in the dark, but she could sense the presence in the room. It was threatening. Evil.

She tried to call to Mary but it felt like something had been jammed into her throat. She couldn't make a sound.

The slithering grew louder, and something close to the ground reflected the faint light of the streetlamp.

Whatever it was, it was big.

She fought for air. Another glint caught the light in the corner. This time it was at eye level, and seemed to be something made of steel. Above it, she clearly saw a pair of eyes, watching her.

A murmur cut through the darkness, causing a panicked sensation to roll up her back and neck.

"Did you think I'd forgotten how you treated me, girl? Did you think I would just let it go?"

He didn't move from the shadows, but she knew it was Logan. She knew by the shifting, demented gleam of his eyes.

"You think you'll get better? You think you'll win over that farm boy?"

She felt the vibration of his coarse laugh. "You're going no place but down. You have unfinished business with the devil. And I'm here to drag you to hell."

She tried to scream, but only a strangled cry escaped her lips.

"Tonight, I'll come for you."

She fell from the bed, crawling toward the door in a frantic attempt to escape him. Slithering followed close behind her.

"Help!" Her voice rasped. She reached toward the door handle, but found her strength sapped. She felt a rush of relief as the door opened and the room filled with light.

"Kathleen? What happened?" Mary rushed in and helped her sit up.

"Logan! He was here to kill me!"

Mary gasped and her eyes darted around the room. She called for Isaiah and he came within seconds. He searched the room completely before he went outside to check the yard and street. He came back in, shaking his head with apology.

"Nobody around."

"He was here!" Kathleen moaned.

"It was just a bad dream, Kathleen. He's not here."

Mary helped Kathleen back into bed and tucked her in. She reached for a cool cloth from the basin of water. Mary tried to console her as she rang it out and gently wiped Kathleen's hot face. "I know those hallucinations you get with fevers can be fearsome things, but it's over now. You're safe, Kathleen."

Kathleen wished she could believe what Mary said. Dream or not, what Logan had said was true. Even if the illness didn't take her life, at some point, something would. It was inevitable. And Logan and the fiery depths of hell would be waiting.

The only reasonable thought she had in the hours and days after the dream was to wish for Joshua. Maybe seeing his face again would make everything right.

If only he would come.

Joshua missed her.

The latest snowstorm had almost done him in. He'd been on his own at the farm for years, but he couldn't remember ever being as lonely as he'd been since Kathleen went to town.

He wondered if she was still angry. It had been two weeks since he'd left her on the doorstep of his sister's home. He stood up to pace in the parlor once again. It was a wonder he hadn't worn a hole clean through it.

Why did I send her away? What if Logan finds her and makes good on his threats? What if Rita lures her back to the saloon? Why am I so stubborn?

He thought about how fun it had been kissing her. He closed his eyes and remembered watching her walk down the path across the bridge to the barn with that mysterious, alluring sashay the woman had no idea she possessed. He thought about her beauty, her scent, her smile.

How he missed her smile.

He was willing to admit all these things to himself. Maybe he'd even told it to Sundi a time or two. But it could go no further. Kathleen had been right. He missed the girl he was pretending she was, not the girl she really was. He didn't even want to think about the real Kathleen. It made him sick to consider it.

He paced. For a good half-hour he went back and forth in his mind. The snow was melting. He could get to town. He should check on the saloon anyway. And it wouldn't be unusual for him to stop in at Mary and Isaiah's for dinner.

Before he could talk himself out of it, he was in the barn saddling Sundi. And he couldn't deny the tremor of excitement he felt knowing he was going to see her again.

He knew something was wrong as soon as Mary opened the door.

"Joshua," she said. He could tell she was glad to see him, but worry edged the lines of her face.

Fear hit him thick in the chest. "Is she alright? Did Logan—" He couldn't finish the sentence.

"No, no, that's not it," she said quickly. "But she's sick, Joshua. The doctor is here."

He felt cold fear. He came inside and looked around for Kathleen. "Why didn't you send for me? Is she going to be okay?"

Mary nodded, though he noticed her brief hesitation. "I think so. I believe she's past the worst of it. The doctor seems to think she'll recover."

Joshua felt a stab of guilt that he hadn't been there. He needed to see her for himself. "What does Luke Thomas know? Nobody in this town really believes he's a doctor. He can't be more than seventeen."

Mary smiled in spite of herself and punched him on the shoulder. "Joshua James," she said with a chuckle. "He's a grown man and he does well enough. You shouldn't tease him so."

"I'm not completely joking," Joshua replied as he ducked under the door of the small room he had helped Isaiah add on to the little house when Mary and Isaiah couldn't seem to stop multiplying.

He wasn't prepared for what he saw. She seemed so tiny in the bed. So pale.

"Hey, Joshua." Dr. Luke Thomas sat at the small desk writing something.

"Luke." Joshua sat down beside Kathleen. She stirred, but didn't open her eyes. "Is she okay?"

Luke nodded. "I think she will be. She's very weak, but her fever broke during the night."

Joshua nodded. "Good." He didn't take his eyes from her face. "The doctor in these parts is a quack."

Luke sighed.

Joshua tucked the blankets around her shoulders as he silently berated himself for not being there. She had needed him. What kind of husband dumped his wife in town because he didn't want to talk about their problems? How selfish could a man be?

"Joshua?" Kathleen opened her eyes, trying to focus on him. They were rimmed with dark circles.

"I'm sorry," he said, his voice deep and gravely as he reached for her hand.

"For what?" She seemed genuinely surprised by his apology. Her voice was so weak and thin he could barely hear her. "I'm glad you're here."

"I am here," he said, pushing damp strands of hair from her forehead. "And I'm not going anywhere."

He hardly left her side for the next two days as she recovered. The morning she was able to stand and come to breakfast, he realized he had lost his appetite.

Not long after, he started to get chills.

Twenty-Nine

Something's missing.

Joshua forced his heavy eyelids open, squinting at the sudden light. His head hurt and his stomach growled like he hadn't eaten in days, and what he wanted wasn't with him in the room. He tried to remember what it was.

Mary appeared in the doorway with a tray in her hands. "Morning, sleeping beauty. You decided to come back to the living, I see." She smirked as she set down the tray that held steaming soup and bread with butter. He grabbed the bread and stuffed it into his mouth.

"That tastes like heaven." He remembered what he'd been missing. "Where's Kathleen?"

"Looks like I won't be spoon-feeding you today along with baby Frank, then?" She put the tray on his lap.

"Where is she?"

"Kathleen wouldn't leave your side. I told her to go get some rest. I had to insist, actually. I told her I could probably manage to keep you from perishing for one night."

"Good thing I woke up or you might have smothered me with a pillow," he quipped as he dove into the soup, slurping loudly and earning an annoyed expression from Mary.

"Your animals are fine, since you asked," she said with a wry expression. "Isaiah and Josh have been staying over there."

"I figured." He shrugged and finished off the bread as Frank crawled into the room. "When did he learn how to do that?" Joshua gestured to the baby with his spoon.

"While you were hiding on your farm trying to avoid your life." Mary didn't miss a beat.

He glared at her. "That right."

"Yes, that's right. And if you keep eating at that rate on your empty stomach you're going to end up right back in that bed, thrashing and moaning your wife's name."

"I didn't moan anything," he said with a snarl as he finished the soup and pushed the tray back toward her. "And I'll take some more of that."

"*Kathleen, Kathleen*," Mary mocked as she moved the tray to the dresser.

Joshua huffed and leaned back against the pillow with his arm behind his head and stared at the cross stitch of the Lord's Prayer hanging on the wall opposite his bed.

"What are you thinking about?" Mary picked up the baby and sat in the rocking chair.

"I just don't know how this is going to work, Mary. Kathleen and I are so different."

"Is that what you told the Lord when you took a sacred vow, in his name, no less, to be her husband, Joshua James?" Mary's gentle voice lessened the sting of her words only a little.

"I don't know," he said, feeling defensive. "I have no idea what God expects in all of this. Is it in either of our best interests to keep this up?"

She didn't answer for a time. He resumed his staring at the wall, morose at the suspicion that Mary wasn't answering because there was no answer.

When she spoke, her voice was very soft. "I know this isn't what you planned, Joshua. I know why you didn't want this, better than anyone else. You know that, right?"

He nodded, looking down.

"God knows it too. His plans aren't the same as ours. Remember the plans he had for Abraham, Joseph, Moses? They didn't understand what he was doing, but they obeyed even when it didn't make sense."

"They weren't prostitutes."

She didn't flinch. "Rahab was. God had a plan for her life. She became part of the lineage of Christ."

He frowned. "But Rahab changed. She believed God and followed him."

"You don't see Kathleen changing, Joshua?" Mary shook her head. "She's come such a long way already. Don't discount that."

"You're right. Her appearance is different and she's taken up more honorable pursuits. But inside, she's the same. Kathleen is so wounded by something that happened between her and her parents she won't even look at the goodness of God or consider him. She's convinced he can't save her, that she's too far gone. I don't ever see her coming around, Mary."

"You came around."

He was caught off guard by her words. It was true. God had pursued him long and relentlessly when he was a teenager with a broken heart, angry and making sure everyone knew it.

"If Jesus could mend your hurts, don't you think he can do the same for Kathleen? Isn't Jesus that kind, that persistent? Isn't he just what she needs?" Mary's voice became a whisper.

"Of course," Joshua said, doubt falling from his tone like chaff blowing into the wind as he faced the truth.

"Then trust him with your wife."

He thought long and hard on her words. Could he look at Kathleen and see a woman Jesus loved? The thought gave him hope.

"Take her home," Mary continued. "Live every day by her side. The difficulty won't go away, you can count on it. She will probably keep refusing God's love, and you will still be reminded of a past you'd give anything to forget. But every night when you go to sleep, get on your knees and pray. Pray for Kathleen. Pray for wisdom. And believe. Believe he's going to do something. And that one of these days, he will. He'll change her heart. And yours."

Thirty

"I can't wait to get my hands in that soil," Kathleen said. She'd been washing dishes, but the garden awash in early spring sunshine caught her attention. Joshua looked up from his breakfast.

"I can start tilling today if you'd like." He grinned as he spoke.

She nodded, feeling the urge to jump up and down and clap her hands with glee. She restrained herself.

After they did morning chores, Joshua met her in the garden with Sundi and pulled the plow from the shed. "Good day for it," he called as he left for the first pass.

She spent the time sorting through the supplies in the shed, carefully inspecting dried seeds and taking stock of the tools Nellie Whitley had carefully put away in their places the last time she planted. Her excitement grew. She had never been responsible for her own garden before, and certainly not one this large. She was breathless thinking about the new life that would grow as a result of her work, and that it would sustain and nourish them.

When Joshua was done plowing, he showed her how to drive stakes into the ground and tie string to make long, neat rows for seeds. She remembered her mama doing the same. She worked through the afternoon until every row was marked off.

When the sun started to set, Joshua came up from the barn as she was putting tools away. He washed at the pump and came to join her beside the picket fence with peeling white paint that surrounded the garden field.

He surprised her by grasping her hand. Without a word, he led her to the swing that hung from the tall oak next to the house. She sat down and he pulled back the ropes with strong arms. He gave her a sturdy push.

"You know you can't plant yet," he said after a peaceful moment. "Frosts don't end until mid-May."

"I know," she said, but her thoughts were no longer on planting. She inhaled deeply of the spring air scented by lilacs and apple blossoms. She looked out over the orchard where lambs frolicked. She remembered happy times in spring, planting with Mama, playing with her sister.

Riding the horses with her uncle – with *him*.

"Where'd you learn how to take care of a garden? It seems to be in your blood." He pushed her higher, and she felt like a little girl again, without a care in the world, believing everyone in her life was exactly who they claimed to be.

"Mama. She loves her garden. She and Jennifer are probably getting it ready about now."

"Jennifer is your sister?"

Kathleen didn't answer. How could she? She didn't know the answer.

"Jennifer is involved with the Anti-Saloon League," Kathleen said after a moment. "She's marched in several rallies."

She didn't miss Joshua's silence as he considered the information.

"Is that why you're afraid to go home?" he finally asked.

"Not really. Jennifer would find it her mission to reform me rather than condemn me."

"So, it's your father. The one you thought was your uncle." Joshua's voice was quiet. She noticed he had stopped pushing her and now stood to the side, his arms across his chest.

Her father. How did she even feel about him? She had always looked up to him, but now, since she had found his letter in the old chest, how did she see him? She'd been so angry at first, so indignant that they had all lied to her. She realized she hadn't taken the time to consider what he meant to her now.

Images of them riding together came to mind. She remembered the Noah's Ark and animals he'd carved for her the Christmas she was four. She could still see herself on the floor of his shop, talking to him while he worked.

Kathleen smiled. He'd been a good listener. She'd always been comfortable talking to him. He didn't speak much, but when he did, he was always honest and direct in his response.

She shook her head. He hadn't always been honest or direct.

She swallowed back tears with the memories. She was determined not to let the beautiful day be spoiled by the wounds. It was time to put them behind her and live for the present. Something told her it wasn't so simple; wounds must be cared for in order to heal, but she was determined to ignore that whisper.

"Come on," she said as she hopped off the swing. She skipped along the muddy path to the barn. She climbed the fence and jumped onto Sundi's back, causing the horse to whinny a protest. She saw Joshua approach the fence and gave him a sly smile.

"You forgot to put the saddle on," he said easily as he leaned on the fence, watching her.

She didn't answer. Instead, she reached down and unlaced her boots, dropping them into the mud under the horse. She directed the mare through the gate Joshua opened for her and went into the field behind the barn, working Sundi up to a trot before she slowly pulled herself up and stood on the horse's back. She extended her arms on either side, her bare toes clinging to horseflesh. She smiled when she remembered the first time she had attempted the trick.

The trick that had made *him* laugh.

"Kathleen Whitley, you're going to fall and break your neck," Joshua said in amused gruffness.

She laughed and let her feet slide down either side of Sundi's flanks. She grasped the mane.

"Hy-ah!" she yelled. Sundi took off over the property fence and galloped across the outer field in wild abandon. She felt the wind in her face as if it was blowing away all the lingering sadness of thinking about her family.

When Kathleen and the horse returned from their romp, Joshua was working in the barn. He seemed quiet while she put Sundi in her stall and watered her. She began to wonder if he was angry with her.

She was about to leave when he spoke.

"I'd like to take you somewhere."

She wasn't sure what to say, but her heart raced in a way that suggested she was either excited or afraid. Maybe both. "Where?"

"My favorite place in the world besides the farm. Evan and I found it a few years back. The fishing's great and you can't beat the solitude."

"I've never been much for fishing," she said, smiling.

"Then I'd say it's high time you started," he said, raising an eyebrow.

She nodded before she turned to leave the barn, but he spoke again. "Kathleen, it's pretty deep in the wilderness. It will need to be an overnight trip."

He paused, and she imagined what he might be saying.

"You okay with that?" he asked, his voice hoarse as she'd ever heard it.

She stood rooted to her spot. Was he asking if she was ready to make their marriage real? Was *he* ready? He was different since he'd brought her home from town, but he hadn't said anything specific.

Of course, maybe he was only asking her if she was okay with them spending the night in the wilderness.

"I suppose so," she said. He set down the planer he had in his hands and eyed her with an expression that only served to confuse her further.

"Get ready, then. I'll meet you here in an hour."

Thirty-One

"Stay behind me. You never know when a cougar or a copperhead might be waiting in the path around the next bend."

Kathleen stepped closer to him. "It's hard to imagine the dangers. It's so peaceful. I feel so safe."

Joshua didn't reply. They had been hiking for a couple hours. Ahead of them, a pleasant creek bubbled a song to the wildlife that lived on the edges. The trees opened their limbs wide enough to let patches of sunlight invade the path. As they journeyed deeper into the solace of the untouched nature around them, Kathleen imagined her troubles getting smaller and more insignificant. Here no expectations plagued her. Logan wouldn't be waiting around the next bend to jump out at her. She need only drink in beauty and survive.

Joshua glanced at her again. He seemed amused by something, but she couldn't imagine what it was. The corners of his eyes crinkled in an authentic smile of happiness.

"So what is it about nature, with all its wildness, that makes a young lady feel so safe?"

She raised an eyebrow. "Are you trying to say I'm in danger?"

"Nope. You're safe with me." He patted his holster at his hip.

"Maybe that's why I feel safe, then," she said softly. He caught her gaze and nodded.

"Where'd you get your gun?" She gestured to the weapon. She'd seen it before. He often brought it to the kitchen table in the evening to clean it. "It's well-crafted. Artistic, even. And if I'm not wrong, it's an antique."

He pulled it from the holster, checked the barrel, and presented her the handle. She took it, surprised by the weight of it. It was a burden that frightened her in an exhilarating way. What would it be like to shoot such a weapon?

"Grandpa carried this gun into Willoughby Run as part of the Iron Brigade. Won the Medal of Honor for his courage."

Kathleen held it up and aimed it. In her mind, she aimed it at Logan. She pretended he was standing at the distant tree, his back to her. Her finger itched to pull the trigger.

"Since when do womenfolk care about guns?" His voice brought her back from her imaginings.

"My mother was a saloon girl and my father an outlaw," she said. The gun fell to her side. "It's in my blood."

He chuckled. "Something tells me the story goes a little deeper." He accepted the gun from her and returned it to the holster.

"It's a beautiful gun. You must be proud of your Grandpa if you carry it."

He nodded. "He was a great man. I miss his wisdom."

Joshua didn't elaborate, but Kathleen guessed he was referring to their situation. To the problem of Kathleen.

As he moved ahead of her again, she caught sight of the pack on his back and the things he was carrying. A bedroll, an old army bag filled with something that clanked as he walked, a tied bundle of sticks. She wanted to read his mind and discover what had brought on this impromptu trip into nature. Was it about fishing? Checking traps or hunting game? Did he bring her along because he felt responsible to keep an eye on her?

As the path widened, he came to her side. Their arms brushed often, and she felt how solid his were. He smelled like grass and wind and sunshine. She felt a pleasant, unnerving jolt as she realized how much she longed to be in the circle of those arms.

"What are you thinking on?" He asked suddenly, making her

jump.

She feigned interest in a grouse hissing and chirping from the other side of the creek. "Just… wondering where we're going."

"That wasn't what you were thinking." He shook his head.

"It was." But she felt her heart flutter, knowing he recognized her lie.

"We're going to my favorite spot on Lake Ramona. I go there when I need to clear my head. It's so deep in the forest I never see another soul."

"We didn't bring any food," Kathleen said and pointed to the bag he carried.

"Plenty of food already there. Fish, berries, clear stream water that tastes like you died and went to glory."

Kathleen didn't bother to mention she would probably never be going to glory.

He eyed her suspiciously. "So where'd you learn to ride like that? The circus?"

She laughed. "I've always loved animals."

The memories swept around her happiness and threatened to undo it.

He nodded as if she should go on.

She shrugged. "When I was little, I used to believe I could read the thoughts of my uncle's horse, Becky. When I was six, he said I could learn to ride her. I spent the next few years riding for hours through the woods, having silent conversations the whole time."

"Your uncle as in your father?"

She nodded and gulped back emotion.

Joshua stayed quiet for a time. Thoughtful. "You know, Kathleen, we're never safe in this world. It's cursed, sinful. Even if we could manage not to mess up our lives, someone else will always come along and destroy what we've tried to build. That's why Jesus said to forgive. Even if it costs us something."

His gentle tone eased the sting of the admonition. She knew he was right, but she had no idea how someone climbed on top of truth like that and owned it. She couldn't just forget what happened.

She shrugged and didn't answer him. He seemed to respect the silence. She wondered why he seemed to understand her so well.

They stepped into a clearing by a small waterfall as the sunlight danced with the drops of water in the air. He stopped and leaned over the edge of the water to fill his canteen. She kneeled to drink and splashed some of the cool water over her face. When she stood, he was watching her. His fingers tentatively reached toward her.

"Your hair almost seems to glow in this light," he said. She held her breath as he considered her.

A rustling next to them stole his attention. He motioned her back and pointed between the bushes next to them. Kathleen gasped when she saw a mother skunk and her young.

They eased quietly back to the main path as the mother skunk watched them with wary eyes. Eventually she turned away and led her babies down the path in the opposite direction.

"Had a tangle with a skunk once," Joshua said. "Never care to repeat it."

That evening they came to a sprawling lake. The trees seemed to bow, paying homage to the gentle waves along the banks. Kathleen heard nothing but birds singing and insects humming.

"I can see why you like it here," she said as she breathed in the peaceful atmosphere.

He set down his pack and started investigating the lower branches of the trees along the edge of the woods.

"What are you doing?"

"Looking for this." He carefully removed an old, dried up bird's nest. "Great kindling."

He started a fire as the sun began to set and the temperature dropped. When he brought out his fishing pole, Kathleen decided to explore.

"Don't go so far you can't hear me if I call," he warned. She wandered away from the fire, wrapping her shawl around her shoulders. She walked down as far as she could on the shoreline of the lake, until she met a fallen tree that blocked the path. When she came back to the fire, he showed her several trout strung together.

"I'd have sat there all day long and never caught a thing," Kathleen said, impressed.

He shrugged. "Not this time of year. They practically jump out of the water onto your plate. Sometimes they even look up and say *Eat me! Eat me!*"

She laughed as he leaned toward her and made a fish face to go along with his high-pitched fish voice. She shivered as the breeze picked up.

"It gets cold during the night this time of year. Hope you don't mind if I sit close," he said, moving closer beside her on the log they were using as a bench. "I don't want us to freeze, after all."

She felt self-conscious as she tried not to smile. "I don't mind."

He cleaned the fish and set them in a small pan he had already set in the coals. Soon they sizzled and offered a smell that had Kathleen's stomach growling. After Joshua prayed, they picked up the fish with their fingers and ate.

"This is wonderful," she said a few minutes later when she pulled the last of the meat from the thin bones. She looked back at the pan, wishing for more.

"Things always taste better when you're good and hungry," he said, but he sounded distracted as he spoke. She looked up and found that he was watching her. Her stomach seemed to flip, and it wasn't hunger that caused it.

"We need to have us a discussion, Kathleen."

Thirty-Two

"We've come a ways, you and I," Joshua began, twisting his handkerchief as he spoke.

Kathleen watched him with curiosity. What was he getting ready to say? That they should go further into their relationship or that they should part ways? She had seen little of Logan since Joshua had taken her home. He had been injured, and the snow had been relentless for a time. But she couldn't expect him to stay away much longer. If Joshua were to let her go, she had no reason to think Logan wouldn't pounce on the opportunity to catch her unprotected.

"I've been praying quite a bit since we came back home," he said. "I've been asking God what to do."

"Has he given you any answer?" Kathleen asked wryly. It seemed childish to expect God to dictate their decisions and schedules.

"He has."

Kathleen was sure he was teasing. "And just how did *God* manage to speak to you, Joshua?"

"Through his Word," Joshua said without a moment's hesitation or a hint of a smile.

"You sound like Mama or Aunt Amelia," she said, picking at the bones of her dinner for any more morsels of meat. He took another fish from the string, cleaned it, and set it on the pan in the fire.

She shrugged. "I confess I never got much out of reading the

Bible."

"You're looking through the wrong set of eyes then," he said calmly, as if her words didn't surprise him. "But he also speaks through his people."

"If you're looking to the Bible and to church folk for answers about you and me, I'm guessing you're trying to tell me you want to end our arrangement," she said, afraid to meet his gaze with her own. "Is that why you brought me here? To tell me you're sending me away?"

Her throat felt tight. She hugged her knees and rested her chin on them, her mind scrambling for a new plan. Where would she go? How would she survive? But he reached a warm hand to her arm.

"Nope."

Her heart started pounding.

"Kathleen, you and I still have some hurdles to jump. I admit I don't even know how it will happen, and it won't be in my strength, I can tell you that. God will have to do the leaping in his time and way. But that's not what I'm getting at. If I'm being honest, I brought you here for one reason."

She closed her eyes as she waited for him to continue.

"Because it sounded awful nice, being alone with you all night."

She opened her eyes and looked at him, surprised. His face was so close to hers she could feel the warmth. His eyelids were heavy and his desire was easy to read. She gulped.

"You're looking at me like you don't know what I'm going to do next," he chuckled.

Do you know what you're going to do next, Joshua Whitley?

Kathleen wanted to remind him once again that desire wasn't the same as commitment. She'd seen desire destroy lives and homes. But in the moment, with his gaze tangled up in hers and his fingers slowly tracing her arm until they reached her neck, she didn't want to think about why he wanted her. She just wanted to be close to him. She let the tension melt away and closed her eyes, relishing his touch. He kneaded the muscles of her shoulders. She sighed away her anxious thoughts.

She could do this. She could let Joshua change her mind about what happened between a man and a woman. It could become a beautiful thing, couldn't it? She could pretend to be the kind of woman he wanted. She'd give him comfort and at the same time she'd keep him from sending her away. Joshua was the sort of man who wouldn't disown a woman after he'd been with her that way. He was honorable.

He came closer, hesitating for a moment as if to ask her permission. His eyes fell to her mouth and she parted her lips in invitation. The objections of Kathleen's mind only grew louder, but in response, she closed the distance between them, stopping just short of making contact. It only took him a breath to decide to make his move.

There was nothing tentative this time. His fingers tangled in her hair as he held her mouth captive with his, with kisses that spoke of need rather than timid attraction. He growled as he pushed her off the log and onto the bedroll by the fire. He kissed her deeply enough to let her know his intentions.

Kathleen was fairly sure Joshua was just as clueless as she was. She'd seen more than her share, but she'd never participated. Now she found herself imitating the things the girls at the saloon had done. She sighed in pleasure as she reached beneath his shirt and pressed her fingers to the flesh of his back.

She heard another growl, and absently wondered how Joshua had made the sound while he was busy kissing every last clear thought from her head.

Further noises told the whole story. She unwillingly pulled back to look across the fire. A black bear cub nosed through the remains of the fish and berries.

"We have company." Kathleen's voice sounded raspy and breathless. She felt the loss as Joshua shifted and sprang into action. He grabbed a stick and waved it in the air, yelling until the creature gave him a final disheartened glance before he ambled away.

Joshua threw the stick in the fire. She waited until he looked at her and made sure he caught her amused expression.

"What are you laughing at? He might have been a cute little baby bear, but you wouldn't want to meet his mama, and I'm sure she's nearby."

"Black bears don't generally attack, do they?" Kathleen teased.

"Mother bears are always dangerous," he insisted. Kathleen watched as he made himself busy clearing the food supplies, washing the dishes and packing them away. When he was done, he stood.

"I'm going for a walk."

He disappeared into the brush. She immediately felt alone. She pulled her shawl tighter around herself and wished for the warmth of his body.

She was worried and she knew she had a right to be. If he hadn't been planning on sending her away before, surely he would now that she had again proved to be a temptation. It wasn't hard to see he was sorry he'd let things go too far.

Thirty-Three

"Lord, what in the world was I thinking?" Joshua leaned his forehead against his clasped hands.

His face burned when he thought about what he'd done to Kathleen. He'd pushed himself on her as if his wants were more important than her comfort. She had seemed to respond, but wouldn't she have been taught to do so in the saloon?

He banged his head against his fists. So much for the headway he'd made in his prayers that she understand the love of Christ. So much for being an example of God's love. He'd ruined everything with his selfishness.

"I'm so sorry, Lord Jesus." He couldn't bow his head any lower, or he would. "Forgive me. Don't let me keep her away from your love."

The memory of Kathleen riding that horse earlier occurred to him again. She'd been so carefree, so lovely. He had wanted her. Wanted to know her the way a husband would know his wife. He felt entitled. He *was* her husband, after all. And anyway, she was used to being desired.

But something had been missing. Something in the exchange hadn't been authentic, just as she had tried to tell him before. And if he had proceeded without the element of the genuine, he was doing nothing more than making use of a prostitute, no matter how well he managed to justify it in his own eyes. Whether it was appropriate by law or not, he knew he'd intended to use her without making a single promise in return.

"I'm sorry," he whispered again. "Jesus, forgive me."

In true Christ-like fashion, the immediate answer gripped his spirit with tender affection he didn't deserve.

Love as I have loved you. Flee youthful lusts. Follow the way of love.

Joshua continued to pray, keeping an eye on Kathleen, who eventually rolled herself up in the blanket and went to sleep. He stayed among the trees, praying God would save a lost soul who needed redemption more than she could possibly understand.

He prayed she'd be saved – in spite of him.

Cold.

Kathleen woke up shivering. Had Joshua stayed in the woods the whole night? She searched her surroundings for him, but only saw the smoldering remains of the fire.

The sight made her think about what had happened the night before. Her face warmed despite her chill, and a tremor of fear coursed through her.

She sat up and pulled the bedroll around herself to keep warm. What had sparked her fear? It wasn't that she was afraid Joshua would hurt her. She knew he was a kind man at heart. She couldn't even imagine him treating her the way Logan had.

The memory of his passion was not a trial to consider, either. He'd awakened her senses. She could have given herself to him. She could have enjoyed the intimacy and taken the memory to the depths of hell where it might have sustained her.

"Good morning," Joshua said behind her. She turned around and saw him standing on the edge of the woods with his hands in his coat pockets. Dark circles underlined his eyes and his voice was tired.

"Morning," she replied. "Did you sleep?"

He came forward and threw more kindling on the fire, poking it with a stick until the flames returned. He didn't answer her question. "Chilly morning."

She nodded, watching him. He gave her a handful of berries and held out the canteen for her to drink.

"What are you thinking about?" He didn't sound certain he wanted to know the answer.

"Just wondering what it meant," she said softly.

"Last night, you mean?"

She nodded.

He sighed and lapsed back into silence for a time. "It meant what you would think it meant, Kathleen."

"I've seen plenty of men do such things for their own pleasure," she reminded him.

He rubbed his palms together and stared into the fire. "I don't see you that way, Kathleen. I promise you that."

She waited for him to explain. He stood up and paced around the fire. Finally, he looked at her. "I've had dealings with a number of saloon girls in the past, mostly because of my job. They are usually bold, disrespectful and defiant of authority. Either that or completely broken and callous."

She nodded in agreement.

"I didn't expect you to be what you've turned out to be."

"Which is?" She couldn't imagine what he meant.

"You're hardworking. You have a spirit and drive that makes you good at everything you set your mind to do."

She watched him.

"Kathleen, I don't know what to do with you," he admitted gruffly with another sigh. "When I thought I knew what you were, it was easier. Now that I… I feel something for you, I'm not sure what to do."

Kathleen tried to hide her smile. "You seemed rather sure last night."

Joshua shrugged with a half-smile, but she could tell he was struggling with his words.

"If I'm not what you expected, and you feel something, what holds you back?" Kathleen knew it was a risk to ask the question. She wasn't sure she wanted to hear the answer. But it confounded her – the way he'd put a halt to things the night before. When she lived in the saloon, she'd never known a man to back down from his passions. Joshua was her husband. Nothing in his faith or the law said he shouldn't do what he wanted to do with her.

So why hadn't he when she was willing?

He didn't answer her question, so she had to guess. "Because you still can't get over who I was. What I did."

She assumed his silence meant she was correct. When Joshua saw her, he saw a girl who'd given her body to other men. He didn't know the truth, because she hadn't told him.

She almost told him. It would make everything easier. Maybe she'd give him the peace of mind he needed to be at peace with their marriage.

But pride blocked the way. She didn't want to have to grovel at his feet, or give him another chance to reject her. Anyway, she'd sinned enough, whether she'd physically betrayed him in the saloon or not.

Besides, Joshua had his secrets as well. Why should she air hers if he was unwilling to do the same?

They didn't talk much as they walked home. When the farm was in sight, Joshua suddenly smiled. "Do you know what tomorrow is?"

"Sunday."

"More specifically," he prompted.

She shrugged. "Sunday, the fifteenth of April, the year 1906."

He chuckled. "It's Easter Sunday."

She considered the news. It brought to mind memories of happier times.

Joshua spoke to her thoughts. "How'd your family celebrate?"

She couldn't help her smile. "We woke up to find the Easter bunny had left treats. Mama would dress Jennifer and me in our new dresses and bonnets and we would join the parade to church. After services my aunt, uncle and cousins would come to dinner and spend the day with us."

She felt the bitterness return and swallowed back the burning in her throat. All her precious memories, tainted by the truth. She had been out of place.

"Gran always made a feast for after church," Joshua said, though he watched her thoughtfully. "Grandpa read the Easter story at breakfast. But only one tradition matters to me now."

"What?"

"Going to church at sunrise."

She raised an eyebrow. "I guess we better go to bed early."

They reached the barn, where they parted ways so he could tend the animals and she could start supper.

"It's worth being a little short on sleep," he called back to her. "And Mary's roast chicken dinner is a nice bonus prize."

Thirty-Four

Some days, a person woke up feeling like it was best to stay in bed. That Easter morning when Joshua knocked on Kathleen's door before dawn, she almost told him she was ill. There was a knot of fear in her stomach she couldn't explain. Was it a sort of premonition of something bad? Aunt Amelia had feelings sometimes, and often she turned out to be right. What if something terrible would happen if Kathleen got out of bed?

She sat on the edge of her bed and tried to think of something pleasant. They would be able to have lunch at the McAllisters'. She missed Mary. It would be fun to see all the women in their new spring dresses, and the little girls with their Easter hats all flushed with excitement.

She realized she wanted to go.

She took special care as she dressed, smoothing out the beautiful white lawn dress Mary and Annie had made her for Christmas. She hadn't worn it yet, but Easter was a time when everyone dressed well, so she wouldn't stand out. It was a daunting task for a saloon girl to have enough courage to don a white dress.

She looked at her reflection in the mirror. She didn't deserve to wear it. It didn't represent her purity. Her sin-blackened heart was as miry as the muddy slop of the pigpen.

But the image in the mirror was lovely. She fingered the delicate puffed sleeves and the gathering of lace that swept across her chest.

184

She eyed her hair next, wondering if she should risk the headache to wear it up for the sake of fashion. She had set her hair in loose rags the night before, so she gathered up the curls into the popular "Gibson Girl" style. She finished the look with a straw hat decorated with lavender and ribbon.

She appeared to belong, even if she didn't. What would it be like to truly fit in?

She went to the kitchen, nervous about Joshua seeing her. Would he be angry she was wearing white?

He stood by the sink, dressed in a fine suit she hadn't seen before. He smelled of soap and had traded his usual stubble for a clean-shaven face. He reminded her of the dashing gentlemen in Aunt Amelia's novels.

He turned and saw her, and his eyes widened. His mouth dropped open, though he seemed quite speechless.

"Do I look that bad?" Kathleen asked, her tone tentative.

He shook his head. "You're... you're a vision." He managed to find his wits and crossed the room to lift her gloved hand to his lips. "Happy Resurrection Sunday, Kathleen."

She felt awkward. When she didn't answer, he leaned closer and inhaled. "You smell good, too."

"Mary made the hat with lavender."

"Mary is trying to ensnare me," he said, narrowing his eyes though the corner of his mouth turned upward. He looked her over again. "First time I was ever tempted to be late for the sunrise service."

She chuckled in disbelief. "Joshua! Shame on you." She wagged a finger at him. Her heart seemed to skip a beat when he caught the finger and kissed it.

"One more thing before we go," he said softly.

She waited, hoping he might kiss her. Instead, he gently removed her hat and ran his fingers through her curls. The pins came loose and fell, clattering on the table. When he had freed her hair of restrictions, he set the hat back on her head and touched the tip of his finger to her nose.

"I won't have you sick on such a day, Kathleen. It doesn't matter what anyone else thinks." He stepped back to grab his guitar from the corner, then returned and offered her his arm. "Besides, I like your hair down."

She nodded and took his arm, letting him lead her to the wagon waiting outside.

On the way to town, Joshua took an appreciative breath of morning air. "It was just before dawn on Resurrection Sunday when the women came to the tomb to anoint Jesus's body. But he wasn't there."

She nodded. Though it made her uncomfortable, she was happy for him in his worship. Even if she couldn't have such a faith for herself, she would never wish for Joshua to lose his. It was an integral part of what made him Joshua Whitley.

They arrived at the church, but instead of heading for the formal spired church doors, he led her behind the church and down a hill to the creek. About sixty worshipers sat on logs or blankets in a semicircle around the pastor.

She felt an odd peace through her turmoil. Joshua spread the blanket on the ground and helped her sit down as the pastor began to pray.

"Lord Jesus, how thankful we are," he said in a tender tone. "How thankful. You finished the task. You did all that was required to save us. You proved your power by conquering death, the grave and hell. Forever! We cling to your promise that we may trust you to be saved from the punishment we deserve. We are thankful you will come just as you left, and we will indeed see you face to face. In the name of Jesus, who rose in power from the dead, Amen."

Kathleen gulped back emotions she didn't want to understand. She realized Joshua had left her side and was standing next to Pastor Merchant, with Evan on his other side. Both the men held their guitars. They began to play a reverent duet, the tones of the guitars dancing together so that Kathleen could not tell the difference. Their gaze wandered back and forth from their own hand to the other's. She could tell they had spent much time playing together. She recognized the song, *Holy, Holy, Holy*. It was a hymn they had sung many times in church back home. She had never considered the words before. Doing so was overwhelming, so she tried not to think about them.

They sang along after Joshua and Evan's hymn, and she found all the songs familiar. She closed her eyes and saw her family members, standing around her, singing along.

> *Was it for crimes that I have done*
> *He groaned upon the tree?*

The words caused the first prickle of heat on her neck.

Her crimes flooded her mind. She'd walked into a saloon knowing it would alienate her from the people she loved. She turned her back on modesty and decency. She provoked a man to twisted obsession and stole the hopes and dreams of a good man who deserved far better than she could ever be.

She was the ugly prodigal, wallowing with the pigs. She might wear white, but inside she was stained crimson with her rebellion and bitterness.

Pastor Merchant stood with his well-worn Bible open in his hand and read from it. *"Have mercy upon me, O God, according to thy lovingkindness: according to the multitude of thy tender mercies blot out my transgressions. Wash me from mine iniquity, and cleanse me from my sin. For I acknowledge my transgressions: and my sin is ever before me."*

The knowledge of her sin rushed at Kathleen like a herd of stampeding cows. What had she done? How much injury had she caused the dear people she loved? And she'd done it all on purpose! She felt the burden of it and struggled to draw a ragged breath. Would God strike her dead right there in the middle of the peaceful gathering?

The pastor continued. *"Against thee, thee only, have I sinned and done this evil in thy sight: that thou mightest be justified when thou speakest, and be clear when thou judgest."*

Kathleen could hang her head no lower. There it was. The reason she had no hope. The reason she would never possess a healing faith as Joshua did. She deserved whatever punishment God had in mind for her.

"Dear people, David provides us a picture in this passage. A picture of ourselves. Not one of us can escape the guilt of our soul. Not one of us has any right to stand before God and claim to be clean. From the mighty to the small, we are all the same in the eyes of God."

Kathleen shook her head in confusion. Her movement caught Joshua's attention. She could feel his gaze on her as the sermon continued.

"This is why we can say with David '*Purge me with hyssop, and I shall be clean: wash me, and I shall be whiter than snow.*"

He paused. Reverent silence rushed over the group, and Kathleen felt something reaching in and around them. It was the pull of something she'd never felt before. Invisible, yet as tangible as her own flesh. When she looked up, she didn't see the pastor. It was his form, but power radiated from his being, and love filled his gaze.

She felt a sudden and urgent need to flee. She didn't belong here. She couldn't stand before God. If he was going to be here, she would have to run away or he would find her and she'd be dragged to hell. She started to get up.

"When our Lord suffered on the cross, he endured the ultimate suffering. Not the crown of thorns pressed into his brow. Not the spikes driven into his hands and feet. Not the beatings, lash by lash, cutting through his blessed skin with shards of bone and metal, over and over, again and again until he was bloodied nigh to death. No, these things are not what caused his greatest suffering."

Kathleen throat constricted. She cringed as she imagined the whip tearing through her flesh, worse than any beating she'd received in the saloon. She froze, hovering in her crouching position, positioned to run.

Joshua touched her arm. "You okay?"

She couldn't answer. Her voice was buried beneath the lump that was threatening to steal her breath. Hot tears broke free and spilled down her cheeks.

"Jesus bore that pain, sinner. The pain that should have been yours. Should have been mine. All the way to Calvary's cross. So far that God, his father, turned away from him. He bore your sin all the way to the grave. Because he knew if *you* bore it, the weight would drag you to the pit for eternity.

"He loves you, friend. He went the distance you couldn't go. He allowed himself to be destroyed, ripped to shreds and broken, though he is Almighty God. Though he deserved their worship, he accepted their cruelty. He did it all for *you*."

Kathleen stared hard at the ground. The pastor *couldn't* mean someone like Kathleen. The hope of such a perfect love was too precious to later discover she was not eligible.

But the picture would not leave her mind. Jesus, beaten beyond recognition. Bloody and struggling under the weight of a cross. She shook her head, but the image stubbornly remained. What had she done? Had it really been *her* sin that drove the nails into his hands and feet?

She recognized her selfishness where before she'd seen herself as a victim. She'd gone with Rita, not because it was her only option, but because she knew it was wrong and it would wound her family. She flirted, knowing full well the men had wives and children at home who were being betrayed. She took over Joshua's life in order to protect herself from the situation she had created.

She saw Joshua's hand resting on the blanket near hers, letting her know he was there. She ached for what she had done to him. She'd forced herself on his goodness. She'd stolen his dreams for a peaceful life with someone like Audrey.

Kathleen couldn't imagine why God would care about her so much that he would provide such a dramatic rescue through Jesus. If he was so good, why would he want her to escape the punishment she deserved?

She felt dizzy. Her thoughts swarmed like angry bees. She held her temple, her vision protesting the brightness that suddenly shone all around her.

She jumped when Joshua put his hand on top of hers. But his touch calmed her. She closed her eyes and tried to keep listening past the ringing in her ears.

"Dear friends, I ask you to consider this illustration: A dungeon has been filled with the vile remnants of mankind. You and I are among them. We wait for reckoning. But light fills the dreariness, and a brilliant figure appears. It is a man. It is Jesus. He steps through, unafraid to spoil his perfect white robe with the filth. Because everything he touches becomes clean and whole. He beckons to you with nail-scarred hands. He is smiling. He exits again, but he leaves the door open wide.

"Some immediately follow. You watch as their condition transforms. They are white. Whiter than snow! They turn and call to you. But you stay where you are.

"Why do you remain, sinner? Do you think you can save yourself? Do you believe you are too far gone to save at all?"

She squeezed her eyes shut. She sensed a presence closer than Joshua's. It wasn't the preacher speaking. His voice was a tool of someone far greater.

"You need only rise and follow Christ. He will do the rest. He will do everything. Rise and follow Christ!"

Her heart began to pound. She fought the urge to stand and run to the pastor. Sobs caught in her throat and she labored for breath. She summoned every last bit of her stubborn pride and fought the onslaught of conviction that had grabbed hold of her and would not let go.

Someone started singing. Other voices from the group joined in, reverent and hushed. The peace contrasted her distress.

> *Jesus paid it all,*
> *All to him I owe.*
> *Sin had left a crimson stain,*
> *He washed it white as snow.*

She could give him no less if it were true he had paid all. She must give herself away. She must surrender control.

Let go.

With the deepest breath she had ever drawn, she made herself stand to her feet. She expected reproachful stares, but most of the worshipers had closed their eyes and bowed their heads. She took a step.

Her feet seemed weighted down. She struggled, lifting one and then the other. As she labored, she realized with a rush of emotion that Joshua was standing at her side, his hand against her back for support. When she looked at him, his eyes were brimming with tears.

Tears for *her.*

Each step became lighter, and by the time she reached the pastor she was all but running. She sank to her knees in front of him and bowed her head.

"I don't deserve it, but if you really think it's possible… I want to be saved."

Thirty-Five

"God, if it's true that you can forgive a soul as black as mine because of the blood of your Son, I ask you to make me clean. In return, I'll give you all of me. Everything. For the rest of my life."

The words had been so simple. She hadn't known what else to say. But the answer had been immediate.

When Kathleen rose to her feet moments later, she felt like a different person. She wore the same clothes, she had the same name and the same history, but everything had changed.

She knew a peace as she never had before. The dark spot on her soul she tried to live with, tried to ignore without success – it was gone. She could still recall every terrible decision she'd made, every hurt she'd caused, but quietness in her soul assured her her debt had been paid.

She turned to Joshua. He had changed as well. Not within himself, but toward her. There was hope in his expression she'd never seen before.

"It's true," she whispered. He squeezed her arm, emotion pulling at his features.

People were watching her. Mary, Isaiah and their children stood nearby. They approached her with well wishes. Little Sally had the most advice, having just gone forward the previous Sunday to be saved. She explained how the Bible said angels rejoice at a sinner's repentance, and that Kathleen now had two birthdays, though this one would always be the more important. Sally also insisted Kathleen should be baptized when the spring flooding in the canal passed. Kathleen was overwhelmed by the information, but she nodded as Joshua and Mary chuckled.

Mary hugged Kathleen. "Never mind, Sally. Aunt Kathleen will figure it out. Just give her time."

"She's got all the time in the world now," Joshua said softly. "All the time it takes to fill up eternity."

"We've had trouble in the train yard."

Kathleen overheard Isaiah speak quietly to Joshua in the parlor. She helped Mary set out snacks for the children before they began dinner preparations.

"Rita Dolsen has been sending girls to the yard during work hours. Fights have broken out."

"I'll look into it. Sheriff Stacy said today at services he'd be leaving on the afternoon train," Joshua replied. "Some days I wish that saloon would burn to the ground."

"Don't worry about it today. This is a day for celebration. Your wife has found the Lord, and there's nothing better than knowing your loved ones are safe."

The conversation ended and Joshua came into the kitchen. "Mary, you're making those potatoes you made last month at the church potluck, right?" He scanned the counter and table, popping a bite of stuffing into his mouth.

Mary rolled her eyes and slapped his hand away. "Kathleen, all you have to do to keep this one around is keep filling his belly. Mark my words."

Joshua reached around his sister to grab another bite. He winked at Kathleen. "She speaks the truth."

Mary huffed and pushed him out of the way. He leaned back against the kitchen counter and locked eyes with Kathleen. The kitchen was small, so they were close. His hand slid around her back and she felt her cheeks flush. The twins were being scolded by their mother for bringing their prized collection of dead bugs to the table, so no one was paying attention.

"Will this feeling ever go away?" she asked him softly.

His smile was the most tender she'd ever seen. "Feelings always come and go; you can count on it. But keep in mind God will never leave you. In the next days and weeks, and for the rest of your days, really, the devil will most likely try to convince you your salvation is a lie. Go right on believing, no matter what. Talk to the Lord. Read the Bible. Memorize the verses that stand out. It's your weapon against the devil. No lie from hell can stand up to the Word of God."

Kathleen nodded as Joshua slipped his hand into hers, weaving their fingers together. His expression held promise. She felt dizzy when she considered the possibilities. But there were still secrets to be shared. Things to be set right. Was she ready? Was Joshua?

"I'll help you," he said softly, as if he was answering her silent question. "You're not alone. I've got something for you when we get home."

She felt a wave of nervous anticipation and looked away. He smiled and squeezed her hand. "I want you to have my Gran's Bible. I use Grandpa's and hers is just sitting on the shelf in the parlor. She'd want you to have it."

Kathleen nodded. Joshua opened his mouth to say something else, but he stopped. They looked at one another in silence until one of the wailing twins who had not gotten his way in the matter of the bugs interrupted the moment.

"Suppose I'll take these hooligans outside to play ball so you women can work your magic," Joshua said, clearing his throat. He let her go.

The children disappeared with Joshua into the warm sunshine to play. Kathleen noticed Mary's eyes following them with uncertainty.

"Are you worrying that they should be sitting still on the Lord's

Day?" Kathleen remembered their previous conversation.

Mary sighed. "I suppose."

"You know, Mary, I've spent my life thinking God's love had to be earned. Your children will know it's a gift, even if they play on Sunday. You're a better mother than you think."

Mary smiled. "Listen to you, Kathleen Whitley, not two hours after finding the Lord."

"I think I was coming to him for a long time. Maybe my whole life. I just didn't realize it."

"I don't think we ever stop coming to him." Mary turned the onions with the other hand on her hip. "Our future is settled, but we have to keep pressing on to know him better, as long as we have breath and a beating heart."

They worked in silence until Mary spoke again. "You and Joshua were standing awfully close a few minutes ago."

Kathleen shrugged and tried to keep her smile in check.

"It's none of my business, according to Joshua," Mary acknowledged. "But tell me anyway."

Kathleen laughed. "Well, the past few days he's been downright friendly, I'll tell you that."

Mary smiled knowingly. "My brother is slow to warm up, but when he decides on something or someone, he'll go to the ends of the earth to see it through."

"I can see how that is true," Kathleen said as she opened cans of beans left over from the canning. "But something still holds him back. Keeps him on guard."

Mary nodded. "Yes. And he better tell you why. Soon."

Kathleen didn't answer. Mary gave her a pointed glance. "You have things to say to him as well."

Kathleen gave her attention to the beans. How did a woman go about telling her husband she was, in fact, a maiden?

"Mary, I don't know how you get chicken to melt in my mouth, but I sure do appreciate it." Joshua pushed back from the table and sighed in satisfaction. "At least if your parenting doesn't turn out well, you've always got your cooking skills."

Mary made a face.

The twins both went for the last biscuit and ended up on the floor wrestling. One of them started wailing. Mary sighed.

"I'm glad they're distracted," Joshua said. "So far I've been kicked in the shins, had gravy poured on my good shirt, narrowly missed a fork to the eye and had an entire mouthful of mashed potatoes sneezed into my face." As everyone laughed, he leaned over and punched Evan, who had joined them for dinner, in the arm. "Maybe that was Evan, actually."

Evan took a big bite of potatoes and made a show of pretending to need to sneeze.

The laughter of the adults caused Jedidiah to experience a miraculous recovery from his injury. He began pouring spoonfuls of peas down the back of Sally's dress. She dutifully screamed.

"Oh, dear," Mary said, her voice lacking conviction.

The children dispersed, to the relief of everyone, and the adults stayed at the table, drinking coffee and eating pie. Mary took the baby to the rocking chair in the corner to nurse. Joshua, Evan and Isaiah became involved in an animated discussion of an obscure passage of Scripture. Kathleen listened, interested for the first time she could remember. She even asked a few questions of the men.

"Kathleen, you were raised in church, weren't you?" Mary asked as she watched from her corner. Kathleen got up and went to sit beside her so they could talk.

"I knew the stories, but I thought they were meant to make me afraid of God. I never considered Jesus, except that he was good and he didn't deserve to be killed. I thought I was supposed to try my hardest to be like him." Kathleen shook her head with regret. "I tried so hard to be worthy. But it seemed like I always ended up failing. I guess, at some point, I got tired of all my inadequate attempts and gave up. I didn't think there was any hope for me."

"You're the prodigal, come home to the father," Mary mused.

"And welcomed back with open arms."

"I suppose I have something I always longed for. A father who calls me his own."

"We had grandfather and we both know the love of a heavenly father, but Mary and I didn't have a father, either, Kathleen," Joshua said. She hadn't realized the men had gone silent and Joshua had crossed the room to stand beside her. She turned to him and saw evidence that the words had cost him.

Mary nodded in agreement. "Without Grandpa, we wouldn't know the meaning of the word."

Kathleen frowned. "Doesn't it make you angry?"

Mary seemed to consider her words for a time. "It makes me sad. Sad that there are men in this world who have children and grandchildren they don't know exist. But I'm not angry. God has always given me what I need."

"Are you still angry with your father?" Joshua asked her suddenly.

Kathleen shook her head and looked at her hands. "I don't know who my father is."

"You're talking about your father and uncle?"

Kathleen nodded. He reached for her hand. "Does it matter? Don't they both care about you?"

She swallowed hard. "Papa always held himself at a distance. He wasn't home much, but when he was, I didn't miss that his relationship with Jennifer was easier for him. With me, it almost felt forced at times, though he never said it outright. I remember wishing my father would be more affectionate – like my uncle. When I came across the truth, written in an old letter in our attic room, it hurt that I could have had the father I needed all along. I felt like he had abandoned me."

Kathleen didn't want to look at their faces and see the confusion. She knew it didn't make sense. But she couldn't act like it didn't matter, because it did. Quite a bit.

"I know you're hurt. I'm not trying to say you shouldn't feel that way." Joshua traced circles on her hand with his thumb. "But what if you decided not to focus on the one big mistake he made? Being a man, I can put myself in his position. From what you told me, I don't think he left you with your aunt and uncle because he didn't love you."

"You're not a father," she argued.

"I'm not," he said with a decisive nod. "But neither are you."

Kathleen hesitated. "When I found out, something went wrong inside me. All the darkness I kept hidden overflowed and everyone saw the real me, the one who deserved to be unloved. The person I have always tried to hide."

"Sometimes that's a blessing in disguise," Joshua said.

"Even if you were unloved, which I doubt, you can't say it anymore," Mary said with a knowing smile.

"Yes, I don't understand why, but Jesus loves me." Kathleen admitted, feeling the peace wash over her once again.

"Of course he does, but I was talking about someone else." Mary gave Joshua a look of challenge. He turned red and glared at Mary. Kathleen didn't know whether to laugh or to leave the room, but it wouldn't matter, because the conversation was interrupted by a gunshot. The echoing sound blast seemed to shatter the fragile joy that had surrounded the day.

Thirty-Six

Joshua sprang to action. "Stay here," he said to Kathleen and Mary as he left the house. "And get the kids inside."

He didn't stay to make sure they followed instructions, but he knew they would. Isaiah and Evan ran behind him toward the saloon. The door was locked and the room inside was nearly empty.

"It's the train yard," Isaiah said, pointing.

They ran toward the group of men standing in the middle of the yard by the tracks. Guns were waving and tempers flaring. Joshua walked into the middle and pulled out his own gun. He held it at his side as a warning. "Do you people realize what day this is?"

A man pointed his gun at Logan, who held a saloon girl by the arm. "I saw her first."

"She wanted a real man," Logan drawled. "What can I say?"

"You no good, lying son of—"

"Alright, that's enough," Joshua interrupted. "Logan, you must be feeling better if you're causing a raucous again. Smith, you said your piece. Stand back and put the gun down." He turned to the girl. "What are you doing in the rail yard?"

She shrugged. "Rita sent me."

Joshua didn't think she could be more than eighteen, yet her demeanor was indifferent and cold. He knew that expression. It had stubbornly clung to the most important face in his world most of his childhood. He'd tried to make her smile. He'd tried to make her soft.

199

For a young boy, it had been devastating to never know his mother's joy.

The girl's outfit reminded him of Kathleen's dress when he had first spoken to her at the saloon. He could see it now, how different she'd been. Kathleen had worn the guarded expression, but it hadn't seeped through to her spirit as this girl. Kathleen had still been soft underneath.

It occurred to him he had no idea how long Kathleen had lived at the saloon.

"Here she comes," Evan murmured beside him. Joshua turned and saw Rita approaching.

She held her brocade skirt out of the mud with an irritated expression. "There better be a good reason for this inconvenience."

"There's no good reason for what's going on in this rail yard," Joshua snapped. "Get these girls back to your place or I'll throw you all in jail for the night."

"You have no right." She shrugged. "There is no law saying these women can't visit with the men on a Sunday afternoon."

Joshua felt his anger surge. He stepped toward her. "I won't have you interrupting Easter dinners with this hogwash."

She laughed. "You should have been a preacher, Deputy. Thank you for the sermon, but you have no grounds to arrest anyone. Do not force me from my place of business unless you have real matters to discuss."

She didn't wait for a response, but glided back along the path to the saloon. Joshua was angry enough to shoot someone. He jammed his gun in the holster to ensure he wouldn't.

"Go home." He directed the men out of the yard. "If you're supposed to be working, get to work. Otherwise, all of you clear out."

He was relieved when they did as he said without argument.

"Where'd Logan go?" Evan spoke next to him.

Joshua fumed. "Can you hurry back and make sure Kathleen is okay? I need a minute."

Joshua allowed Isaiah and Evan to walk ahead of him so he could take a few deep breaths and regain control of his temper. He prayed for strength, and knew he was going to need it when he heard a spiteful voice behind him.

"You still got that pretty filly at home, Whitley?"

Joshua's anger returned and multiplied. He turned to face Logan.

"She still owes me a night. She was all paid for when she ran," Logan said in an insolent drawl. "And I got a new lease on life these days, Deputy."

Joshua took a deep breath. And then another. "Get out of my sight before I do something you regret," he said quietly.

"We're just having a conversation," Logan said, obviously missing Joshua's barely controlled wrath or possessing some sort of death wish. "I paid, fair and square, and the last place I saw my property was at your farm."

"Listen up, you filthy pile of horse dung." Joshua took several steps closer, until he was close enough to Logan to see the stubble covering his chin. "You're gonna want to stay as far away from Kathleen as you can, or I will not hesitate to take out this gun and end your sorry life. Believe me when I tell you, I would spend the rest of my life in jail to protect her, without a moment's hesitation. Think on that before you try anything."

Joshua seethed at the loathsome laughter that followed his words. Foreboding clutched at his chest as he made his way back to the McAllister home.

Kathleen was standing on the porch, her arms wrapped around her middle. "I was worried."

"It's okay," Joshua said, trying to sound more at ease than he felt. He guided Kathleen to the door. "But I do want you to take extra care from now on."

He saw fear flash in her features. "Why?" she asked in trepidation.

"For my sake. The men down there are rough and I don't like the thought of decent women walking around alone until things settle down or we get that saloon closed up for good."

Kathleen stood still on the porch as Joshua went inside. Had he realized he was referring to her as a "decent woman" now?

Joshua and Kathleen went home to the farm washed in the warm rays of the late afternoon spring sunshine. They didn't speak much, but he held the reins with one hand and slipped the other around her shoulders, inviting her to lean against his shoulder. She reveled in the gesture. Just as they were turning into the barnyard and Kathleen was fairly sure life was about as beautiful as it could possibly be, Joshua sat up and grunted in displeasure.

"What's this?"

She sat up as well and saw the vultures gathered on the path in front of the barn. Joshua jumped down and went to shoo them away and investigate. Kathleen hopped down and followed him.

"Is it one of the chickens?" She could see a bloody carcass. Her stomach turned.

"Stay back, Kathleen."

She stopped short at the tone of his voice. He walked back to her and she saw his eyes had taken on the angry glint again.

"What is it?"

He reached a palm to her face. "I think Logan's been here."

She tried to breathe. "What did he do?"

"It's the kitten."

Kathleen gasped a sob. "No." She pushed around him to see, but he tried to hold her back.

"Don't look, Kathleen. Just go to the house and I'll take care of it."

"I have to!" She gave him another push and went to the bloodied mess of what used to be her spunky, affectionate little orange and white-striped cat. He'd been decapitated.

"I'm so sorry, Kathleen," Joshua pulled her into his arms. She pushed away from him and ran for the house.

Kathleen spent the rest of Easter Sunday evening sobbing on her bed and wishing she'd never entered that saloon in the first place.

How much pain could one bad decision cause?

"Jesus, please forgive me for not taking care of Ginger. It's my fault. Everything is my fault. I try and try... but I always fail."

Monday morning following chores, Joshua told Kathleen to pack a lunch and come with him to town. She sent him a questioning glance, but she did as he asked without a word. She didn't seem to feel much like talking yet. He had heard her crying herself to sleep the night before. It made him sick to consider what Logan had done to her beloved cat. He hadn't missed the warning contained in the unthinkable act. He was desperate trying to think of how to keep Kathleen safe. He wondered if it was time to start thinking about leaving town, though he couldn't imagine leaving his beloved farm. What was the right choice? What did God want him to do?

He dropped Kathleen at Mary's and went to the Sheriff's office. He wasn't surprised to find several notes pinned to the door. He took them inside to read, though he figured he knew what they said.

As he expected, every note was a complaint about the saloon girls down at the train yard. Mrs. Cooke sent him fair warning saying she was planning a march on the saloon that morning. He was half-tempted to turn a blind eye. But that would only mean more trouble when Rita grew irritated enough to retaliate.

He glanced at the desk in the back office belonging to Sheriff Stacy. If he didn't hold the man in such high esteem, he might be tempted to entertain a bitter thought. He was doing the man's job while the sheriff lobbied in Columbus for prohibition. He had mixed feelings about the quest the sheriff was on. Joshua was as tired of the saloon as the rest of them, and he had more reason from his past than most to want an end to the reach of the saloon's influence. But he doubted banning strong drink was the answer. People always found a way to satisfy their greed. He also had entertained the notion a time or two that the sheriff might not be telling him the whole story about what he was doing in Columbus or what had happened to drive him away from Dempsey.

Militant singing interrupted his musings. He pled for patience as he headed to the saloon.

Quite a crowd of supporters and spectators had gathered for Elizabeth Cooke's temperance crusade. Joshua could tell emotions were strong on either side. Two of Rita's men stood on the front walk and fired shots into the air, intended to scare the women off. Joshua saw hatchets in some of the women's hands. He had to push his way through the crowd to stand in front of the angry group.

"Time to head home, ladies," he called, wishing it would be that simple and knowing his words would have little impact.

"There have been saloon girls in the train yard all night!" A woman sobbed as she spoke. Joshua could guess that her man or her son had been involved. "If we allow them to invade our town, there won't be a decent place left! We've all heard of the untamed West, how evil overtakes towns."

"This ain't the West, ma'am."

"We voted to close the saloon on Sundays. You must make them honor the law!"

Joshua rubbed his eyes with one hand. "It *is* closed on Sundays."

"But they just open the back door and anyone can go inside," another woman said. "What good are laws that are not upheld? Where is Sheriff Stacy in all of this?"

"You know where he is," Joshua replied. "He's in Columbus fighting for prohibition. You all sent him off with a parade, remember?"

His sarcasm wasn't well-received.

"Go home." He held up a pair of handcuffs as warning.

"I'm sorry, Deputy," Mrs. Cooke, who had been quiet, suddenly spoke. Her voice wavered like the words cost her something. "We answer to a higher authority. Arrest me if you must, but the saloon will be smashed today."

She raised her hatchet as the other women cried and cheered.

Rita's man answered by pointing his gun at her chest. "Don't think I won't, lady."

"You'll hang for murder if you do." Joshua pointed his own gun at the man.

"We have a right to defend our property." Rita appeared behind her man holding the gun. She held a young girl by the arm. The girl wasn't dressed like a saloon girl.

"Let her go, Rita," Joshua demanded, alarmed. The girl shook with obvious terror and made him think of Kathleen.

"She came to me in need of a home. I need a new girl to sing, since you stole my top performer, Deputy."

"What's your name?" Joshua spoke directly to the young woman.

"Victoria." Her voice was timid.

"Why are you here, Victoria?"

The girl's eyes darted to Rita's face. Joshua saw Rita's grip tighten on Victoria's arm, making her wince.

"Her family left town without her. I offered her a home." Rita seethed as she spoke, daring Joshua to become involved.

Joshua watched them evenly. He was sure Rita was lying, but he didn't expect the girl to say so. Had Victoria been sold to Rita? She couldn't be more than fifteen.

"Are you trying to say you're going to marry this one, too, Deputy?" Rita laughed.

Mrs. Cooke chose that charged moment to leap forward with her hatchet, shattering the glass of the window. Shards rained down on Victoria and Rita, cutting exposed skin. Rita cried out and let go of the girl.

Meanwhile, Rita's man took aim at Mrs. Cooke. Joshua shot his gun at the post beside the man and aimed the next one at his heart. The man slowly let go of the gun and put his hands in the air, though he smirked the entire time. Joshua used his handcuffs on the man and took Mrs. Cooke by the arm.

"I'll be back for the girl. Leave her be, Rita." Joshua tucked the man's gun into his belt and led his prisoners down the street to the jail, while Mrs. Cooke was applauded by the adoring women.

"By the time you get back, it will be too late." Rita called.

Joshua whirled around. "I will come back for her, and she will be standing right here where I left her and ready to see the doctor about her cuts."

"Will you trade her for Kathleen? I wouldn't mind getting my star back. I'm willing to trade." Rita narrowed her eyes, resuming her hold on Victoria.

Joshua heard the veiled threat. "Let her go, Rita. Victoria, please follow me as best you can."

He didn't look back. He didn't want there to be a chance Rita would see his fear. He realized with a start that he was more vulnerable than he'd ever been. For if Kathleen was harmed, it would be a stake through his own heart.

He was realizing a simple, yet profound truth. He loved her. He loved his wife.

Thirty-Seven

Joshua met Kathleen back at Mary's at lunchtime and they sat on the front porch to eat. He told her of the events of the morning. She sighed, already feeling spent from the sorrow of losing her pet so violently.

"Is poor Mrs. Cooke still in prison?" Kathleen asked.

"No, she was enjoying her martyrdom too much. I let her go after an hour or so. I let Rita's man go, too. He hadn't technically done anything."

"Rita is good at deflecting proof of wrongdoing away from herself." Kathleen set down her sandwich, unable to eat.

Joshua watched her for a moment. "This don't change what happened to you. You're as saved as ever. Don't forget."

She braved a smile. "I know."

He frowned and looked back at the jail. "I have someone else at the jail, though she's not a prisoner. I'm not quite sure what to do with her. As Rita so thoughtfully pointed out, I can't marry all the girls that fall into her web."

Kathleen gulped back the lump in her throat. "Who is she?"

"Name's Victoria. She can't be more than fifteen. Rita got her claws in her and claims she owns her. I have her locked up to protect her from Rita."

"Where is her family?" Kathleen asked.

"I can't be sure, but I'm thinking they were the ones that sold her to Rita."

Kathleen shook her head. "How awful. We must help her. She could stay with us and help on the farm until we figure out what to do with her."

"I don't mean this the wrong way, but I can't have two of you out there. It's too tempting for people who mean harm. I'm going to talk to Pastor Merchant. He's taken folks in before. He took in Evan when he was a teenager and on his own with no family."

Kathleen hadn't realized Evan had lost his family. She thought about the gentle giant of a man who seemed kind and devoted. "I guess everyone has a past."

"It's true." Joshua gave a nod. "What do you have there?"

Kathleen looked down at the paper beside her on the porch step. "I… wrote to my family."

"That's great, Kathleen," Joshua said, and she knew he meant it. "Do you want to read it to me?"

"I suppose." Kathleen began to read aloud.

"Dear Mama,

I hardly know where to start. I'm not sure how to say I'm sorry. You have been a dear and faithful mother, and I had no right to treat you like I did.

I have two things to tell you. I am married now. My husband is Deputy Joshua Whitley. He has gone out of his way to see to my safety. He is a good man with a kind heart.

This is not to say that I have erased the consequences of my sins. We have many obstacles we are trying to overcome because of my choices.

This leads me to the other news I have. I recently attended the Easter service at our church and God revealed his love to me. I should have seen it so long ago, but it took me ruining my life to see that Jesus was the remedy. He has forgiven me. I am cleansed.

You are in my thoughts. I pray you, Papa and Jennifer can forgive me even though I don't deserve it.

All my love,
Kathleen."

Joshua smiled as Kathleen looked up from her letter. "It's good. Post it."

She folded it and laid it in her lap, feeling uncertain. "I don't know if I can find the nerve."

"You can. You've got a new source of power these days." Joshua reminded her. He looked back at the saloon.

She felt his mood darken. "You're angry."

He sat back. She saw him make an effort to relax. He slid his arm along the back of the bench behind her. "Not at you. It's just that woman thinks she can get away with anything."

Kathleen nodded. "Rita won't stop until she gets what she wants. She doesn't care who she hurts."

Joshua was quiet for a long moment as he considered her. "Would she hurt you again?"

Kathleen felt his perceptive eyes on her face and knew she couldn't lie. She suspected he already knew the answer anyway. "I have no doubt."

Joshua sighed and rubbed his chin with his palm. Kathleen noticed he did it often when he was worried. She caught his hand with her own, smiling shyly. He squeezed her hand and reached with his other to trace her jaw. "You even look different."

She wasn't sure how to respond, though she wanted to. When she dared to meet his eyes again, she saw tenderness.

She had known his desire, she'd received his anger, but she'd never seen that look of enthralled gentleness before.

209

Was it love?

Could it be he loved her, in spite of the way things had started? Could Jesus untangle their marriage and make it right?

He leaned closer and kissed her. It was quick, but it was the sweetest gesture she had ever known.

He stood, still holding her hand. "Let's go inside."

"We aren't going home?"

He shook his head and started to explain why, but then he stopped and gave her a second look. He smiled when he caught her meaning. She felt her face flood with heat.

"I better stick close tonight. There's bound to be trouble." He frowned as if he wasn't happy with his decision, and pulled her close to kiss her forehead. "I'm going to take care of the animals. I'll be back soon. Stay inside."

She nodded, watching him unhitch Sundi from the wagon and ride out of town.

She closed her eyes, breathing in deeply and knowing peace. "All those years of clinging to lies, believing I had gone too far, yet it only took a blessed moment for you to wash me clean," she whispered. "Thank you, Jesus. Help me be a good wife. Help me fix what I've broken. Don't let me waste a moment."

"I never pegged you as mad, yet here you are, talking to yourself." Rita stood at the edge of the boardwalk, watching her.

Kathleen stumbled back toward the door, reaching for the handle.

"I know you're trying to devise a way to trick your husband into thinking you are good," Rita scoffed in a low voice. "You don't think he can see you're trash? Give him time. He'll figure it out."

Kathleen considered Rita. Rita's graceful charm and beauty took nothing away from her intimidating demeanor. But as Kathleen considered her, she realized Rita seemed smaller now. Kathleen didn't fear her the way she had. Why should it matter what Rita said or did now?

"I was praying," Kathleen said softly. "Now I'm joining my family. Excuse me."

"Family?" Rita scoffed. "They are no more your family than I am. This is a charade, Kathleen. You're just pretending. You're going to wake up one day soon and realize you can't have this life. You don't deserve it. Your place is in the saloon."

"I know I don't deserve it," Kathleen agreed. And for the first time since she'd known Rita, she wondered what guilt Rita carried. Had she ever longed for more? Wished to undo her choices?

"It's not about what we deserve, Rita. It's only about Jesus. He died and rose again to forgive our sins when we seek him in repentance."

Rita shook her head with condescension. "A religious experience doesn't change who you are. You were born into this life, and it will pull you back, it's only a matter of time."

Kathleen remembered Logan, and a tremor of uncertainty shook her. She opened the door, but Rita stepped forward and grabbed her arm, her long fingernails biting Kathleen's skin.

"You tell that interfering husband of yours if he does anything to break up the business my girls have at the railroad, I'll personally see to it that Bill Logan gets exactly what he keeps pestering me for. *You.*"

It was dark when Joshua returned to town. He noticed Kathleen's hand trembling when she brought him a cup of tea. He took off his jacket and hung it by the door. "Kathleen? What happened?" He took the tea and set it on the table so he could hold her arms and study her face.

"Why did I think this could be?" Kathleen whispered, tears in her eyes. Her words scared him. Mary crossed the room and grabbed her hand.

"What happened?" Joshua felt the familiar rage and took a deep breath.

"Rita," Mary said.

"She threatened me. She threatened you, too, Joshua," Kathleen answered.

Joshua narrowed his eyes as he felt the wrath seep into his spirit. "What did she say?"

Kathleen hesitated. "If you, Isaiah, Evan or anyone else try to stop the girls at the train yard, she'll make sure Logan knows where to find me."

Mary huffed in disbelief. "That's ridiculous! She can't honestly think Joshua would allow anything to happen to you."

Kathleen met Joshua's eyes, and he knew what she was thinking.

"Rita gets what she wants," he said. He paced to the window, pulling aside the curtain and glaring down the length of Main Street. The lights and sounds coming from the saloon contrasted the dim quiet of the rest of the town.

"I've already applied to the train office in Columbus for reinforcements to keep the girls off the property," Isaiah said. "I could try to stop them. Say we can handle it ourselves."

Joshua considered it. He did. But it was the same as conceding defeat. He couldn't let Rita or Logan use Kathleen to dictate his actions. It wasn't right.

"I can't let her send girls to the train yard," he said. He turned back to Kathleen. "But know this, I will do everything in my power to keep you safe. I promise you."

"I know you do. But you're only a man, Joshua. Even forgiven sins have consequences."

He knew Kathleen was right, but she probably didn't realize he would be lying in a pool of his own blood before he'd let Logan anywhere near her.

"You're safe with me."

Mary went to bed, leaving them with blankets and pillows to sleep on the floor of the small parlor in the front room. Joshua watched her try to find a comfortable position on the hard floor for a moment before he reached for her and pulled her to his chest. She sighed and relaxed against him.

"Thank you," she said, her soft voice muffled as she spoke against him.

"Kathleen, I've been thinking." He took a deep breath as she leaned back enough to look him in the eye. "I know, I know, dangerous pastime. But it's time we talk."

She was silent. He plunged ahead with his speech he'd been reciting to himself the entire ride in from the farm. "I've been holding things back from you. But I'm seeing I can't call you my wife and lay beside you at night if I'm not willing to tell you the truth."

"You don't have to tell me anything you don't want to." Her voice was small and fearful. Did she not want to hear his story? He wasn't exactly itching to tell her; he hated the thought of what he'd lived through. But he'd argued long and hard with the Lord, and he'd lost. It was time to tell her the truth.

"I had plenty of reason to question God about marrying you. It wasn't just because of where I found you."

Kathleen waited without speaking. Part of him hoped she'd stop him, but she didn't, so he took a deep breath and went on. "It was because of my ma."

He felt her curiosity, but she still said nothing.

"Kathleen, I know I've held you at arm's length. But I want you to know, I think I'm almost ready to move on. We both know you aren't who I was praying for. But you couldn't be, not after everything that happened to me when I was a boy."

He paused and wondered if the frown on her face meant he was just confusing her. "I have to be willing to accept you the way you are. I'm just as much a sinner as you or anyone else, Kathleen, only my sin is pride."

Her eyes shone, kissed by the moonlight from the window. Her lips parted slightly as she considered him. What else could he do? He brought his mouth to hers. He was ready to speak with something other than words. Words were too hard.

"I've been wrong, Kathleen," he whispered a moment later as he drew back. "So wrong."

Thirty-Eight

Kathleen opened her eyes the next morning and saw Lou, inches from her face, staring at her.

"Oh! You scared me!" Kathleen smiled and kissed the little face.

"Unca Josh be back," Lou announced with a careful voice.

"She's been waiting to give you the message for nigh unto a half-hour," Mary called from the kitchen where she was frying eggs with a fussy baby on one hip.

Kathleen sat up and pulled the toddler into her lap. "Thank you, Lou."

As she snuggled with the little girl, she thought about what Joshua had whispered to her in the darkness.

He had hinted of his secrets. But she had kept hers. She wasn't sure why. Was she also being proud?

She got up and went to Mary to relieve her of the baby. "I'll change him. Seems like you have an assistant for the day."

"You won't hear me complaining," Mary laughed as the twins ran through the kitchen, knocking Lou over in the process. Lou started howling.

"Oh, dear," Mary said in a mild tone as she turned the pancakes.

The older children were fed and sent off to school. Mary put the baby down for a nap and gave Lou some paper and a pencil so she could draw at the table.

"This must be your favorite time of day," Kathleen said as she helped Mary drag out the metal washtub for laundry.

Mary cast a disparaging look. "I don't believe there's a woman alive partial to the washing."

Kathleen gathered the box of Lux soap powder and the washboard from the small cupboard in the corner of the kitchen. "I meant the quiet."

"Oh yes, quiet is always welcome." Mary laughed as she gathered the pile of clothes in one basket and grabbed the pail of dirty diapers on her way out the door to the backyard.

They worked all morning, Mary at the washtub over the fire and Kathleen at the wringer machine. By lunchtime, their backs were aching and all the clothes were blowing in the breeze of the warm spring day.

Mary sighed as she eyed the pail of diapers. "I'll care for these. You go in and check on Lou."

Kathleen nodded and went inside, stretching her aching muscles. It was good to do something that took her mind off the turmoil. She looked in on the baby and saw that Lou was happily playing on the floor. She went out on to the front porch, hoping to see Joshua walking back for lunch. Her gaze traveled to the saloon. Was Joshua there, dealing with more trouble?

She didn't see him, so she turned back to the door, but a call behind her made her stop and turn around. Evan ran across the street toward her.

She smiled as he reached her, looking up at him as he caught his breath. She'd never stood so close to him. She had to admit, if he wasn't so friendly, she'd be afraid of him. Evan was handsome, but big as a grizzly, with shoulder-length brown hair and the shadow of a beard to lend to the illusion.

"Isaiah asked me to come by and check on you, Mary and the kids."

"We're fine," she said. "How are things at the train yard?"

Evan shrugged. "Rita sent girls. Isaiah's trying to keep them out. The men aren't so keen on them leaving. The situation is tense, and it's only going to get worse before it gets better."

"I can't help feeling responsible."

"It's not your fault," Evan said. They stood in silence for a moment until Kathleen started to say goodbye so she could go back inside.

"I... uh, I need your help," Evan said, capturing her arms with his big hands to stop her. "There's an ice cream social at the end of the month at church, and I was hoping to ask Beatrice – Miss Walsh – if she might go with me."

Kathleen nodded. "What do you need from me?"

He smiled sheepishly. "It's just that I don't know how to dance. I've tried to learn before but I'm so big and my feet are so clumsy. Surely you know how to dance. I mean, you did work in a saloon."

She looked away, embarrassed.

"I'm sorry, I sound like a bumbling idiot," he said, laughing and hitting himself in the forehead with his palm.

She shook her head. "I don't do that anymore."

He nodded. "I didn't mean to suggest that you did. But I don't know who else I could ask. You're my best friend's wife, and I don't think Josh would mind. You're my only hope! I'll be lost if I can't take her. Sam White has been eyeing her, and I know he's going to get to her before me. I can't let that happen."

"Of course I'll help you," she said with a smile.

They went through the basic steps a few times until he could make it through a waltz without stepping on her toes. He seemed grateful. "I'm mighty beholding. If Miss Walsh and I end up getting hitched, it will be all *your* doing, and I won't forget it."

She laughed. "I hope it works out. Truly I do."

She had hardly turned away when he spoke again. "If it's not too forward of me, do you suppose it would it be okay for me to hold her hand? And I'd sure like to sneak a kiss, but she's awful shy."

"You could ask Joshua," Kathleen said.

He chuckled. "You know Joshua well enough to know that if I asked him to help me kiss a girl he'd tease me till the cows come home and then throw me in the creek for good measure."

She giggled. It was true, and they both knew it.

Kathleen did want to help him. She'd noticed his affection for the piano player since she'd first gone to church and it was obviously genuine. But she suspected he was asking her because she had worked in the saloon.

"Well, whether you believe this or not, the only experience I have is with Joshua. And you and Joshua are different." Kathleen remembered when Joshua had kissed her the first time. He hadn't asked her permission, and he hadn't exactly been a gentleman about it. She hadn't minded, but perhaps Miss Wash might feel differently. Kathleen hadn't spent much time talking to her, but she had sensed Beatrice was a nervous person.

"I've never laid eyes on anyone as beautiful as Miss Walsh." Evan sent a wistful smile in the direction of the church, where they could both hear her playing a medley of hymns.

It was true Beatrice was a rare beauty, with lovely dark hair and eyes. Kathleen felt the need to say something. "If you don't mind me asking, how did you come to be so enamored of Miss Walsh? Have you known her long?"

Evan smiled, watching the church like it was a mirror of his memories. "No. She hasn't been in town too long. She's lovely and talented, and there's something about her, I don't know..." He stopped suddenly and looked at her. "My parents and baby sister died when I was twelve. I've been on my own since then, though Joshua's grandparents and the Merchants looked out for me some. The way I feel about Beatrice gives me hope that I might not always be alone."

Empathy tugged at Kathleen's heart. She'd had no idea Evan had such sadness buried beneath his easy-going demeanor. She felt honored to be trusted with his burden. "I'm sorry to hear about your family."

"I guess I didn't know much about what love was until I met Beatrice. Everything I do, I do because I want to be able to offer her a good life. She's always polite, but I can't get her to stop holding me at a distance, you know?"

"Oh yes," Kathleen said softly, thinking of her relationship with

Joshua. "I know what you mean. I believe if Miss Walsh could only see the depth of your affection for her, she'd surely be yours in a heartbeat."

Evan smiled. "I hope you're right."

Kathleen didn't have the heart to tell him she doubted it would happen. As much as Evan was determined not to be alone, Beatrice seemed desperate to remain that way.

Joshua spent the morning at home doing chores. He returned to town only to find Rita's girls were at the train yard again, and this time they were luring men back to the saloon. Joshua was beyond tired and frustrated, and disgusted with the sickness infecting his town.

The remaining girls at the train yard saw him coming and left without being told. He was relieved, but he stayed around to give the men another warning about consorting with the girls, and to promise the ones who had left their job to go to the saloon would be dealt with harshly. He looked for Evan, but he was nowhere to be found.

"Maybe if you'd do your job once in a blue moon, these men wouldn't be sauntering off to the saloon," he muttered to the missing foreman. He went to find Isaiah in his office inside.

A few minutes later he was headed back to the jail, knowing Rita would probably pay him another visit. She wasn't one to let things go any more than he was.

He caught sight of Evan in the street outside the McAllisters'. He was about to yell something about his friend shirking work in the middle of the day when he noticed Evan was leaning over a much smaller figure. Was he talking to Miss Walsh, of all people?

He chuckled, eager to give his friend a good ribbing later. Maybe throw him in the creek.

Rita was waiting in his office. "Mr. Whitley, you can expect me to uphold my end of our deal."

His mood quickly darkened. He'd never been so tempted to

thrash a woman. "There's no *deal*. You leave my wife alone or things will get very bad for you."

He took a big step closer, hoping to make her feel his threat, because he meant it. The thought of Rita conspiring with Logan to hurt Kathleen made him angrier than he'd ever felt in his life. He wouldn't admit it to the likes of Rita Dolsen, but the thought also scared him to death.

Rita didn't speak for a moment, but he didn't like the triumphant smile pulling at the corners of her mouth. "How much do you really know your wife, Deputy?"

She focused her piercing black eyes on him and took a step toward him, closing the remainder of the distance. "Doesn't it bother you, what she was? What she did? Who she did it with?"

"I'm warning you, woman. Get out."

"I'm sure you tell yourself the past is the past," she continued, ignoring his threat. "But what if the past... is the present?"

He sighed loudly. "What in tarnation are you talking about?"

"Honestly, I'd expect it from Kathleen. She can't change who she is. But isn't Evan Masters your close friend? I probably should have told you of their past when you first took Kathleen from the saloon, but I assumed you knew. You seemed so determined; I didn't think it would stop you to know those two had a history together."

"Evan Masters wouldn't go in the saloon if you paid him."

Rita laughed haughtily. "Deputy, there are very few men in this town who haven't secretly made use of my establishment, no matter what they might say publicly. Even your beloved sheriff has more ties to the saloon than you might imagine."

"That's a lie."

"It's not. Why do you think he allows us to continue to break the law to stay closed on Sundays? Where do you think the funds come from that keep his office running smoothly and keep him living in comfort? Didn't you realize he was collecting quite a tidy sum from the saloon in fines every week?"

Joshua took an unsteady breath, staring at her as white hot rage threatened to erupt from his person like lava spouting from a volcano. "What exactly are you saying?"

"I'm simply trying to explain to you that most men are not what they appear to be outwardly. If you don't believe me, see for yourself." Rita stepped back and calmly gestured toward the door.

He pushed past her and went back into the street. Fear and anger mingled in his chest until it hurt to breathe.

He saw them. Evan and Kathleen were standing together outside Mary's house. And Kathleen was smiling. Smiling! As she dishonored him in broad daylight with his best friend.

He was so livid he saw spots. He lost all sense of reason and stomped toward them, fumbling for his gun. When Evan saw him, he stepped away from Kathleen, holding up his hands with a panicked expression. Joshua assumed it meant he was guilty.

"Hold up, Josh," Evan said. "What's wrong?"

"What are you doing with my wife?"

Evan looked at Kathleen with genuine surprise in his eyes. "I was checking on them, and Kathleen and I got to talking. She was helping me."

"Oh, I saw how she was *helping* you," Joshua said with spite. "How could you? We've been friends since we were kids. You knew everything. Everything that happened to me. Yet here you are making use of my wife in public where anyone can watch."

Joshua's finger flirted with the trigger. He was tempted to forgo all sense and pull it. After all the betrayal he'd endured in his life, surely he was entitled to one act of retribution.

For the wrath of man worketh not the righteousness of God.

The Scripture, in Gran's voice, flooded his angry spirit like water dousing a fire. He lowered the gun.

"Was it just a game to you?" He stared hard at Kathleen. How could he have been so taken in by a pretty face? "Did you want to make sure I fell for you before you made a fool of me?"

"I haven't." Her voice was small and timid. She stepped away from Evan. "He was just asking my advice on courting Miss Walsh. That's all, Joshua."

Evan took a step toward him. "Josh, think about it. When did we ever give you an impression something was going on?"

Joshua hesitated. He gripped the gun so hard his fingers ached. Was he misreading things? Was Rita lying? Evan was right; he'd never had a cause to doubt them before. He took a deep breath and tried to calm down.

"And still they make a fool of you," Rita spoke behind him. "These two had a relationship that went on for months in the saloon."

The heat returned to Joshua's face as he turned around.

"Mr. Masters was a regular visitor late at night after you had gone home to your farm. He came to see Kathleen quite a few times. Spent many an evening alone with her in her room."

Joshua's breath was ragged as he breathed in.

"She's lying!" Kathleen cried in protest. "I never spoke to Mr. Masters before the night we were married, and he was never in the saloon."

"Honestly, Josh, you're going to believe Rita Dolsen's word over us? Don't you think if I'd had a habit of going in the saloon you would have known about it?" Evan said in exasperation.

Joshua didn't speak. He couldn't. Confusion, anger and a sharp ache in his chest prevented it. He felt as if he was on the edge of some precipice, and they were about to push him over.

"If you require proof, my staff will tell you the same." Rita's voice was calm. Unconcerned that his life was unraveling. Again.

"If they did, they'd be lying," Evan scoffed and came straight toward Joshua. Joshua raised the gun again.

"You know me!" Evan took another step. "Why would I ruin my chances with Beatrice for the *saloon*? I wouldn't do it. Rita's trying to manipulate you. Don't let her, Josh. She's already manipulating so many of the men in this town. Don't let her get to you, too."

"As I recall, you requested Kathleen most nights," Rita said to Evan.

"Go back to your hell-hole!" Evan turned on her, roaring with ferocity that made both women flinch.

Rita gave Joshua a final, pointed glance before she stepped away from Evan and followed the path back to the saloon.

Joshua didn't look either of them in the eye as he spoke in a barely controlled tone. "If I see either of you for the rest of the day, I just may shoot you."

He shoved his gun back in the holster and walked back into the jail.

Thirty-Nine

Joshua stood in front of the desk he had just ransacked. He'd pried open a locked drawer and pulled out the papers that kept track of the favors and money owed between Sheriff Stacy and the saloon. The dates went back for years. It may have started out as an innocent indulgence on the sheriff's part, but it was clear that by now, Rita owned him. He was her puppet, forced to do her bidding or be outed to the town, his family and his church for his iniquities.

Joshua paced. He fought the restless desire for revenge. Why had he expected more from the sheriff? From Evan? From Kathleen? Rita was right about Kathleen. Saloon girls didn't change. He'd never seen it before, yet he allowed himself to be taken in by her pretty face and her apparent dramatic conversion.

He should have known better. He learned the hard way, when he was nine and watching his mother walk away without even a backward glance. He'd promised himself he'd never let anyone else do that to him again. Yet here he was. And there wasn't a thing he could do about any of it.

Pray.

"You want me to pray? Fine. How could you let this happen again?" He spoke aloud. He was ashamed of the tone he was taking with the Almighty, but it seemed to overflow out of him without his permission, like a pin had pricked the skin of his pride and his hurt and all the darkness just below the surface was seeping out. "Every woman I care about turns away from me."

He stopped pacing and sank back into the seat behind his desk, his head buried in his hands. "Don't you care? Why didn't you just give me what I asked for? Why did it have to be her?"

I will never leave you or forsake you. I know your pain. I've felt it, more than you ever will. Give it to me.

Joshua stayed in the jail until evening shadows started to fall. He didn't know what else to do.

"Joshua?"

He looked up at Mary, standing in the doorway. She crossed to him and put her hands on his shoulders.

"Kathleen and Evan didn't do anything and you know it," she said in soft admonition.

"Rita says they have a history."

"You don't believe Rita would lie to get her way?" Mary answered immediately.

"You didn't see them, Mary. They were all huddled together... it wasn't hard to see what was going on."

She scoffed. "You saw what you wanted to see."

"Why in the world would I want to see that?" He stood up, feeling the anger resurface.

Her voice softened again and she sighed. "It doesn't make a bit of sense, Joshua. Gran would be ashamed of you being so quick to blame your loved ones."

"Rita was right about Sheriff Stacy. He's betrayed Dempsey, just like Evan and Kathleen betrayed me."

Mary scoffed. "I don't know about the sheriff, but the only one who betrayed you is long gone. You're going to ruin everything hanging on to your grudge against her."

"How can you forget, Mary? How can you trust anyone after what she did to us?"

Her eyes were thoughtful. She brought her hand to his cheek.

"You were so young. So trusting. None of us realized your pain."

Mary watched him for a long moment before she spoke again. "The memory of her walking away from us, down that path and out of our lives forever – it's like a knife to my chest. So I don't revisit it. But I haven't forgotten. Anyway, what she did has nothing to do with Kathleen. Kathleen is only more convenient."

"They're the same." Joshua crossed his arms over his chest.

"They are not." Mary turned toward the window and stared out into the dark street. "You have a choice. You *can* let this go, Joshua."

He shook his head and pushed against his desk so it loudly scraped against the floor. "I don't have a choice. I never did."

"You're just feeling sorry for yourself. That's why you feel trapped. But you're not. I know because God helped me out from under the burden."

"It's not the same."

"Joshua, I have every reason and more to hold on to the bitterness. You know I do. I was coming of age. You know what was happening to me in that place."

Joshua shook his head, loath to think of it.

Mary's voice broke, and she took a ragged breath before she spoke again. "You have to choose to forgive Mercy. Not because she deserves it, but because we deserve to have you minus all the bitterness."

Joshua refused to look at Mary. He didn't want to consider what had happened to her in the saloon.

Mary was quiet for a long time as she looked out the window. She finally spoke in nearly a whisper. "Think how far Jesus chased you and me into the darkness. The filth he walked through to get us out. You can be like him. You can love that way, too. Don't waste this chance."

Joshua sat back down and stared at the floor.

Mary sighed. "Whatever you do, you can't say Kathleen is the same person as Mercy. It's just not true. And you're being even more unfair to Evan."

He heaved a long sigh. "Whether or not they did it doesn't

matter," he said sullenly. "Maybe this just made me realize everything I was trying to pretend I had accepted."

He looked up at her. "Mary, I haven't."

Forty

As Kathleen expected, Joshua refused to see her or take her back to the farm with him. She was sure he was done with her.

She missed her home. She missed the animals and the peace Joshua's grandparents had left as a gift. It spread all over their home like a warm blanket for any cold wanderer that came inside. The second day she was living at the McAllisters' again, she told Mary she was going for a walk. When she saw Logan at work in the train yard, she turned the other way and walked all the way through the woods to the farm. She sat in the barn with the animals and poured out her heart. They watched her and listened to her tell her story. A barn kitten that bore a resemblance to Ginger rubbed against her leg until she picked him up and cuddled him in her lap.

"I've been a fool to think Joshua could love me in any lasting way." Her whisper seemed to echo off the quiet rafters of the barn. "I've lost him."

When she had to leave before Joshua found her there, she went back to Mary.

"Kathleen, you can't just walk off like that! I was worried! I already sent little Josh for his pa!"

Kathleen nodded as she fell into Mary's arms and cried. "I know, Mary. I'm sorry. I was careful."

Mary held her, though her own house needed tending and her children were running wild. "God knows what he's doing, and it will get done as he sees fit."

Kathleen finally dried her tears and set her mind to helping. She needed to think of a plan. She needed to accept that the beautiful dream was over and figure out her plan to go on alone. She considered going back to Little Sicily. She had never garnered the courage to post her letter, but she could face her parents. All of them. She could ask for forgiveness. Hadn't the prodigal son done the same and been welcomed with open arms?

But they weren't God. Their love might have limits where God's love did not. Joshua's did, after all. Could she endure their rejection? Would God be enough when she realized she was truly alone?

She asked Mary, who had an immediate answer. "I don't know your family, Kathleen, but if you were my girl, I'd be so glad to see you well and whole, I wouldn't be able to contain my joy."

Kathleen felt overwhelmed at the thought of going home. Tears stung her eyes, already weary from so many tears. Mary peeled potatoes and sang.

> *Then gentle patience smiles on pain*
> *And dying hope revives again;*
> *Hope wipes the tear from sorrow's eye,*
> *And faith points upward to the sky.*

Kathleen went to the farm again. She couldn't seem to stay away. She confided in Mary to keep her from worrying and checked to be sure Rita and Logan were occupied. She left in the afternoon when Mary was able to sit on the front porch and sew or read, so Mary could keep her eye on the saloon. They agreed that if either Rita or Logan headed in the direction of the farm, Mary would send Evan or Isaiah.

Kathleen could tell Joshua had been avoiding the task of washing his clothes, so she spent the morning scrubbing and hanging laundry.

When she finished with the wash, she went to the garden and feverishly weeded around her growing plants. The painstaking but dull task freed her mind, and she began to think about the soil as her life. God had granted it, but she had to make the effort to rid her heart of anything that would threaten the tender growth God was causing.

She was wondering how it could be done when something Joshua had said occurred to her.

It's my Gran's Bible. I use Grandpa's and hers is just sitting on the shelf in the parlor. She'd want you to take it.

She washed up at the pump and went inside to the parlor. She scanned the spines of all the books until she finally located the black leather-bound Bible. She opened it, surprised to find Gran had covered every margin and free space with notes, prayers, explanations and question marks. She'd underlined verses, sometimes with two or three lines for emphasis. Her neat script was easy to read in even the most cramped spaces. Kathleen hugged the Bible to her chest, eager to take it back to town and spend the evening reading.

She prayed God would give her direction. She prayed with all her broken heart that Joshua would forgive her. But she also prayed God would grant her peace should Joshua turn her away.

She might have to say goodbye to this life and this home she had fallen in love with. She needed to be prepared.

Joshua could smell her.

He'd spent a week ignoring Kathleen and Evan. He hadn't acknowledged them in town or church. He'd hoped avoiding them would lessen his pain, but it continued to eat away at him. His solitude seemed to strengthen the infection in the old wounds that refused to heal.

He was kidding himself to think he could avoid her. Her scent was all over his clothes and his house – that inimitable essence of a female, enhanced with lavender and soap. It was going to drive him mad if she kept coming to the house during the day. He hadn't missed the clean laundry folded neatly in his drawers. The weeded garden flourishing. The funny way she arranged the feed bags and water pans in the barn. That confounded bonnet of hers hanging stubbornly on the pegboard by the kitchen door.

He missed her every waking moment. When he closed his eyes at night, he remembered all the times they'd been close. The lovely invitation of her lips, her hair smooth as silk slipping through his fingers. He was sure he could live a thousand lifetimes and never know a thrill compared to the one that possessed him when he held her body close to his.

He was standing in the kitchen one morning, days and a lifetime after everything had changed, when he heard the kitchen door open. He whirled around, wanting to see Kathleen standing there more than anything he'd ever wanted in his life.

"Go away," he growled when he saw Evan. He looked away, trying not to care about the sorrowful expression twisting his friend's features.

"No, I won't go away. Not until you listen to me. You've had time to cool off. I know you're upset, and I know what you think you saw. But you're wrong."

"I'm not willing to take that chance," Joshua said, dumping the rest of his coffee in the sink and setting the mug on the counter. He pulled on his gun belt and slammed his hat on his head.

Evan barred the door, his arms across his massive chest. "Your wife and I were talking, Josh. That's all that was going on. You're making yourself look like a fool by ignoring her and making her stay with Mary. You're also putting her in greater danger because she sneaks back over here most days."

Joshua stepped back and pushed a chair at the table so hard it fell with a clatter. The relief of his anger didn't come, so he turned back to Evan and drew back his fist. He punched Evan so hard in the jaw, his friend fell back against the screen door and bent the frame.

Evan stood up and tried to close the warped door. He rubbed his jaw. "Feel better?"

"Not even close." Joshua went to the other side of the kitchen and stared out past the porch into Kathleen's garden.

He heard Evan cross the kitchen and stand behind him. "I'm not saying what I did was right, Joshua. Maybe I should have thought better of being personal with your wife. Asked you first. I'm sorry."

Joshua felt the weight of the offense lessen, but he didn't answer.

"I didn't intend to hurt you, but if you're going to stay mad at anyone, let it be me. Kathleen was only being polite. You have to open your eyes and see this for what it is. Rita is trying to destroy what you and Kathleen have built here. You're giving her what she wants."

Joshua glared hard at the floor. He knew Evan was speaking the truth. But he recognized the dose of humility it would cost to get himself out of this hole he'd dug.

He turned and left the kitchen, letting the broken door shut with an awkward bang.

Late that night as he lay in bed, the dream came again. The memory. His mind filled with the images he never allowed himself to think about in the daylight. He saw the young woman on the bed and heard her cries as she was mistreated and mocked. The shameful scenes played out before him as he huddled in the corner, tearing at the wallpaper in a desperate attempt to give his attention to something else.

Time in his dream-world shifted, and he was no longer the child cowering in the shadows. He was older, standing on the back porch, feeling Grandpa's hand, firm on his shoulder. He watched her walk away. She didn't wave. She didn't smile and say she'd be back for him soon. She just walked away without even an explanation.

He opened his eyes and saw the soft glow of moonlight on Gran's curtains and heard the breeze rattle the branches of the oak tree outside the window. The dream faded away, but the memory remained.

Why should his mother have looked back? Joshua was the ugly product of her rebellion and a man's payment. He didn't blame her for wanting to get rid of him. But he was afraid. He'd wanted to tell her he would try harder. Be more useful. Stay out of the way when he wasn't in school.

But she didn't give him a chance to explain.

"I'm sorry, son. If I'd known you and your sister existed, I'd have come for you long ago." His grandfather's voice was gruff as he stared after his daughter's fading form. "I'm sorry for what you've been through."

Joshua might have expected the next years to be easy ones, but they weren't. He couldn't seem to convince himself he was in a safe place. He was always looking over his shoulder, trying to appease his grandparents out of fear that they would send him away. He'd had to learn how to trust people.

He closed his eyes and remembered. Grandpa teaching him how to run a farm, assuring him that one day it would all be his. He recalled carrying jars and jars of preserved produce to the root cellar for Gran. He smiled when he remembered how she'd chided him for killing the big black rat snake that lived under the shelves. He'd thought he was doing her a favor.

"And just what is going to eat all the mice now, young man? I guess it will have to be you."

He'd brought her a kitten from the barn the next day just liked he'd done for Kathleen when she had found the drowned mouse in the kitchen. Gran had laughed. Gran's laugh was a medicine, calming his fears and restoring his peace when it was difficult to find.

Grandpa had tried to get him to talk about his life at the brothel. But it seemed like Joshua's mind had chosen to lock up the secrets and throw away the key. They continued to fade away until that part of his early childhood could only be remembered in dreams. He remembered folks taking Mary and him to church, and he remembered being the child in school that all the kids stayed away from and all the adults whispered about. But he didn't think about the things that went on inside the saloon, or the depravity he heard from behind the thick velvet curtain in his mother's room at the brothel. Grandpa said it was a blessing his mind was letting it go. He made Joshua memorize Scripture, and Joshua was glad for it. Having the Word in his mind had changed his life.

Joshua saw the beginning of dawn breaking outside, so he gave up the idea of sleeping and got up and dressed. He went downstairs to start the coffee and go to the barn, but the picture on the mantle in the parlor caught his attention. He went and picked it up.

It was a small picture, but it was the only reminder he had of what Gran and Grandpa had looked like. The sight caused a constriction in his chest.

"I miss you both," he whispered. He studied the younger version of himself. He could see the distrust in his eyes. He'd been so quiet. So sure everyone was going to disappoint him.

But God had changed all that. He'd made all things new. Just like he'd done for Kathleen at the Easter service.

"Kathleen isn't Mercy," he said aloud. The words were a revelation. Kathleen wasn't anything like his mother. How could he have assumed she was?

"Who is Mercy?"

He whirled around and saw Kathleen standing at the parlor door. The sight of her filled him with exhilaration. Everything about her was sweet and lovely, and he wanted nothing but to hold her.

He put back the picture and turned toward her.

"Who is Mercy, Joshua?" she asked again, folding her hands over her apron as she waited for his answer.

"Mercy is my mother."

Her lips parted in surprise. She looked so intently into his eyes he was afraid she was going to see straight through his soul and be scared away. He crossed the room and grabbed her hands, just in case. But as he touched her, he wanted more of her. He reached for her waist and tried to pull her to him.

She chuckled with uncertainty and pushed him back. "Wait, Joshua. Let's talk."

He made an effort to subdue himself. They sat down on the settee and he crossed his arms to keep himself out of trouble.

"Will you tell me about her? Your mother? Will you tell me about your childhood?" She asked the words so gently and sweetly he found he couldn't refuse.

"When Mercy was growing up with my grandparents in Michigan, they lived near a mine. Grandpa was the foreman." He stared hard at the floor. "When she was barely thirteen, one of the miners... assaulted her."

"Oh, how awful," Kathleen said.

"After that, she was different. She left home when she was fifteen, saying Gran and Grandpa couldn't love her, and no man would ever want her. She ended up in a brothel. They didn't know where or they would have tried to bring her home. She'd only been there a year when Mary was born. I came along a few years later."

Kathleen shook her head. "It's amazing that either of you lived to see your first day, Joshua. Most girls in that position are forced to make sure their babies are never born."

He nodded, knowing it was true enough. "Honestly, Kathleen, I don't remember much of my childhood. I have no idea how she protected us, but it must have been God, because she managed to give birth to both of us, and we lived in the brothel until Mercy took us to Grandpa and Gran and left us there."

He must have been frowning at the carpet pretty hard, because she reached for his hand and pulled it to her lap to cradle it between her own.

He held on tight, grateful for the gesture. It only took that moment for his anger to dissipate.

"Kathleen, I came away from my childhood convinced of two things. If I married, it was going to be a woman opposite my mother in every possible way. And I was going to do whatever I could do to close the saloons and brothels for good. That's why I took the position of deputy."

"It all makes sense," she said, her voice soft. Sad.

He remembered what he hadn't said. "Kathleen, I've been a fool." He gave up the last of the anger with a resounding exhale. "I know you weren't doing anything with Evan."

"I wasn't," she agreed. "But I would give anything to go back and not give you a reason to doubt me."

He rubbed his chin and frowned. "I don't know how to get past what you are. Or what you were, rather. I've prayed and prayed, and I've tried to look at you without seeing all the other men that used you. But it hurts me."

He was being more honest than he wanted to be. He didn't want the truth to create a wall that separated them further. It was a gamble when he wanted her so much.

But he couldn't keep secrets any longer. It was time they were said.

"Joshua," she said slowly, so softly he had to strain to hear her. "I should have told you long ago. I can't prove it to you, so I will understand if you don't believe me."

She took her time before she spoke again. But when she said the words she looked him straight in the eye. "I've never... been with any man in the way you think I have."

He was shocked. He couldn't speak. She was right – if she'd told him the truth before tonight, he wouldn't have believed her. But he doubted she would lie when he'd just bared the deepest truths of his soul to her.

She looked down at their hands. "I'm not saying I haven't sinned. I've done things that would make me blush to speak of now. I saw more disgusting behavior in those two months than anyone should witness in a lifetime. But the truth remains. I am still a maiden."

"You were only there for two months?" He hadn't thought to ask. He couldn't remember the first time he saw her, but now that he thought about it, it hadn't been long before everything happened.

She nodded. "Rita was pressuring me, especially after Logan took an interest and became so insistent. But I had the advantage of being Clara McCloud's daughter. She had enough of a reputation that men would come just to hear me sing. But I know for certain it wouldn't have lasted much longer if you hadn't saved me." Her matter-of-fact tone seemed ironic against the revelation she had revealed.

"You've... you've never...?"

"No," she said, and blushed. She looked away with an embarrassed smile. And there it was, the proof she didn't think she could offer. He could see it written all over her lovely face.

He had no intention of belaboring the conversation. He grabbed her arm, pulled her up with him, and swung her into his arms.

"What are you doing?" She laughed in surprise, throwing her arms around his neck.

"What I should have done the first day you were here." He headed for the stairs.

"Joshua," she protested, her cheeks as red as apples. "It's morning! We have chores! Maybe… maybe tonight?"

"Kathleen Whitley, you are my wife and if I want bedtime to be now, bedtime will be now." He clomped up the stairs.

She giggled and offered no further argument. He kicked open the door of his room and tossed her on the bed.

Before he even got his boots off, there was a knock on the door.

Forty-One

"What are you doing here?" Kathleen stood in the kitchen and listened to Joshua speak to the man at the door. When she had seen who it was, she ducked around the corner and hid.

"We need the law at the saloon. There's been a brawl and Bill Logan killed a fellow." Ames, the bartender, spoke gruffly.

"Of course he did. Where's Logan now?" Joshua grabbed his hat and jammed it on his head.

"We locked him up at the jail. Rita is having the girls clean up the mess."

Joshua found Kathleen before he left. "I suppose you heard that. I'll be back as soon as I can." He kissed her cheek. "As sad as it is that someone had to die, at least this means Logan won't be causing us any more trouble."

It was an inconceivable thought. She hardly knew what to do with herself. She was free for the first time since she'd left home.

She reached a hand to her hair and looked down at her work dress and stained apron. She was relieved she'd have a chance to clean up a bit before he came home.

She donned the white lawn dress she'd worn at Easter and brushed her hair until it shone. She made a stew from Grandma Nellie's recipes and put it on the stove to simmer while she mixed biscuits.

By the time she was ready for Joshua to return, it had only been enough time for him to have reached town. She knew she would have to wait, so she brought out Nellie Whitley's Bible and began to read in Luke where she'd left off the day before. She had been reading the story of the Prodigal Son.

> *When he came to himself, he said, How many hired servants of my father's have bread enough and to spare, and I perish with hunger! I will arise and go to my father, and will say unto him, "Father, I have sinned against heaven, and before thee, and am no more worthy to be called thy son: make me as one of thy hired servants."*
>
> *And he arose, and came to his father. But when he was yet a great way off, his father saw him, and had compassion, and ran, and fell on his neck, and kissed him.*
>
> *And the son said unto him, "Father, I have sinned against heaven, and in thy sight, and am no more worthy to be called thy son."*
>
> *But the father said to his servants, "Bring forth the best robe, and put it on him; and put a ring on his hand, and shoes on his feet: And bring hither the fatted calf, and kill it; and let us eat, and be merry: For this my son was dead, and is alive again; he was lost, and is found.*

Kathleen felt a lump in her throat as she considered her own story. Her own father. Would he respond to her like the father of the prodigal son did if she were to go home?

She read Gran's scribbled notes in the margin, which made tears sting her eyes. Were the words a sign from the Lord?

Dear Lord Jesus, bring my wayward child back to my arms. I love her, Lord, I want my Mercy home. Bring her back to your fold.

The clock on the mantle chimed the hour. Kathleen looked up in surprise. "Heavens, the animals!"

She didn't have time to change before heading to the barn, so she made up her mind to be extra careful not to ruin her dress. The pungent aroma of horse and straw tickled her nose, reminding her of every time she had entered the barn before to care for those animals. Joshua's animals. Her animals.

Theirs.

Esmerelda pushed her nose against the wooden gate in her pen until Kathleen came to milk and feed her.

"I don't know about you, old girl," she said as she stepped around manure and carried the milk pail out of the stall. "But I think it's going to be a fine evening."

The cow stamped her foot in response.

"Now, now," Kathleen said as she glanced out the back door into the east field. She reveled in the rolling meadows of green grass. The purest blue sky, now tinged with hints of pink as the afternoon grew long.

She sat on the milking stool, facing the wall. She idly watched the ducks on the hill by the pond as she milked. She could hardly believe this beautiful, peaceful home was to be hers. Always. Not because she had done anything to earn it, but because of the man who had offered his life to share with her.

She considered what might have become of her if she had spent another day in the saloon. How different her life would be now, if she were even still breathing. The thought reminded her that Logan was no longer a threat. She was safe.

Kathleen's thoughts were interrupted by the quiet sound of footfalls on the straw behind her. The sound chased away the darkness she considered, and a smile pulled at the edges of her mouth as she waited for Joshua to make his presence known. A thrill spread through her, making her feel warm when she remembered the taste of his kisses and the secure fortress of his arms. She wanted Joshua to take her home and make her his. Forever.

Hands reached around and covered her eyes. She laughed and turned to throw herself into his embrace.

"Hello, darling."

It was not her beloved's voice. She opened her eyes and saw the snarling, repulsive face of Bill Logan. She cried out as he grabbed her by the arms.

"I'm glad you're so happy to see me," he jeered, pulling her against his chest even as she struggled to get away. "And look at you, all fixed up and pretty for me."

A sickening feeling hit her in the pit of her stomach. "No," she screamed, vainly trying to loosen his hold and get away. In a moment, all her dreams would burst, as fleeting as the lifespan of a soap bubble floating delicately on the breeze.

He grabbed her by the hair and dragged her across the barn to an empty horse stall. She cried as he pushed her to the floor and climbed on top of her.

I drove this man to do this horrible thing. It's my fault. I deserve to suffer.

As quickly as Kathleen thought the words, other words filled her mind. One of the first verses she had memorized after her conversion.

It is for freedom that Christ has set us free. Stand firm, then, and do not let yourselves be burdened again by a yoke of slavery.

She could not be resigned to whatever Logan had in mind. She would not allow him to steal what rightfully belonged only to her husband. To Joshua. The Spirit came alive in Kathleen's spirit and flooded every part of her with light and power. She screamed, kicked and fought with every ounce of strength she possessed.

Her struggle didn't make her free. In the end, Logan was stronger than she was. And for the rest of her days she would have to try to forget what happened in those next moments.

Kathleen opened her eyes when she heard Joshua's voice. Her brain felt slow. Foggy. Every part of her body ached and her spirit felt as if it lie bleeding, dying on the straw of the barn floor. Had she been kicked by the cow? Did she fall from the loft?

She struggled to remember why she wasn't happy to hear Joshua's voice. Why she didn't want to answer him – didn't want him to see her.

The swirling madness of memory returned in a slow cascade and shame caused her to huddle farther into the corner. She wrapped her arms around her legs and tried to whimper a wordless plea for Joshua to stay back. But her voice would not make a sound. She was hoarse from her cries for help.

"Kathleen?" Joshua called. She heard the worry in his tone. He had probably already searched the house for her.

She could call out to him. She could let him take care of her. She could simply never tell him the awful truth. Joshua could go to his grave thinking she was his and his alone.

I fell from the hayloft, she could say.

She hugged her arms around herself and felt a warm stickiness. She lifted her hand and saw the deep red stain soaked into her white dress. Then she felt the pain, and realized Logan had cut her. He'd left her there to bleed to death.

I fell on the pitchfork, she could explain.

Joshua would believe her. He loved her. But he might not love her anymore if he found out what had happened. And then what could she do? Would her family want her back now, ruined as she was?

Kathleen knew dishonesty couldn't save her. She couldn't run from this. Joshua deserved to know the truth, even if the truth separated them forever.

"Kathleen, are you here?" Joshua's voice became more desperate.

The answer seemed clear. She needed to get back to the house without him seeing her. She would take his gun while he slept, and point it at her head. Pull the trigger. She wouldn't face God's judgment, would she? She was safe. There was nothing to fear.

There was plenty to fear in this new version of her life.

"Please, Kathleen, please tell me you're here."

She heard the panic in his voice, and her heart seemed to twist inside her chest. *Don't waste your concern on me, Joshua. It's based on something that isn't true anymore.*

"Oh, Lord, where's my wife?"

Kathleen could see Joshua now. He stood in the center of the barn, turning in a circle as he surveyed every corner, every opened door into the farmyard. His hands were tented over his mouth and nose; his hat had fallen on the floor, forgotten in the face of his fear.

She felt an overwhelming need to shift. The pain in her bruised hip burned. She cringed as the silence of the barn exaggerated the sound of the crunching of straw beneath her twisted leg.

He was there in the next moment, staring at her with horror in his expression. Had he read the whole story in her eyes?

"Joshua," she whispered. It sounded like a plea. A plea for mercy.

"What happened?" He asked in disbelief as he quickly opened the latch of the stall and fell to his knees beside her. His eyes took in the bruises and scrapes, the straw in her matted hair. The blood dripping from her hand where she held her wound. "Kathleen, did someone do this to you?"

He reached for her, but she shifted away from him, sending a wave of overwhelming pain to her wounded side. She cried out. He stopped, his eyes wide and wounded.

"No!" she moaned, pushing away his hands. "Don't touch me!"

She saw his face the moment the truth dawned on him. He started to breathe faster. His eyes turned to steel.

"Was it Logan?" His voice was a heated whisper. "When I got to town I realized I'd been lied to. I couldn't find Logan, Rita or Ames anywhere. I came back as fast as I could – they must have planned this."

She watched him fight for control. Kathleen had never known Joshua to wear rage like a garment, not even when he thought she and Evan had betrayed him. But now his eyes burned with fire as he realized what had happened there, on his barn floor, with his wife.

Would he finish what Logan had started? Would he put her out of her misery?

Her tears burned her eyes, aching to be released, but she would not allow them. She waited while Joshua drew a quick breath, his gaze focused on her blood soaked dress. He reached again, and this time he easily lifted her into his arms. Kathleen gasped in pain.

"You're hurt bad." His voice was gruff, and his hand was red with her blood. He started for the house. "God, please let her be okay."

He heaved her all the way to the house and set her down on the long butcher's block in the kitchen. The very place he'd set her the night she had run through the woods and found his farm. The night he'd stitched her leg. Would he have allowed her in the door if he knew what kind of trouble and disappointment she would bring to his life?

"I'm sorry," she said, her voice raspy. Tears flooded her eyes at the injury in his expression. He couldn't hide it as he turned away to adjust the lanterns to full strength.

She felt him hesitate before he unbuttoned her dress. He eased the sleeve away from the shoulder and began to unlace her corset.

"Tell me what happened."

A long silence followed his query.

"I was doing the barn chores," she said in a very small voice. "Logan came up behind me and grabbed me by the hair. He forced me into the stall. He had a knife."

Kathleen glanced at Joshua, hoping he would gather the rest of the information himself and not force her to speak it. She couldn't bear to say the words. She watched him tremble as he breathed in and out through his nose.

She stared hard at the floor. "After, he… he stabbed me. Left me there."

Her voice was so quiet he had to lean close to hear her. His breath hitched as he pulled the fabric away from her wound and she cried.

"How could I have let this happen?" He turned away from her and slammed his fist into the glass of the hutch. It shattered.

"It's not your fault," Kathleen said. "I should have found a way to escape."

Joshua washed his hands at the sink before he took care of her wound. He tried to stop the flow of blood, but after two soaked hand towels, he shook his head. "This will need stitches. I'm going to take you to town to Doc. He should examine you for other injuries anyway. I'll give you some laudanum for the ride into town."

She shook her head, but had no strength left to argue. He watched her for a long time without saying anything.

"This isn't your fault," he finally said, with effort. He held the cup of medicine to her lips. After she managed to drink it down, he cleared his throat and looked away from her. "I need to know, Kathleen. I think I know, but I have to be sure. Did Logan do to you what I'm thinking he did?"

Kathleen knew what he meant. And she knew she had to tell him the truth. "Yes."

With her admission, she began to shake with silent sobs that would not be put off any longer.

Joshua turned away, his gaze catching on the rifle hanging above the door. "I'll kill him."

Forty-Two

It was time for Kathleen to leave.

She felt peace knowing it, though her decision hadn't been easy. It had been born of the pain that made her feel like she was drowning inside.

Sunday morning, Joshua didn't want to leave her alone. He hemmed and hawed about going to church without her. She insisted he should go, but before he left, he went around and bolted every door and taught her how to use the shotgun he propped beside her bed.

"If for some reason he shows up here, don't ask any questions. Shoot him on sight. I wouldn't leave you, but things in town are out of control. The sheriff showed up last night and I'm going to have to arrest him and get help from Columbus. And I have to find Logan."

She heard the hard edge of his voice and wanted to cry. It had been over a week since it happened, and Joshua's anger had only gotten stronger. It consumed him. She could tell it was quickly becoming hate, and it was the main reason Kathleen had decided she must leave.

When he left, she slowly packed her things and walked to town. She walked past the church, trying to ignore the words of the hymn that floated from the church building on the gentle calm of the breeze.

May thy will, not mine, be done
May thy will and mine be one.
Chase these doubtings from my heart,
Now thy perfect peace impart.

Her resolve was almost undone. She wanted to be with Joshua. She wanted back what had been stolen from them.

It had been too much to hope for, spending her life as Joshua's wife.

She felt the tragedy with her entire being, for as she walked away, she knew for sure she did love him. She could recognize it. She loved him enough that she couldn't force him to live out his days with her. He wouldn't make the decision for himself, so she would make it for him. She would set him free to live the life he deserved.

Joshua would be angry at her. But in time he would come to see it was for the best. She would give him this gift.

Kathleen stood inside the courthouse in Columbus, awed and intimidated by the solemn grandeur. After inquiring at the desk, she was directed to the office of the attorney responsible for matters of marriage contracts.

An older man with a white beard, spectacles and a pleasant smile opened the door.

"Mr. Schott?" Kathleen stood in the doorway. "I'm hoping you can assist me."

"Of course," he stood back and welcomed her into the office. "Please sit down."

He smiled kindly as he sat across from her. She hated to tell him her business. Would he be so accommodating after he heard her story?

"How can I help?" he asked, folding his hands on his desk.

She hesitated, feeling like she was confessing to a crime. "I need to have my marriage annulled."

She waited for him to respond, shifting as her still-healing wound began to ache.

"I see." He fingered his beard, considering her. He reached for a pencil and sifted through neatly stacked papers until he found what he was looking for.

"Name and date of birth?"

"Kathleen Able Whitley. June 5, 1886."

"So you are twenty years old. And your husband?"

"Joshua James Whitley. He's four years older."

"Now," he said as he finished writing and sat back. "Tell me your story."

"Everything?" She bit her lip. She hadn't planned on sharing anything about the saloon or Logan's attack, but it made sense he would need such information to make a judgment in her case.

"I'm afraid that to legally annul a marriage, we need to establish a clear reason to do so."

She nodded, resigned to the task. She would speak the words, this once, to give Joshua the gift of freedom. "Joshua is the deputy in Dempsey. We were married because Joshua was trying to protect me from a man who wanted to hurt me."

"I know of the good deputy," Mr. Schott said. "The sheriff and I have spoken. He is here in Columbus often, trying to close the saloons in Ohio and working toward establishing prohibition laws."

Kathleen didn't mention that Joshua would have to arrest the sheriff for his crimes against Dempsey.

"Sheriff Stacy has always spoken highly of his deputy." The man watched her carefully.

"Oh yes! Joshua's character is beyond reproach."

"I see," Mr. Schott continued. "Does Deputy Whitley also wish for annulment?"

"I'm sure he does after all that's happened." Kathleen wiped tears from the corners of her eyes.

Mr. Schott handed her his handkerchief. "Mrs. Whitley, did both of you agree to annul the marriage at the beginning?"

She frowned. "Honestly, sir, I wasn't thinking much at the time.

I was just hoping to survive the night. We never discussed our plans."

The man hesitated and cleared his throat. "Forgive me for the indelicate nature of this question, but I must ask. Was the marriage consummated?"

Her cheeks felt hot and she twisted the handkerchief in her lap. "No."

"But you lived together? Alone?"

She nodded.

He made a few notes and then gave her his attention again. "You see, Mrs. Whitley, a marriage must meet certain requirements to be nullified. There are specific rules about consummation and cohabitation, and it will be up to the judge whether he deems your situation appropriate to void your union without a legal divorce."

She felt overwhelmed. "I figured I just needed to sign something."

He watched her for a long moment before he turned the form toward her and handed her his pen. "I would advise against this, Mrs. Whitley. At least talk it over with Deputy Whitley first. From what I know of the man, he would make a fine husband."

"He is a good man." She tried to keep her voice even as she quickly signed her name on the line. "But he deserves far better than me, Mr. Schott. Far better."

Kathleen felt no peace after she left the courthouse. Her turmoil only increased. She doubted her decision as she stood on the busy street in downtown Columbus. What would she do now?

She had only enough money for a night in a hotel and meals for a day or two. The only skills and experience she possessed were fit for a dance hall or a saloon.

Her gaze fell upon a sign opposite her on the street. *The Harmoneon* was advertised as a concert hall for gentleman. An unartistic representation of a nude Venus revealed the intent of the establishment. Frantic piano music aired tempting promises in a code men would understand as they passed by.

A sign in the front window caught her attention. *Wanted—pretty girls to wait tables. Apply within.*

Her spirit plummeted to the ground at the thought, but what other option did she have? If she wanted to eat, she would have to go inside.

She started across the busy street.

Forty-Three

Joshua stared at the documents in utter disbelief. He'd assumed the package from a law firm in Columbus was about Sheriff Stacy, who was to be transferred to a prison in Columbus to await his trial. Joshua had thrown it on the kitchen table to deal with after chores. He hadn't thought about it again until after he'd cleaned up his supper dishes.

Kathleen wanted to end their marriage.

He yelled in frustration and kicked the chair closest to him so hard it fell back on the floor with a clatter. It had been torture enough that she'd left him without a clue where she was going. He had searched everywhere, including Rita's saloon. Rita had mocked him, saying he shouldn't have expected anything else from a girl like Kathleen. Rita had suggested he would find Kathleen in a saloon or a brothel, because that was the only place her kind could go when it was all said and done.

After he'd met dead ends looking for Kathleen, he had resumed his search for Logan, who had apparently had enough good sense to leave town after assaulting Kathleen. Joshua decided that finding and killing Logan was the only thing that would make everything right again. He *would* kill him. It was only a matter of time.

But how could Kathleen just give up on their marriage? Push him out of her life and move on to deal with her wounds by herself? Did she think he blamed her?

Did he blame her?

He stood and groaned long and loud in frustration. "Lord, why would you let that wretch hurt her after she'd given her life to you and asked for your mercy? You could have stopped it. You could have stopped it from happening!"

He sank to the floor and let his head fall back against the leg of the table. "I just want her home. I want her safe."

Part of him was hoping God would answer his questions then and there in the kitchen of his farm. But God seemed silent. The world was dark and unfair, and Joshua didn't know if he could keep living on his own and putting up with the bad behavior of other people. He'd had enough.

He'd just had enough.

Joshua managed to pull himself together enough to do morning chores and go to town. He eyed the post office as he passed it, imagining himself mailing the marriage dissolution papers. Could he go through with it? It was obviously what she wanted. He'd stared at the form for a good hour the night before. He finally signed them, but added a note of frustration in the margin, saying it wasn't his choice and he thought their marriage still deserved a chance.

Either way, Joshua couldn't be married to a woman he couldn't find. And he wasn't sure where to start looking.

"Hey, Josh," Evan met him on the boardwalk in front of the jail. He clapped a sympathetic hand on Joshua's back. "I was just seeing to the sheriff's needs."

Joshua nodded. "Appreciate it. I can hardly stand to look the man in the eyes."

"Has he given a reason for what he did?"

"He says Rita lied and blackmailed him. I know it wouldn't be the first time she'd have done something like that, but it's hard to believe him with that pile of papers and cash in the drawer."

"I'm sorry, Josh. I know you trusted him. We all did."

Joshua nodded and moved to go inside.

"Found any sign of Logan?" Evan followed Joshua into the office, having to bend over to walk through the doorframe, he was so tall.

"I think he knows better than to show his face around here. I'll have to hunt him down."

Evan nodded. "Count me in."

Joshua tossed the envelope with the form on his desk and hung his jacket on the peg. He cast a glare in the direction of the cells where the despondent Sheriff Stacy waited for justice. He pulled the curtain across the room so he didn't have to look at him.

"What's this?" Evan picked up the envelope.

"Kathleen sent it. Documents to end our marriage." Joshua sat down in the chair behind the desk.

Evan looked at Joshua in surprise. "You signed them?"

Joshua shrugged. "Doesn't mean I'm sending it."

"Do you have any idea where she went?"

"If I did, I wouldn't be sitting here staring at your ugly mug." Joshua leaned back in his chair.

"She can't be that far away. We could send wires to the nearby towns. Someone might have seen her," Evan said. "I have a few minutes. I could stop by the telegraph office for you."

Joshua exhaled and swiped his chin with his palm. "It'd be like finding the needle in the haystack."

"Well, you have to start somewhere," Evan said, his tone slightly impatient. "Why did she go in the first place? Did she leave a note?"

Joshua wondered if he should give Evan the final detail. It was unspeakable. It made him sick thinking on it. He had told Evan and Mary that Logan attacked Kathleen, that he'd cut her. But he hadn't given them the whole story.

He sighed and covered his face with his hands. "Evan, Logan didn't just cut Kathleen."

Evan narrowed his eyes, first in confusion, then in disbelief. He shook his head and punched his fist in his hand. "Josh, I'm really sorry."

"Me, too. And no one's sorrier than Kathleen. But the only person who should be sorry is Logan. And he will be when I put a bullet in his chest."

"Which is why I'm going to help you find him, so you don't end up paying for his sins. We'll turn him in, not kill him in cold blood."

Joshua shrugged. "I'm sure he'll give me a reason." He pulled his Smith and Wesson from the holster and held it up for effect. "I'm counting on it."

"Josh, revenge doesn't take away the pain," Evan said. "Only time and the good Lord can help with that. You know I know what I'm talking about."

Evan's words carried great weight. Even with Joshua's broken past and painful present, he knew his story paled next to Evan's. Evan had learned through experience, and he was right. Joshua couldn't rush a resolution. Letting his emotions run the show would only make things worse. Joshua pushed his gun back into the holster, thankful for Evan's quiet admonishment.

Their conversation was interrupted by a knock on the door. Pastor Merchant gave them an apologetic greeting. "I'm sorry to interrupt. Joshua, there is a man at the church asking about Kathleen."

Forty-Four

Kathleen had stood outside the "concert hall' a good half-hour before she decided to delay the inevitable. She had taken a room at the boardinghouse, but she had a clear view of the saloon from her bedroom window. It taunted her as if it knew she didn't have enough money for another night.

Her only other option was to go home to Little Sicily. She would have to face her family and beg for their mercy and understanding. Maybe they would give her a roof over her head or at least find her a job. It would be humiliating, but she wouldn't need to go back to the saloon.

And yet, she had come from the saloon. Perhaps it was her destiny, as it had been her mother's.

Purposeful singing floated on the air through her open window, interrupting her thoughts.

> We're coming, we're coming
> Our brave little band
> On the right side of temperance
> We do take our stand!

The group of women came marching down the street. Kathleen saw the barrel of water they carried between them. She sympathized with whoever was going to be on the receiving end.

254

"We are here today to denounce the evils of the demon alcohol! It has ruined many a family and enslaved the men of Columbus!" The leader of the women called as she perched herself on the stairs of the saloon, surrounded by her followers.

"I speak now to the women of this den of sin," she said, turning to the saloon girls wandering the porch waiting for customers. "Come to your senses! May our administrations wake you from your evil slumber so that you realize you must leave this place and never return!"

At her cue, two women lifted the barrel over the head of the nearest girl. It was cumbersome and they struggled to hold it high enough, so the girl was able to duck away.

"Stop this right now!"

Kathleen's heart beat faster at the sound of the familiar female voice.

"Of all the foolish behavior I've seen, this takes the prize. Why do you think dowsing these poor girls with scalding water is going to make them want to come out of this place and live among you?"

The temperance leader leaned over the railing to shake her finger at the woman who had spoken. "We are on the Lord's errand!" she cried.

Kathleen could only see the top of the hat of the woman who opposed them, but the sound of her voice filled Kathleen with a bittersweet yearning for home. "Have any of you ever taken the time to listen to these girls' stories? To find out if they were even given a choice in being here? If you're here for that purpose, I applaud you. Are you willing to take steps to ensure their freedom and to see to their needs while they find a way to make a new start? I invite you to do so with enthusiasm."

The woman paused, surveying the girls on the porch who were trying to pretend they weren't listening and they didn't care. "Otherwise, you are simply taking up space on a crowded street corner and you should go home to your knitting."

Kathleen chuckled in spite of herself. She could not contain her curiosity any longer. She ran down the stairs and out into the street.

She slipped through the crowd to the side of the saloon so she could peek at the woman without being seen.

The crowd began to disperse as the woman resolutely climbed the stairs to the saloon door. Kathleen listened from below.

"I'm sorry to bother you, dear," she said, presumably to one of the saloon girls on the porch. "You only need to say the word and I will do whatever I can to help you. I'm inquiring after a girl named Kathleen. Kathleen Able. Is she living here?"

Kathleen covered her mouth with her hands, tears filling her eyes at the confirmation of the woman's identity.

Aunt Amelia.

Kathleen moved back so she could see her face. Amelia looked weary, but every bit as graceful and practical as ever. Kathleen wanted to run into her arms. To ask how long she'd been searching. Had she been looking this whole year she'd been gone? Did her parents or Uncle – did they look for her as well?

"Sorry. Don't know a Kathleen. There are quite a few saloons in Columbus, though."

"I will visit them all if I must. We must find our Kathleen." Aunt Amelia patted the girl's shoulder as she turned away. "Thank you, dear."

"I wish my family would come looking for me," the girl called after her.

Amelia turned and grabbed her hand. "Dear one, even when our family fails us, Jesus is ever ready to forgive and restore. We can go somewhere and talk if you'd like. I could buy you some supper."

The girl pulled her hand away. "Too late for me."

Amelia watched the girl turn and disappear into the saloon. When Amelia turned and came down the stairs, she passed Kathleen so closely Kathleen could smell her familiar lavender lotion. She wanted more than anything to run to her. Amelia wore a sensible but elegant blue traveling dress and a fashionable hat, all revealing her true nature. She was ever poised, but she held within a thousand secret dreams and thoughts at any given moment. Kathleen had always looked up to Aunt Amelia. She'd felt a connection to her.

She'd have made a good mother.

Kathleen couldn't bring herself to call out. She was ruined now. She didn't want to bring that shame upon her aunt. If she went into the saloon, maybe she could spare everyone else a world of hurt.

She felt her throat constrict. *Please, God. Give me another way. If I still belong to you, show me the way out.*

"Kathleen?"

She gasped and turned at the voice. Aunt Amelia stood before her, shock and joy sharing company in her expression. In two strides, Amelia had Kathleen in her arms.

"My dear, dear Kathleen," Amelia pulled back only enough to take Kathleen's face tenderly with her gloved hands. "We've been looking everywhere! Thank the Lord you're safe. Oh, praise Jesus!"

Kathleen couldn't bear to look her aunt in the eyes. "I don't deserve to be found."

Amelia paused. She looked at Kathleen as if she was studying her for clues. "What happened?"

Kathleen didn't want to tell her aunt such a sordid tale. But this was Aunt Amelia, who had always listened, who had ever been filled with gentle instruction and unfailing love. Kathleen knew she was safe.

"I was working at a saloon."

"Here in Columbus?"

"No. A small town west of here."

Amelia watched her and waited for her to continue.

Kathleen felt her lip tremble. "I've done things I'm ashamed of. You shouldn't even be touching me. I'm unclean."

Aunt Amelia hugged her tighter. "Oh, my dear girl."

Kathleen let her aunt lead her across the street to a vacant bench in front of the boardinghouse.

"Why did you leave your family, Kathleen?"

Kathleen swallowed with difficulty when she remembered how she had felt when she learned the truth.

"I found the letter."

"The letter?" Aunt Amelia's tone was uneasy, as if she knew

what letter Kathleen meant.

Kathleen nodded, glancing at her aunt's face.

"In the trunk in the attic room? Under the baby things?" Aunt Amelia asked.

Kathleen started to nod until she realized what her aunt had said. "No. The letter was on the top."

Amelia's eyes swam with tears. "I wish you'd found the other letter, dear girl. Who was this letter from?"

"From my father. My *real* father. Sent to Mama when you were away for your mother's funeral."

Amelia sighed. She caught Kathleen's hand and held it tightly. "Did you ask your mother to explain?"

Kathleen shrugged sullenly. "My *aunt* explained."

Amelia shook her head. "We should have told you."

"I don't blame *you*," Kathleen said. Both of them were quiet.

"Why did he leave me in a home that wasn't truly mine?" Kathleen heard the bitterness in her voice, the same bitterness she thought she had let go. Now that she could know the answers, the questions plagued her.

Aunt Amelia dabbed tears from the corners of her eyes. "You probably feel your father abandoned you. But he was only thinking of you. He thought it would be cruel to take you from the only home you'd ever known. Kathleen, it was a decision he didn't make lightly. He agonized over it long after we were married and the boys were born."

"It was the wrong decision," Kathleen said.

Amelia nodded. "That's clear now, but it wasn't then. And your uncle is not easily talked out of a decision he has already made."

"My father," Kathleen corrected.

"Your father."

Kathleen leaned forward and covered her face. "I was so angry when I found out. I wanted to hurt him. I wanted to hurt all of you." She took a deep breath, releasing all the doubt as she exhaled. "But Joshua helped me see my problem was my sin, not the mistakes of others. My selfishness got me into the mess I was in."

Amelia watched her through misty eyes. She could see the hope in her aunt's features.

"I asked Jesus to forgive me. Wash all the stains from my sin away. He did," she smiled through her tears. "He did, Aunt Amelia. He washed it all away."

Amelia reached for her and hugged her as tightly as she could. "My dear, dear Kathleen. Praise the Lord!"

Kathleen stayed in the warm embrace of her aunt for a long time before she sat up straight and returned her aunt's teary smile.

Amelia handed her a handkerchief. "Now, who in the world is Joshua?"

Kathleen's smile slipped. "He was my husband."

Amelia's brow furrowed in confusion. "Was?"

Kathleen summoned the courage to answer the question. "It's over."

She offered no further explanation. She didn't want to consider what she had lost when she sent those dissolution papers to Dempsey. Aunt Amelia only watched her in thoughtful silence.

"Is my father here?" Kathleen asked in a small voice.

Amelia squeezed her shoulders. "*Both* of your fathers have been very busy looking for you."

Kathleen wasn't so sure it was true. Her Papa had never been one to be distracted from his work very long. And her true father had given her away.

"William has been scouring the towns around Columbus. He's to meet me here in two days."

"Scouring them for what?" Kathleen asked.

Amelia laughed softly. "For you."

Kathleen took in the information. "He's looking for me?"

Amelia nodded. "We've been looking for you since the day you left. We started by writing letters. When school let out for the boys, we left them with Amy and Connor and traveled around asking about you. On a hunch, William went to the saloon in Columbus where your mother lived. A woman told him you'd been there and you'd taken the photograph of your mother. She said you left with a woman she thought might be a brothel madam. We've focused our search on saloons since then, but there are so many of them."

Kathleen heard the sorrow in her aunt's tone and felt shame. "I'm sorry."

"But for the grace of God go any of us," Amelia said resolutely. "I'm just relieved you are safe. And that God has saved you! How I've prayed."

Kathleen didn't doubt it, and she was grateful. She squeezed her aunt's hand.

"Dear Kathleen, will you come home now?" Amelia asked hopefully.

Kathleen took a deep breath and released it, along with her lingering doubt. She summoned a smile. "I think I'm ready."

Forty-Five

Amelia took Kathleen to the Grand Southern where she was staying. While Kathleen's attention was taken by surveying the beautiful foyer, Amelia went to the front desk to tell them Kathleen would be staying with her.

Kathleen turned in a full circle to take in the whole of the grandeur. It was surreal. So different from the farm. She felt a momentary twinge of guilt. She should be on the farm, doing her chores and making supper.

When Amelia returned, she was holding a slip of paper. "Telegram from William," she explained. "He wants me to take the next train to Dempsey. Apparently, he ran into your husband."

Kathleen felt faint as she boarded the car at the Scioto Valley Traction station in Columbus. She felt even worse when the train took off out of the station, so fast she could hardly comprehend the scenery flying past the window. She held on to the wooden armrest of the padded seat and closed her eyes.

"Everything will work out for good," Amelia promised.

There could be no fooling Aunt Amelia. She had always been able to sense other people's emotions, sometimes before the person even realized it themselves. But she also knew her aunt had no idea about the things Kathleen had seen. The things that had happened to her. How could she admit the truth to the people most capable of crushing her with their rejection?

She tapped her foot anxiously as questions flooded her mind. Would her father be angry when he heard the story of where she had been? He had every right to be. At the very least, maybe he would accept her once again as his niece.

And Joshua? Would he want to see her now, ruined as she was? Was he relieved she had left? Could she face him knowing they were no longer husband and wife, and they would never share a home or a future?

She blinked back tears and tried to form a speech to her father. She remembered the Prodigal Son.

I have sinned against God and against you. I am no longer worthy to be called your daughter. Please forgive me, and let me be your niece again.

A gentle voice in the recesses of her mind reminded her she was no longer lost. She had been washed. But she wrestled with doubt. Had what Logan did to her erased the experience she'd had on Easter? Did God's forgiveness have certain limits? Was he too holy to look at her now?

What seemed a hundred years later, and yet before she had fully prepared, the train screeched to an abrupt halt outside the Dempsey depot.

Kathleen glanced out the window and saw a tall figure leaning against the side of the brick building. His hands were in his pockets, his hat low over his eyes. Her heart lurched.

Amelia patted her hand and went ahead of her, toward the steps. When William saw her exit the train, he smiled and took several steps forward to meet her. Kathleen hung back, watching the couple reunite as other passengers brushed past her.

William embraced Amelia and kissed her, winding his arms around her and locking his fingers behind her back. They shared private words. A frown settled on his face as he glanced up at the train. Could he see her through the window? Was he unwilling to see her?

I have sinned against God and against you. I am no longer worthy...

She took a step down. Then another. Her hand trembled when the attendant held it to assist her final step to the ground.

When she found the courage to lift her gaze, her father was watching her, as if he could not believe his eyes. She waited for disappointment to alter his expression. Instead, a grin appeared.

And then he started running.

He apparently had no thought for the other passengers around them. He weaved through the people standing between them, until he had crossed the distance and grabbed her, swinging her into his arms and his powerful embrace.

"Kathleen!"

At his breathless word, she put her arms around his neck and hugged him back. He was as strong and solid as he had ever been. His whiskers tickled her face as they always had. But always before, he had been Uncle William. She had made herself hold him at a distance. She had felt awkward for loving him as much as she did.

Now she hugged him like he was her father. And he hugged her like she was his daughter. And they couldn't hold each other tightly enough.

When he set her down long moments later, he laughed through tears that had gathered in his eyes.

She took a deep breath and lowered her gaze. "I have sinned against God and against you. In unspeakable ways. I was angry and I wanted to hurt you. I'm still trying to understand the reasons, but I believe God has forgiven me. I know I'm not the Kathleen that left Little Sicily, but I'm asking you to forgive what I did and where I've been. At least let me be your niece again..."

He shook his head, smiling as if her words made no sense. "Kathleen, there is nothing you could have done that would be worse than anything I've done. You have always been my daughter, even when you didn't know it, and you always will be, no matter what happens to either of us. I'm the one who should be apologizing."

"You might not feel that way if you knew everything," she said with great remorse.

He reached for her chin and gently made her look up at him. The skin around his eyes crinkled joyfully. "My beautiful, beautiful girl, you look so much like your mama right now. I remember the day we both held you in our arms for the first time and stared into your eyes, wondering how in the world we were going to keep you safe and loved forever. I am glad you're safe now. And so is your mama, in her home beyond the skies."

Kathleen relaxed in his embrace. What a feeling it was, to be held in her father's arms. Accepted. Forgiven. Loved.

Forty-Six

"So is your wife coming back?" Evan leaned against the fence as Joshua came out of the barn. Joshua frowned at him and walked toward the house.

"She's not my wife anymore."

Evan followed him. "That man you met in town, though, he's her father?"

Joshua glared at Evan, but he nodded. "Why do you care?"

Evan shrugged. "Just wondering. I was hoping it meant she was coming back. You miss her."

"I do miss her," Joshua snapped. "But it's not my choice. She left. She went to the trouble to draw up papers to end our relationship. Our marriage is over, Evan. What can I do?"

"Maybe she was giving you the option. Maybe she wanted you to get her back."

Joshua sighed as he threw open the back door. "I'm no good at playing games. Why aren't you in town dogging Miss Walsh? You won't win her if you're here worrying about my problems."

Evan shrugged, dejected. "Miss Walsh told me to stop following her around. She isn't interested."

Joshua glanced at his friend's features. "Sorry to hear that."

"At least she said the same thing to Sam." Evan sighed. "I've been looking for Logan. I thought I saw him head into the woods this morning so I came here looking for him."

"Are you sure it was him?"

Evan shook his head. "Nope. I just wanted to make sure, especially if Kathleen was going to come home."

Joshua kicked a flour sack he'd left on the floor in the kitchen. He was having trouble keeping up with the inside chores. "No one ever said she was coming home, Evan. She's here to see her father."

Evan crossed his arms over his chest and stared out the window. "Doesn't seem right. Everyone can see plain as day you two are made for each other."

"Did you come here to make me feel better?" Joshua huffed. "Because I'm about to go drown myself in the creek."

Evan chuckled. "Sorry. What's her pa like?"

Joshua sniffed and passed a palm over his chin. "Tall."

"Wow, it's like I can see him standing here. You should be a writer or something."

Joshua made a face. "Taller than me, not as tall as you. 'Course, ain't too many men as unreasonably gargantuan as you."

"Jealous?"

"I'm a respectable six feet. Why'd I be jealous of you having to bend down so you don't get your pretty hair wet in the clouds?"

Evan stood up to his full height. "You could grow out your hair if you want it to look like mine, you know."

"Why in the world would I want to look like a girl? Bible says men should have short hair."

"I never read that. And besides, Jesus had long hair," Evan argued.

"He did not. Nowhere in the Bible does it say Jesus had long hair."

"He does in all the pictures," Evan shrugged.

Joshua sighed loudly as he poured himself and Evan cups of steaming hot coffee. "Nobody drew a picture of him when they were actually looking at him. Nobody sat him down for a photograph, either. So don't be telling me you know what Jesus looks like."

"Isn't that the same thing you're trying to tell me?"

"That's not what I was saying at all."

Evan smiled. "Joshua, if you miss her, just say so. You don't have to be ugly."

"I'm not the ugly one." Joshua sipped his coffee loudly and stared out the back door.

Evan chuckled and watched Joshua with interest.

"What?"

"You seem like yourself again for the first time."

Joshua pushed open the back door and grabbed the slop bucket to take to the pigs. "It's only because I'm settled on the fact that I'm going to make Logan pay."

Evan's smile faded. He followed Joshua out the door and down the path toward the barn, but Joshua ignored him.

He scrutinized the surroundings, looking for possible clues that Logan had been there. Every day that went by without Kathleen, he wanted revenge more. He daydreamed about standing over the man's dead body with a smoking gun in his hand. Logan was going to get what was coming to him.

Vengeance is mine. I will repay.

Joshua ignored the voice of the Spirit just as he had ignored Evan. He knew he was out of line, but he felt justified. God would forgive his grudge, considering everything, wouldn't he? And even if he felt guilt, Joshua's plans to end Logan's life weren't going to change.

His thoughts unexpectedly returned to his meeting with Kathleen's father that morning. He'd seen the family resemblance, for sure, but Mr. Morehouse was intimidating in his rugged demeanor and appearance. He hadn't seen a gun, but the man sure seemed like the gun-slinging type.

Son, I've made mistakes. Kathleen's been hurt by one of them. I've been looking under every rock between here and Cincinnati because I can't bear the thought of her being in trouble. She's my little girl, Mr. Morehouse had said.

Joshua hoped Kathleen's father would take her home and keep her safe, since Joshua was incapable of doing it. He'd proven that well enough.

"Look up yonder." Evan elbowed him in the ribs. Joshua lifted his gaze and saw them. Mr. Morehouse with an unfamiliar woman on one arm and Kathleen on the other. They were coming down the path from town.

Joshua swallowed, feeling nervous at the sight of Kathleen. He wouldn't let himself hope. "She's probably just picking up something she left before they head out." He handed Evan the slop pail. "I'll be in the barn if they need me for anything."

Evan gave him a reproachful stare as Joshua pushed his hands into his pockets and turned in the direction of the barn.

"Yellow-bellied fraidy-cat," Evan called after him.

"Least I mind my own business," Joshua answered without looking back.

"You're a coward. You need a good dunk in the creek," Evan said loudly.

A few moments passed as Joshua stood in the barn. He could hear them talking, but he couldn't hear the words they were saying. He knew he should go to her. But the image of her on the floor of the barn stall, bleeding, crying, cowering from his reach like she was too filthy to touch – it haunted him.

He'd failed her. He didn't want to do anything else to hurt her, and if he stayed in the barn, she'd go home with her family. She'd be safe.

He watched them from the window, even though he knew it made him a coward, just like Evan had said. After a few minutes, Kathleen left the group to head toward the house. He assumed she was gathering the remainder of her things. She turned back once and looked toward the barn. He wondered if she was yearning for what they had lost.

Joshua was feeling some powerful yearning himself. He watched her walk, watched her long blonde curls bounce with her movement. He wanted to run to her and hold her tight. Never let her go. He wanted all the history between them to be rewritten. He wished they could have a clean slate and a new life together. He wanted it more than he had ever wanted anything.

He turned back to arrange the feed bags. They were all thrown together in a mess, leaking feed everywhere. The chickens loved it, but he missed the order Kathleen had kept in the barn. He spent a good ten minutes reorganizing, but it still wasn't the way she had done it.

"Joshua!"

He heard the concern in Evan's voice, and his heart started racing. He took off toward the house as fast as he could go. When he came up the hill he saw Evan and Morehouse searching the vicinity with worried expressions. The woman he assumed must be Mrs. Morehouse trembled, her hands over her face.

A cold sweat broke out on Joshua's forehead.

"She's gone," Evan explained. "She went into the house for just a few minutes, and she's gone. We can't find her anywhere."

Joshua slammed his fist down on the porch rail. "It's gotta be Logan. He'll head for the woods. Let's go."

"I need a safe place for my wife," Morehouse put a hand on the woman's arm.

"Door left of the fireplace in the kitchen. Stairs lead up to a bedroom closed off to the rest of the house. No one would think to go up there."

"Let me come with you!" Mrs. Morehouse insisted to her husband. "I can help!"

"Not this time, love," he said, pushing a strand of hair away from her face. He kissed her with gentle insistence. "If Kathleen comes back, you need to get her up to that loft and bar the door."

She only met his gaze for a moment before she nodded. "I love you."

"I love you, too, woman. Now go be safe."

The men ran for the pasture behind the barn and the path that led into the woods. Joshua motioned for them to split up. He traveled along the northwest trail that led to the rail yards. He didn't want Logan getting on a train and out of town. He could hear Evan and Morehouse rustling through the brush on either side of him.

Gunfire erupted. He heard bullets whiz by his ear and realized he was the target. He jumped behind a tree and tried to ascertain where they were coming from.

"Joshua!" he heard Kathleen cry.

"Get down!" Joshua yelled to Evan and Morehouse.

"So this little strumpet is worth every one of your lives?" Logan called from somewhere beyond the bend in the path. Joshua thought he saw movement behind the gathered limbs of an old Buckeye tree, under the draping of the branches sagging low with leaves.

"Come on out, Logan. It's over," Joshua shouted.

"She was supposed to die. I wanted it to be slow, but you found her too soon. Rita was supposed to keep you busy. So now I'm here to finish the job," Logan said. "It can't end any other way."

Joshua wondered why Logan hadn't killed her immediately, but he wasn't going to question it. Maybe God was lending a hand until Joshua could get to her.

"Come on out and we'll talk about it."

"How many of you are there?"

Joshua heard the uncertainty edging Logan's voice. He called back. "Enough that you don't stand a chance of walking away from this. You let her go and come out now and I'll tie you up and take you to jail instead of blasting you to hell like I want to."

Logan didn't need to know Joshua had no plans to let him live. The thought of a bullet in Logan's chest satisfied him. He'd never been so sure a man needed to die.

"If I come out, you'll kill me." Logan called his bluff.

A sound nearby made Joshua look up. Evan signaled that he would sneak around from the back. Joshua narrowed his eyes, trying to tell Evan he better be careful.

Evan grinned.

Joshua continued to talk, keeping Logan's attention from what Evan was doing. "You're a sorry piece of trash, Logan. You're making me realize I should have killed you the first day you set foot in my town."

"I was having the same thought about you, Deputy," Logan said in a mocking tone.

Joshua heard the sound of a scuffle. He ran toward the tree he thought Logan was behind just as a gunshot rang out. Joshua almost tripped over Evan, who was lying on the ground, holding his side. Blood seeped through his fingers.

"Too easy," Logan said with a smirk. He held a handful of Kathleen's hair as she half-kneeled beside him, whimpering. "So it was just the two of you, wasn't it? Shame. Now all three of you will die."

It was an odd moment for a revelation, but it occurred to Joshua that big moments in life happened fast. Before a body prepared. Before one could collect his thoughts and think things through. Sometimes life was completely changed – or lost – in split-second reactions.

Logan lifted his gun and took aim in the same moment Joshua did. But Joshua instinctively knew Logan had a moment's head start.

"Hey!" Morehouse's voice called out. Logan turned the other way in surprise and shot his gun. Joshua took careful aim, not wanting to take a chance on shooting Kathleen, but another shot rang out before Joshua had the chance to pull the trigger. Joshua watched Logan fall to the ground with a bullet square in the middle of his back.

He looked at Evan on the ground, holding his smoking gun.

"I wasn't about to let you do it," Evan said before he fell back on the ground with a groan.

"You alright?"

"I'm fine. Just a scratch."

Joshua nodded and looked back. Kathleen's face had gone white as she stood next to Logan's body. Joshua remembered he'd heard Logan's gun go off. Had Kathleen's father even been wearing a gun?

Dread made him feel cold all over. He ran to Kathleen's side and looked into the brush. "Where'd he go?"

Kathleen didn't answer. She just stared, still and pale as a ghost.

Joshua went on down the path. "Morehouse? You okay?"

The sound of shallow breathing caught his attention, and he saw Morehouse on the ground, holding a wound in his abdomen from

271

which blood flowed freely.

"Daddy?"

The word tumbled from Kathleen's mouth without her conscious thought when she stepped forward at Joshua's beckoning. She saw the blood soaking her father's shirt and sank to her knees beside him. He reached for her hand, and when she held it she could sense how weak he was.

"I'm going for help," Joshua said, but William stopped him with a slight shake of his head.

"It's too late, son, we're too far out," William said. "I... I need to say something, and you need to listen."

Joshua kneeled next to Kathleen. She felt his arm go around her waist.

"First of all, Kathleen, I need you tell the boys to be good and take care of their mama," William began, causing Kathleen to start crying. She held his hand and leaned over, against his shoulder. Her father took a deep breath. "And then you tell that wife of mine – you tell her she's stronger than she thinks she is, and she's going to be okay."

Kathleen shook with sobs. Joshua held her tighter.

"She's going to say she won't." Her father gave a breathless chuckle, and when Kathleen sat up to look him in the eyes, she saw his tears. "But you tell her I said she will."

Kathleen nodded briefly, her tears flowing.

"And you, young man," William turned to Joshua. "I got one job for you, but it's an important one. I can't do it myself, now, though I'd like nothing better. You're going to take care of my little girl."

Joshua stared sadly at the older man. He gave a short nod, though Kathleen saw hesitation.

"Please," she cried. "Please don't die. Not now."

"Little girl, I don't mind dying. Especially for you. Your ma did the same for me, so it's only fitting." William's voice was getting slow. Sleepy. He reached a trembling hand to her cheek. "I'll tell you what she told me. You live for love. Find out what God wants you to do and do it with everything you got in you."

Her voice trembled. "I'm sorry for what I did. I'd do anything to go back and change all of this."

"Don't be sorry." His voice was fading. She saw peace spread over his features, as if the pain was lessening and heaven was already beginning the process of collecting his spirit. "We all have a path we need to take to get to Jesus. I wouldn't want you in any other direction. This is right."

The three of them were silent for long moments as William struggled for breath. Finally, he gave her fingers a light squeeze.

"Kathleen, don't you ever doubt your pa loved you."

With a quiet exhale, he was gone.

Forty-Seven

Kathleen wondered how any of them could be calm. She even heard quiet laughter in the dining room, where neighbors and church members crowded to partake of the luncheon Amy Able had set out on the sideboard.

Couldn't they all see her father in his coffin in the parlor? How could they eat? Socialize? Her stomach protested against the smell of food. She had no words for those who offered her their condolences for the loss of her uncle.

He was my father.

Joshua stayed by her side. She felt his presence, though he didn't say much. She appreciated that he was there, that he didn't act as if everything was okay. He sat on the settee, leaning his head on his hand, staring at the coffin. Or at Kathleen. She wished she could hear his thoughts.

Every time Kathleen looked at Amelia, Kathleen had fresh tears. She would never forget the image of her aunt, as she came up the path with Evan and Joshua carrying William's body. Amelia had gone white, staring at them like a statue. She'd backed away from them, as if she could outrun the pain they were bringing her. As Amelia had been confronted with the truth that her husband was gone, and she had recognized that there was no hope that he'd live, she had crumpled into a heap. Kathleen had held her.

"I can't do this!" Amelia had cried out, over and over again.

"He told me to tell you that you can. That you're stronger than you think." Kathleen had said the words as they both cried together.

Now, as William's family sat huddled in the parlor, Kathleen figured the boys and Amelia were the only people feeling the pain she was feeling. Mama, Papa and Jennifer were sad, to be sure, but losing a brother or an uncle was not at all the same as losing a husband or father.

Amelia sat beside her, her eyes red-rimmed and swollen. She dabbed them with a handkerchief Kathleen recognized as one of her father's.

"How are you doing?" Amelia asked, squeezing Kathleen's shoulders. Amelia gave her a brave smile that didn't seem to reach her eyes, yet was brimming with genuine concern.

Kathleen looked at the boys. Her half-brothers. Harvey was fourteen, Samuel eleven and Ian eight. All too young to lose a father. They stared blankly at the coffin as they tried to make sense of what was happening.

"I don't know," Kathleen answered.

"I know what you mean," Amelia sighed. A more genuine expression of loss replaced her attempt at a smile. "My heart is broken."

Amelia was only thirty-seven. Youth still clung to her features; only the tiniest lines had started around her eyes and mouth. She was alone, and responsible to raise three boys to adulthood on her own. Kathleen could barely remember the time before her father had married Amelia. She could always tell they had loved on a grander scale than most.

"Treasure every moment," Amelia whispered, glancing at Joshua as she said the words. "Don't hold back. In the end, it will hurt, and every day you're given won't seem like enough, but you'll never regret loving each other."

Kathleen shook her head. She stood abruptly and crossed the room to her father's coffin. She saw that Joshua stayed in his seat, but Amelia followed her.

They stared at the dear face, so still, so peaceful.

"He's with Jesus," Amelia said suddenly, as if the thought had just occurred to her, as if William had whispered to her from beyond the veil. "He gets to be with Jesus, Kathleen. Oh, but I'm jealous."

Kathleen didn't know what to say in response, but the thought gave her comfort. She realized one day she'd be there, too.

Amelia took a deep breath and led Kathleen away from the casket, out of the parlor and onto the front porch.

"Now tell me about you and Joshua." Amelia sniffed and wiped away the newest tears.

"I don't think it's going to work with Joshua," Kathleen said quietly.

Amelia watched her. "Tell me why."

"Because I'm ruined," Kathleen said, defeated.

She felt her aunt's gaze focused on her. "Kathleen Mae Able-Morehouse! You have been bought with a price! The very Son of God gave his life for you! Never call ruined what he has called clean."

"Aunt Amelia, even if I'm clean to God, it doesn't make me clean to Joshua," Kathleen said, shame filling her once again.

Amelia's eyes softened. "Give him time. I've seen the way he watches you, Kathleen. I know that look well. He'll come around."

Kathleen didn't answer. They moved back into the house. She felt Joshua's eyes on her. When their gazes met, he seemed to capture her so she could not look away.

She realized she didn't want to be without him. Not ever.

"Some weather," Joshua muttered, glancing at the clouds. When had summer come upon them full force? The humidity made him feel breathless. Humidity and grief.

Kathleen looked away and didn't answer. He wished he could bring back her father. He hated that she'd lost him just as they'd made things right. And it had to hurt that her father had died to save Joshua's life. He would never forget the image of her standing before her father's coffin, small and fragile and wounded. It wasn't what he'd wanted for her.

But here they stood, at the train station in Little Sicily. He needed to get back to Dempsey. Isaiah was standing in as sheriff until Joshua returned, but Isaiah had a business to run and babysitting Rita's saloon was a full-time job.

Joshua didn't want to go back alone. But he didn't feel like he could ask Kathleen to leave her family while they were all hurting. They still had healing to do. Did she even *want* to come back with him? Since the day she'd been attacked by Logan, she'd been different. Reserved. Maybe she didn't trust men anymore. He couldn't blame her. Maybe she no longer wanted or needed his love.

He frowned. It pained him something awful to leave her. He did love her, more every day and more the longer he considered it. He wanted her on the farm, doing her horse tricks in the field with Sundi or kneeling over her garden plants with tender care. He wanted her flushed and smiling, fussing over special meals as he came into the kitchen.

He wanted a thousand kisses to look forward to, and that would be a good start. He wanted to hold her in his arms at night when the dreams troubled his sleep. He wanted to wind her long, pale locks of hair around his fingers while they sat in the orchard arbor and watched the sunset. He wanted to see his babies take their first breaths in her arms, blinking up at them with Kathleen's features all mingled together with his in the beautiful circle of life.

Tell her, you lily-livered coward, he could almost hear Evan say.

Kathleen didn't ask him to stay. She didn't ask to go with him. Wouldn't she say something if it was what she wanted? His frown deepened. He wouldn't do anything that gave her more pain. If she needed to be with her family, he wouldn't ask her to leave.

He supposed that was what love was. Sacrifice. He'd learned that all too well in the last few days.

If you love someone, you give up what you want if it's not the best for them. Lord, help me let her go.

The train whistle blew and the conductor called the riders to board. Kathleen folded her hands in front of her and watched as people began to climb onto the train headed toward Columbus.

"Listen, Kathleen," he said, not sure what he was going to come up with, but knowing he had to try. "I know there's been quite a bit of bad. I get it. And whatever you need, that's what I want for you."

She lifted her eyes to meet his, revealing an uncertain hope. Or maybe just confusion at his ambiguous words.

He was out of time. He grabbed her hand and lifted it to his lips. "You know where I'll be if you need me."

He didn't look at her again as he grabbed his bag and headed for the steps up to the passenger car. He tried to put her out of his mind, praying the Lord would give him strength to let her go. Praying her Savior would protect her and heal her many wounds.

She needed that kind of care before she'd ever be ready to receive his fumbling, imperfect attempt to love her.

Forty-Eight

It wasn't fair, but it was strangely comforting, how quickly life returned to normal. Faster than the hurt went away.

Kathleen sat in front of her father's gravestone, her gaze memorizing every etching of the letters on the white stone. Her chest ached with sadness, but the pain was, in some strange way, sweet. She traced the lines with her finger.

William Morehouse
Loving Husband and Father
In the Presence of the Lord
1861-1906

"Hey, sis."

Jennifer sat down beside her, crossing her legs under her skirt. She reached for a dandelion and blew the seeds into the air. Kathleen watched her, envious of the blush of innocence on her sister's cheeks.

"I guess it makes sense now, why we've always been so different." Jennifer played with the flower until it was stripped bare of the wispy seeds. "I'm so sorry you lost your father, Kathleen."

Kathleen nodded. She appreciated Jennifer saying the words, though it was probably hard for her to admit someone other than Papa was Kathleen's father.

"Did you know?" Kathleen asked quietly. "You were about six when I came to live with your family."

"No, I didn't know. I don't remember a time you weren't there," Jennifer said with a shrug. "We're still family, Kathleen. Nothing is going to change that. And I don't mean you'll be my cousin from now on. You will *always* be my little sister."

Kathleen didn't answer, but she felt the lump in her throat get tighter.

"And I assume Mama and Papa feel the same way," Jennifer continued. "You still have us."

"Even after everything I did?" Kathleen whispered. "Do you realize where I've been, Jen? You're in the Anti-Saloon League. You are fighting to close the saloon I lived in."

Jennifer shook her head. "I'm against what those places do to men, and to boys, and to women just like you, Kathleen. Being against what hurt you isn't the same as being against you."

Kathleen felt her lip tremble. "Thank you."

Jennifer hugged her. "And now I have an important question."

Kathleen smiled at her sister's lighter tone. "What?"

"You've been with us for two months. I've been so glad to have you back, so don't get the wrong impression when I ask this, but… why in the world are you still here?"

Kathleen chuckled. "I thought you said you were glad I was here."

"I am. But next month I will be marrying my sweetheart and moving to Toledo. We have to grow up, Kathleen. Make our own lives. Mama, Papa and Aunt Amelia don't expect you to stay here forever." Jennifer raised her brow expectantly.

Kathleen smiled and shook her head. "Just say what's on your mind, Jennifer."

"Okay, I will," Jennifer said. "You were married a few weeks ago, Kathleen. *Married.* You know that when you make a promise like that, God expects you to keep it."

Kathleen frowned as she grasped what her sister was saying. She looked down at her hands. "I hadn't thought about it that way."

"Did you promise to love, honor and obey your husband?" Jennifer watched her with a serious expression. Kathleen nodded.

"And did the minister say you were man and wife?"

"Yes."

"What makes you think a slip of paper with your signatures erases all you promised each other in God's presence?"

Kathleen considered Jennifer's words. They sat in silence for long moments. "He didn't ask me to come home with him."

"Maybe he thought you didn't want to go back to Dempsey."

Kathleen hesitated, but she finally spoke the words. "Jennifer, do you know what happened to me? Before I found Aunt Amelia and my father in Columbus?"

Jennifer's expression clouded. "Do you mean in the saloon?"

Kathleen heard the doubt in her sister's uneasy tone. She took a deep breath and tried to manage the onslaught of terrible images.

"Nothing happened in the saloon. Nothing that ruined me." Kathleen tried to be delicate, recognizing her sister's innocence. She didn't continue until Jennifer nodded for her to do so.

"There was a man who became obsessed with me. He wanted to have me. It's why Joshua married me in the first place – to protect me from this man. Joshua kept me safe for a long time. But eventually, this man found me. He had his way with me and left me for dead in my husband's barn," Kathleen explained softly.

Jennifer grasped her hand. "Oh, Kathleen," she whispered.

Kathleen stared hard at her father's headstone. "Joshua and I have never... well, you know. And I fear he thinks of me as ruined now."

Jennifer contemplated Kathleen's predicament in silence. Kathleen sighed, feeling a measure of relief. It lessened the burden, sharing it with someone.

"Kathleen, I think you need to find out for sure."

Kathleen frowned. "I can't go back there and risk him telling me to leave. It would hurt too much."

Jennifer nodded in understanding. "Sometimes we have to do the very hard thing, Kathleen. You can't just spend the rest of your life not knowing for sure if there was a misunderstanding between the two of you. I watched that man – that very handsome man, if I might add – and he looks at you with tenderness. The same way my Arthur looks at me. You need to be brave. Go to him, and ask him if you can come home."

"Oh, Jennifer." Kathleen's voice faltered. "Do you know what you're saying?"

"I know the Bible says prodigals should go home."

Kathleen felt her heart begin to pound. "It says they should go home to God. But Joshua isn't Jesus. He's got a past he's trying to live with, and I might be the worst choice he could make."

Jennifer watched her thoughtfully for a moment. "Or the very best."

Forty-Nine

Joshua began the day by falling to his knees beside his bed and praying. Praying for the saloon to be closed. For his family to be kept safe. For health and strength to take care of the farm and all of Dempsey. For Kathleen.

He prayed God would protect her. Heal her. Give her faith and courage to know what came next.

He asked God to bring her home.

After breakfast, he pulled on the jacket hanging by the kitchen door. Fall was fast approaching; the evening had a chill. It would be harvest time soon.

He stuck his hands in the pockets as he went down the porch stairs, and his fingers touched something. He brought out the velvet jewelry box and opened it. He had found it in Gran's dresser drawer a few days back and he'd taken to carrying it around.

When I'm gone, you go ahead and give my ring to the woman you want to spend your life with. You keep it safe, Joshua James. Only give it to the one your heart can't do without.

Joshua closed his eyes and almost saw her dear, wrinkled face. Her crinkly smile lighting up glassy blue eyes that seemed as beautiful and clear as they had ever been, even when the rest of her body was failing.

He stuffed the box back in his pocket. He wasn't sure why he kept it so close. He should probably give it to Mary.

Yes, that was what he'd do. Take it to Mary.

Later that afternoon, after he came home from town, Joshua set out for the orchard, determined to harvest apples to sell in town instead of letting them go to waste as he had in past years. Kathleen had opened his eyes to the bounty his farm was capable of producing.

He started working, but it wasn't long before he found himself on the porch steps, staring out into the cornfields bathed in the light from the sunset.

He kept trying to convince himself it was settled. He'd be fine. Kathleen would find her way and he would find his, and they would both be okay.

But he knew it wasn't the truth. He missed her more than he'd ever missed anyone or anything his whole life long. Nothing was right on the Whitley farm without Kathleen Whitley.

"Lord," he said, rubbing his face with his palms. "Give me faith."

Scenes played on his mind. Kathleen offering up her harvested bounty for the good of the ones who had suffered. Her enthusiasm as she learned to keep house and do chores. How she'd helped Mary and made herself useful while he was being unreasonable.

He remembered the image of her standing on that horse, arms thrown to the wind. He heard the sound of her laughter as an echo in his mind, a sweet tone that faded away and disappeared.

The ache burned in his throat again. "I love my wife."

But there was ugliness to consider. Kathleen's innocence had been stolen. Maybe she wouldn't be able to give herself to him because of what had been taken from her. Would he be able to love her, to live with her, even then?

He recalled her lovely features as he'd held her. Kissed her. Felt her respond to him. He tried to imagine what might have happened if he hadn't been called to town on a fool's errand that day, but his mind rebelled against the thought.

Maybe the problem's not with Kathleen.

He felt the treachery. The betrayal. Flashes from earliest memories, when men used his mother and left her broken in spirit and wounded in body. He saw Mercy walking away. Not even turning to wave goodbye.

"I keep blaming Kathleen for the things Mercy did to me," he whispered to the Lord. It wasn't exactly a revelation, but for the first time, he saw it from Kathleen's perspective, and he could see why she stayed away. "No wonder it was too heavy for her to bear."

As he lifted his face heavenward, the image of his mother, defeated, cynical, uncaring and unfeeling toward her own flesh and blood – that faded. Instead, he saw Kathleen. He saw her smile, though it would probably always be marked by a certain sorrow. He saw her eyes cast downward in meek sweetness, her cheeks blushing at him. For him.

He knew in that moment he wanted her back. He was ready to let everything else go and live for her. He was ready to trust again.

Movement caught his attention, and he looked on the horizon. He shaded his eyes with his hand and squinted.

He saw a figure in a white dress, with hair that glowed like strands of sunlight.

His heart thumped wildly. He stood up, taking several steps down the path. He stumbled along the low path and up the hill to the barn. When he turned the corner around the barnyard, he saw her.

Kathleen stood, waiting, as if she was unsure she was welcome. She smiled tentatively, pushing back the hair that hung loose around her shoulders.

She had come home.

An incredible surge of affection ignited his spirit. A second later, he was running.

Fifty

Be strong and of a good courage; be not afraid, neither be thou dismayed: for the Lord thy God is with thee withersoever thou goest.

Nellie Whitley had underlined Joshua 1:9 in her Bible with a heavy hand. Now, as Kathleen stood at the edge of the woods and looked out over the farm, she remembered it. If it weren't for the courage God had been giving her every step of this trip, she wouldn't be standing there. She wouldn't have come if she didn't have faith that God would always be there, even if Joshua chose not to be.

Before she was sure she was ready to face him, he was standing by the barn. She smiled, nervous. Hoping he wouldn't be angry she'd come. Praying he wouldn't send her away. For a moment he only stared at her. He seemed dumbfounded. His hands were on his hips and his eyes narrowed in disbelief, as if he wasn't sure she was really standing there.

I am not worthy to be called your wife. But at least let me call you my friend.

She took a step toward him, hoping he would move from his spot, but when she lifted her gaze again, she realized he was running.

Toward her.

It didn't take him long to reach her, and she felt his strong arms go around her. She felt his heart in his embrace. He knew what he wanted. *Whom* he wanted. And for the first time in her life, Kathleen knew she was exactly where she was supposed to be.

"I know I'm not what I was when we shared a life, Joshua. Something was taken from both of us." She pushed back and spoke the words that needed saying.

He shook his head. He took her face between his hands and studied her as if he was memorizing every detail. Taking her in, making her a part of him. He slowly and deliberately leaned forward and kissed her forehead. Her cheek. Her chin.

"Please don't ever leave me again," he said before he kissed her the way she wanted him to.

"I thought…" She tried to speak. The words would not form.

He smiled. "Don't think."

He watched Kathleen as if he knew every part of her. Every darkness of her soul. He knew her rebellion, her anger and bitterness. He knew the way she had manipulated herself and her loved ones in order to hurt them. He knew she had put herself on display and invited a man's obsession. And Joshua knew what had happened in a dark corner of the barn.

He knew everything, and he still loved her. She was certain of one thing, even though a hundred questions circled her mind.

She was home.

"We should go inside."

It didn't occur to Kathleen until Joshua spoke. They had been in the same spot, sharing tender words and kisses for quite some time. She would have been happy to stay there for the rest of their lives. But she allowed him to take her hand and lead her across the field.

She heard the pigs and glanced toward them. The sight of their mucky sty and disgusting existence made her chuckle.

Joshua turned, smiling. "What?"

"How did you stand me when I was wallowing in the mud with the pigs?"

He shrugged. "I've spent enough time there myself to know folks don't always mean to end up there. You just needed a chance to climb out."

"I'm grateful you saw something in me I couldn't see in myself."

He squeezed her hand and led her to the house, pulling her into the kitchen and throwing his hat on the table. His coat dropped to the floor, and then his hands were on her hips and he was pushing her back against the butcher's block. She welcomed his kisses, though she was tentative at first. She could only think of Logan's attack, and how painful and humiliating it had been. But this was different. It felt completely different. This wasn't an evil man taking his pleasure at her expense. This was her husband, expressing his love.

Her husband...

"Joshua," she gasped as he started kissing her neck and reaching for the buttons on the back of her dress.

He stopped immediately and looked her in the eye. "I'm sorry, Kathleen. Am I moving too fast? We can wait. As long as you need."

She laughed aloud and then covered her mouth with her hands. He stared at her with an odd expression.

"Joshua, we *have* to wait! We aren't married!"

He cleared his throat and took a step back. He held up a finger, motioning her to wait. He left the kitchen and went out in the courtyard. A moment later she heard the pump going, and him gasping at the shock of the cold water. He came back rather wet and sheepish.

"Now, then." He picked up his jacket off the floor and pulled out a small box, which he opened. She gasped at the beautiful antique ring. He removed the ring with fingers too large for the task and threw the box on the table.

"This was Gran's. She wants you to have it." He grabbed her hand and pushed the ring onto her finger.

Kathleen smiled. "What are you saying, Joshua Whitley?"

"What do you think I'm saying?" he huffed, his face still dripping. "I'm asking you to marry me, Kathleen Mae Able Whitley Morehouse... Whitley. Almost."

She laughed. "How did you know my middle name?"

He shrugged. "From the annulment papers."

She giggled and stretched her arms out to surround his neck. "I think I'd just like to be Mrs. Whitley. As soon as possible."

"The sooner, the better, as far as I'm concerned," he said. "But first, I need to tell you the whole truth. About me. Just so there aren't any secrets."

She nodded, sobering at his serious expression.

He stared at her. "I love you, Kathleen."

"I love you too, Joshua."

He cleared his throat and sighed. "I know I told you this part, but bear with me. My ma was a prostitute in a brothel. I was a very unfortunate accident."

Kathleen smiled sadly and squeezed his hand. "That sounds a bit like the way my story started."

He considered her words. "You're the only one besides Mary who could say the same."

"I suppose so," she said. She sensed he needed to say more, so she led him out to the steps and sat down. She waited for him to continue. He didn't sit. He leaned against the porch rail and stared across the path to the orchard.

"I lived for the first nine years of my life in and out of the saloon. Sometimes my mother found us decent folk who would take us in for a while. Other times she hid us in the saloon. When we were old enough, we were given chores to do and expected to keep out of the way."

"It sounds like a hard life for a child," Kathleen murmured. He nodded, and she saw his jaw clench. "You don't have to tell me anymore, Joshua."

"I do. It's important you know the whole story."

"Then tell me."

"When I was nine, my mother showed the first concern for us she ever had when she snuck us out and brought us to Grandpa and Gran. I don't know how she managed it, but she didn't stick around to see how we felt about it. She walked away, back to her life, without even saying goodbye. But it's what happened next that made the whole thing so hard to forget."

He stopped and looked up, his expression dark. Kathleen could tell whatever the next words, they would be spoken at a price.

"Not long after, a man beat her with an iron bar. She died."

"Oh, Joshua. I'm so sorry."

It all made sense to her now. It was why he had spoken those first kind words, why he had chosen to save her life, why he had been so hurt when he thought she had been with Evan. He loved her, in part, because she reminded him of his mother. But he had struggled to love her for the same reason.

"I've wondered sometimes," he said, his voice gruff. "If maybe I could have saved her had I still been there."

His quiet words were carried away in the breeze, for she had no answer.

"Kathleen, I blamed you for a whole lot of mess you never made. When you left and sent those papers, I felt like that boy again, losing his mother all over. But you didn't leave because you were selfish or too cowardly to leave that life." He looked her directly in the eye. "You left because I sent you away. Simple as that. It was my fault. And I'm sorry."

She shook her head, hoping he knew she didn't agree, since her voice refused to work.

"I want you to know it's different now. I don't care what happened when you were in that saloon. And I sure don't blame you for what happened in the barn. You are clean, Kathleen. Jesus washed you, whiter than snow."

He took her hands and lifted her up. Held her close to him. "I accept you, Kathleen. With joy. As you were, as you are, and as you will one day be by the grace of God. And I hope you'll do the same for me."

Epilogue

Three days later, just enough time for Little Sicily relatives to make their way to Dempsey after receiving the news by telephone, Kathleen walked into the church she had come to love, wearing Mary's beautiful satin wedding gown, which Mary had willingly given her since the confounded thing would never fit her again anyway.

Her papa brought her down the aisle to meet her beloved deputy farmer, who stared open-mouthed as if he had never seen such a sight before in his life.

"Do you, Kathleen Able Morehouse, take Joshua James Whitley to be your husband?"

"I do."

"Do you, Joshua Whitley, take this woman, Kathleen Able Morehouse, to be your wedded wife?"

"I do." Joshua glanced at the pastor. "And I mean it this time."

Evan poked him in the side and the congregation laughed. Pastor Merchant smiled and nodded his approval.

"Then by the power vested in me by the Lord God Almighty and the state of Ohio, I pronounce you man and wife – again. And this time, what God has joined together, let not man ever separate. Joshua, *this* time, give your bride a kiss."

"You better believe I'll give her a kiss," Joshua mumbled as he scrabbled with Kathleen's veil. He quickly found her cheeks with his hands and her lips with his own.

"May I present Mr. and Mrs. Joshua Whitley!"

They walked down the aisle as Beatrice played a rousing processional and Evan watched her with obvious yearning. Meanwhile, the twins tore up all the paper bows Mary had painstakingly attached to each pew.

When they had greeted their guests, Joshua turned to Mary with a firm hand on Kathleen's waist.

"Thanks for all your hard work, sis. See you later."

"Oh no, you don't!" Mary shook her finger in his face as he tried to turn and walk away. "I have prepared a lovely wedding supper and you are going to march yourself to the churchyard and eat it, Joshua James Whitley. There are traditions to be kept. Presents to be opened! You can't just waltz out of here –"

"Mary, you may not want to see this, but Jedidiah's throwing rocks at the stained glass windows." Joshua pointed. Mary groaned in frustration and turned away at the sound of breaking glass.

"Let's go," Joshua pulled Kathleen's hand and led her to where Sundi waited with the wagon. He had just helped her up to the seat when Mary returned with a twin's arm in each hand.

"Come back here this minute! I'm ashamed of you, Joshua! What are we supposed to do with all that food?"

"Why don't you eat it?" Joshua slid his arm around Kathleen, who gave Mary a helpless, amused expression. Before any more words could be spoken, he turned the horse resolutely toward the Whitley farm.

Before noon, with the sun still high in the sky, Joshua carried his bride over the threshold and up the stairs without a single glance to the right or left.

The rest can be summed up quite simply. Not in happily ever after, of course, but in the Lord's gracious promises kept.

Jesus led them all the way.

The End

justice netwOrk
END INJUSTICE FOR ALL

It is my great privilege to share with you this interview with the **Justice Network,** founded by Tanya Dennis and Susan Panzica and tirelessly dedicated to eradicating the problem of modern-day slavery and sex trafficking:

Miranda: At the turn of the century, with groups like the Anti-Saloon League and Carry Nation smashing saloons and picketing, it's easy for us to look back and see they were going about their fight in the wrong way. We don't want to cause more trouble or get in the way of God's working. What are some ideas for people to start getting involved in their own communities that will truly benefit the people who are being harmed by human trafficking?

Tanya: This is a great question. Just as some of the characters in your book spread condemnation rather than hope, we can often cause harm when trying to help. These unintended consequences often come through lack of understanding. Many take action before seeking to understand the situation fully, before know the dangers, before thinking through the solutions and what happens next.

Justice Network's mission statement is "to educate, empower, and equip our friends and neighbors to become abolitionists." The first step toward helping is education. If we want to be effective in our efforts, we must understand what's really going on. We have a number of fabulous resources on our website — www.Justice-Network.org — from films and documentaries to books and websites.

I encourage people to search for like-minded organizations in their local areas, too. Find people who are doing something good and join them.

Miranda: We confess our hesitation can mirror Joshua's when he was faced with the question of how far he was willing to go to help Kathleen. How do we answer to our fears about getting involved in the messy parts of other people's lives?

Tanya: It is important to distinguish the source of our fears before listening to them or going against them.

Fear can be a good thing. God gave us fear as a means of protection. Human trafficking is a very dangerous business and fighting it can be war. Quite literally. Joshua was a law enforcement officer. He had authority that most of us do not possess. If you're not in law enforcement, be very careful. Do not engage until you have had proper and adequate training.

While some fear comes from God, some comes from a lack of faith. I think this is the heart of your question. Just as God gives us fear to avoid unwise circumstances leading to dangerous situations, He also gives us the strength to overcome unfounded fears. The safest place to be is always in the center of His hand and will. If He calls you to something — to a situation where you can serve, where you can help, where you can love — it is far safer to walk in that calling than to go against the will of our righteous God.

Love is messy. It's not safe, but it's always worth the risk.

I always find my strength solidified through Bible study. Consider those we meet through Scripture: Moses, Joshua, Esther, David,

Deborah, Rahab, Ruth, Nehemiah, the Apostles ... Jesus Himself! I could list forever the people who have faced fears and overcome! Each and every one of these fought social injustices. They rallied against the norms of safe society to chase the will of God. And that will is to love Him and love others. We can't go wrong pursuing that.

Miranda: How can we teach our children to be abolitionists?

Tanya: When I started working against human trafficking, our children were 7 and 9, far too young to understand the extent or details of the issue. But they understood justice. They understood fairness and equality. And they understood human value. So I talked to them in those terms. I explained that God wants us to love others, no matter what their appearance, circumstance, or history. I explained what slavery is and explained that God wants us to do whatever we can to stop it and to help those caught in it.

Most of us will not be involved in busts and rescues. We'll be involved in education and restoration. There are many, many ways to get involved in this and many ways you can involve your kids in it, too.

PRAY. Only God can change the hearts of people and only God can restore the lives of the broken. Prayer is our #1 weapon against injustice.

EDUCATE YOURSELF AND OTHERS. Read books on the topic and the solution. Talk about the issue. Raise awareness. Seek to inform.

SHOP FAIR TRADE. People often think human trafficking is just about sex trade. It's not. Huge portions of major industries run on the backs of slaves and child laborers. Coffee, chocolate, and fashion are the top three offenders. Buying fair trade ensures that the items we consume are not fueling slavery around the world. Learn more at www.fairtradeusa.org.

GIVE. Organizations cannot run without support. Seek out rescue and restoration initiatives in your area and see what they need. Gifts may be monetary, but they could also be clothing, food, educational tools, personal items, or just cards of encouragement.

ACT. Justice Network started with prayer and then a film viewing to raise awareness. In two short years we had reached a national impact networking through educational events, training sessions, hospitality support, and restoration efforts. Seek out an organization or ministry in your area. If you can't find one, start one. Start small with what God has already placed within your reach and see where He leads.

Miranda: You mentioned fair trade. Some argue that supporting fair trade or boycotting companies who use child and/or slave labor takes jobs away from people who are surviving on them. Is this a misconception?

Tanya: Fair trade doesn't eliminate jobs at all! Rather it serves as an advocate, making sure workers are paid for the jobs they do. Families absolutely do need these jobs and fair trade is the only way to ensure that they can survive with them. Without fair trade, there are no consistent economic regulations or floors for prices. That means the one with the lowest prices (typically with the highest education and exposure) gets the money. This consistently leaves those already in poverty deeper in poverty, exploited by those who have resources. The poor keep getting poorer while the rich get richer.

Fairtrade isn't about charity; it's about fairness. It is about rethinking the relationship between producers and consumers. Fair trade makes sure that, establishing mutual honesty and respect, producers can make a decent living within healthy working environments.

Miranda: Now tell us more specifically how we can pray for this movement.

Pray for the safety of those on the front lines of rescue teams. Pray for peace and strength for their families. Pray for salvation of the victims. Pray for restoration and healing for the survivors. Pray for the pimps to know God. Pray for the Johns (those buying). Pray for the mothers so entrenched in poverty they see no choice but to sell their children. Pray that hearts will be changed and lives redeemed. Pray that governments will do all they can to protect life and to promote equality and justice. Pray that God will make Himself known in undeniable ways and that He be glorified through our efforts. Pray that those who fight will find rest in His perfection and that we will not grow weary in doing good. Pray that we will see an end to slavery in our lifetime.

Miranda: What can we do to support Justice Network?

Tanya:

1. Follow us online. We're on facebook and twitter. We have a monthly newsletter and a weekly blog.
2. Tell others about us and encourage them to follow as well.
3. Join our efforts. We have a number of events and opportunities, both local and virtual.
4. Donate.

Miranda: Are there other groups like yours we can support?

Tanya: YES! The largest international organizations include International Justice Mission (IJM) and A21, but smaller local groups are popping up all over the country. Check out our website for Network Partners.

Miranda: What does God say about helping those in slavery and trafficking?

Tanya: Oh, God says a LOT about social justice! The founders of Justice Network are currently writing a book on the subject. Be sure to follow us for release dates. In the meantime, here are a few of my favorite verses on the subject:

"He has told you, O man, what is good; and what does the Lord require of you but to do justice, and to love kindness, and to walk humbly with your God." – Micah 6:8 (ESV)

"Learn to do good; seek justice, correct oppression; bring justice to the fatherless, plead the widow's cause." – Isaiah 1:17 (ESV)

"To do righteousness and justice is more acceptable to the Lord than sacrifice." – Proverbs 21:3 (ESV)

Acknowledgments

Thanks to my editor Tanya Dennis (tanyadennisbooks.com) for her expert help on so many levels, and for a friendship that seems to thrive though we live so far apart. I am blessed to call you a partner in writing. Here's to blonde heroines!

Thanks to my husband and my opposite. Thanks for being supportive, and loving me in your calm, logical way.

Thank you so much to Olivia, who graced us with her beauty to capture the essence of Kathleen on the cover of this book. (As well to the lovely Megan on the front of *Where We Belong*!) And to Kathleen Kirtland, who accomplished it with her expert eye and her camera.

Thank you to you, my readers, for believing that a worthwhile Christian historical romance can come from an Indie author. Thank you to so many who have supported me by telling their friends online and in person, who have written reviews and looked forward to this sequel. It is for you that I have been called to this ministry, and I promise never to lose sight of that fact.

About The Author

Miranda Shisler started writing stories when she learned to read. From that point on, she could usually be found either reading or writing.

She pursued music education and vocal performance at Cornerstone University, but after marrying the love of her life and starting a family, she clearly felt God's call to a writing ministry.

These days, she is busy homeschooling her four children, serving in the music ministry of her church, reading all the quality fiction she can get her hands on, and spending her evenings quite literally writing her heart out.

Connect with her online!

mirandashisler.blogspot.com
facebook.com/authormirandashisler
pinterest.com/mirandashisler/ (See the *Whiter Than Snow* board!)
goodreads.com/mirandashisler

Please remember this series is an Indie project so *you* can have the highest quality reading experience. You can help Miranda (far more than you might think) by doing a quick review for *Whiter Than Snow* on Amazon and Goodreads today!

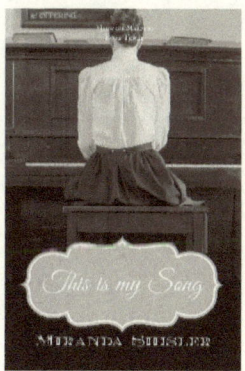

Beatrice Walsh would give anything to go back in time and somehow prevent the tragedy that happened to her family in Chicago twelve years before. Her life and the lives of countless others were devastated by the Iroquois Theater Fire of 1903.

Beatrice believes that the injuries she suffered in the fire will eventually claim her life, so she has decided to spend the remainder of her days alone, finding her solace in the piano.

Evan Masters has had enough of being alone, since he's been that way since he was hardly more than a boy. He has held an interest in the mysterious piano player since the day she came to Dempsey, but so far all of his overtures have been met with rejection.

Can Evan convince Beatrice to rejoin society and take a chance on love? Can Beatrice trust God and allow him to use her broken song to tell the story of his grace through her life?

THIS IS MY SONG
MAY 2017

www.ingramcontent.com/pod-product-compliance
Lightning Source LLC
Chambersburg PA
CBHW021209250626
47155CB00008B/2744